A LOST KINGS MC NOVEL

TELLER'S STORY: PART TWO

AUTUMN JONES LAKE

Copyright 2017 Autumn Jones Lake

BEYOND REASON:
TELLER'S STORY, PART TWO

(LOST KINGS MC #9)

by Autumn Jones Lake

Teller finally has his ride or die girl, but a devastating secret from her past threatens to sabotage their future.

COPYRIGHT
BEYOND REASON: TELLER'S STORY, PART TWO
(LOST KINGS MC #9)
by Autumn Jones Lake
Copyright 2017 – All Rights Reserved.
Print Edition
Digital ISBN: 978-1-943950-22-5
Paperback ISBN: 978-1-943950-23-2

Edited by: Ellie McLove
Cover Designer: Letitia Hasser, RBA Designs
Photographer: Meagan Harding
Makeup/SPFX Artist: Liv Zak
Cover Model: Jaxon Human
Formatting: bbebooksthailand.com

This is an original work of fiction by Autumn Jones Lake. Published by Ahead of the Pack, LLC.
AutumnJLake@gmail.com

About Beyond Reason

WHEN THE MOST TOXIC PEOPLE COME DISGUISED AS FAMILY, WHO CAN YOU TRUST?

Betrayal by blood cuts the deepest.
Teller's found his ride or die girl. The light Charlotte brings to his life has touched the darkest parts of his soul. But a devastating secret from her past resurfaces to threaten their future.

Every truth can be erased with one lie.
When a sinister truth is exposed, it forces Charlotte to question everything about herself. Even whether she's worthy of Teller's love.

The darkest betrayals never come from your enemies.
With Teller's love roaring louder than the lies, Charlotte can finally put her demons to rest. But has too much damage been done for her to prove her loyalty to the Lost Kings?

NEWSLETTER

If you'd like infrequent updates about what I'm working on, sign up for my newsletter! I promise not to bug you unless it's important!
http://eepurl.com/bOZj95

SOCIAL MEDIA

Sign up for Autumn's Newsletter
eepurl.com/bOZj95
BookBub
bookbub.com/authors/autumn-jones-lake
Goodreads
goodreads.com/AutumnJonesLake
Instagram
instagram.com/autumnjlake
Facebook
facebook.com/AutumnJonesLake
Twitter
twitter.com/AutumnJLake
Lost Kings MC Ladies Facebook Group
facebook.com/groups/LostKingsMC
Pinterest
pinterest.com/autumnjoneslake
www.autumnjoneslake.com

THE LOST KINGS MC SERIES READING ORDER

Although Teller's story can be read as a stand-alone or first in the series, I think you'll get the most enjoyment from reading the series in order.

ACKNOWLEDGMENTS

Wow, I feel like I just wrote one of these! Thank you again to Liv Zak for making this cover happen. Thank you to Meagan and Jaxon for the beautiful photos.

I need to thank Liz Kelley and Amy Addams for their excellent feedback.

Thank you, Kari, Cara, and Virginia for being the best crit partners ever. And for not smacking me when I backed myself into deadline hell on this book—even though past Autumn gave you permission to.

Tanya, Daniele, and Jezzie thank you for your help and feedback.

The Lost Kings MC Ladies. Our little group keeps growing and growing. Thank you for your questions, and enthusiasm for my guys! I love hanging out with you.

My awesome readers, I love your notes and messages. Some days I can't believe how lucky I am and I have you to thank for that.

Mr. Lake, I told you I'd make you like Teller!

GLOSSARY

I debated whether or not I should include the glossary in this second part of Teller's book. I mean, you (probably) just read Beyond Reckless and there's a glossary in there. But then I figured if you did want to look something up, it would be annoying to have to grab another book to do it. So here it is. Updated to include new revelations from Beyond Reckless, just so you don't feel like you're reading the same thing over and over. Perhaps a few other important details are thrown in.

THE LOST KINGS MC

President: *Rochlan "Rock" North.* Leader of the Upstate NY charter of the Lost Kings MC. His word is law within the club. He takes advice from senior club members. He is the public "face" of the MC. Much to his annoyance, Rock is seen as the "father figure" in the club, especially by the younger members.

Sergeant-at-Arms: *Wyatt "Wrath" Ramsey.* Responsible for the security of the club. Keeps order at club events. Responsible for the safety and protection of the president, the club, its members and its women. Disciplines club members who violate the rules. Keeps track of club by-laws. In charge of the club's weapons and weapons training. Will challenge Rock when he deems it necessary. Outside of the MC, Wrath owns a gym, Furious Fitness. He is experienced in underground MMA-style fighting.

Vice President: *Angus "Zero" or "Z" Frazier.* In most clubs, I think the VP would be considered the second-in-command. In mine, I see the VP and SAA as being on equal footing within the club. Carries out the orders of the President. Communicates with other chapters of the club. Assumes the responsibilities of the President in his absence. Keeps records of club patches and colors issued. Z also co-manages the MC's strip club, Crystal Ball.

Treasurer: *Marcel "Teller" Whelan.* Keeps records of income, expenses and investments.

Road Captain: *Blake "Murphy" O'Callaghan.* Responsible for researching, planning and organizing club runs. Responsible for obtaining and maintaining club vehicles.

Prospect: A prospect is someone who has stated a clear intention of being a full patch member of the Lost Kings MC. The Lost Kings vet their prospects for two or more years. To vote a prospect in as a full patch member, the vote must be unanimous. Not all prospects will become full patch members. Some will realize the club is not for them. For others, the club will realize that the prospect is not a good fit for the club. Prospects are expected to show respect to all full patch members and do whatever is asked of them. Malik may or may not be a prospect for the Lost Kings MC in the future.

OTHER MEMBERS

Cronin "Sparky" Petek: Sparky is the mad genius behind the Lost Kings MC's pot-growing business. He is rarely seen outside of the basement, as he prefers the company of his plants.

Elias "Bricks" Serrano: We saw Bricks and his girlfriend throughout the series. One of the few members who does not live at the clubhouse, he performs a lot of general tasks for the club.

Dixon "Dex" Watts: We've also seen Dex throughout the series. He co-manages Crystal Ball with Z.

Sam "Stash" Black: Lives in the basement with Sparky and helps with the plants. He came out of the basement to help out in *White Knuckles*. Other than that, we're not really sure what he's up to downstairs.

Thomas "Ravage" Kane: We got to know Rav and his snarky humor a little bit better in each book. Ravage is a general member who helps out wherever he is needed.

"Sway": President of the downstate charter of the Lost Kings MC. We've seen Sway off and on sine *Strength From Loyalty*. He's such a fun character, I figure he deserves a slot in the glossary.

Grinder: Rock's mentor. Grinder is an older member who we met briefly in *Corrupting Cinderella*. He's been incarcerated since before Rock took over the Lost Kings.

THE LADIES OF THE LOST KINGS MC

Hope Kendall, Esq.: Nick-named *First Lady* by Murphy in *Corrupting Cinderella (Lost Kings MC #2)*, Hope is the object of Rock's love and obsession. Their epic love story spans four books: *Slow Burn, Corrupting Cinderella, Strength From Loyalty*, and *White Heat*.

Trinity Hurst: She was the caretaker of the Lost Kings MC clubhouse and the brothers. She and Wrath have a long, tattered love story full of lust, fury, and forgiveness in *Tattered on My Sleeve (Lost Kings MC #4)*. She and Wrath are also featured in *White Heat (Lost Kings MC #5)*. They finally tie the knot in *White Knuckles (Lost Kings MC #7)*.

Heidi Whelan: Teller's little sister. Heidi is a recurring character in each of the books from *Corrupting Cinderella (Lost Kings MC #2)* on. She also has short stories in *Three Kings, One Night (Lost Kings MC #2.5)* and *Between Embers (Lost Kings MC #5.5)* she is a major character in *More Than Miles (Lost Kings MC #6)*.

Charlotte Clark, Esq: Teller's girl. She was first mentioned in *Corrupting Cinderella (Lost Kings MC #2)* and we briefly saw her in *Strength From Loyalty (Lost Kings MC #3)*. *Beyond Reckless* and *Beyond Reason* are the books dedicated to her burgeoning relationship with the brooding Treasurer of the Lost Kings, Teller.

Swan: Lost Kings MC club girl and dancer at Crystal Ball.

Willow: Bartender at Crystal Ball.

Lilly: One of Hope's best friends and frequent "booty call" of Z. She appears in books 1-5 and is the focus of two short stories in *Three Kings, One Night* and *Between Embers*. While she sent Trinity a wedding present in *White Knuckles (Lost Kings MC #7)*, we haven't "seen" Lilly since *Between Embers (Lost Kings MC #5.5)*. Where, oh where, can Lilly be and will we ever see her again?

Sophie: Hope's former best friend. We haven't seen her since *White Heat (Lost Kings MC #5)*.

Mara Oak: Friend of Hope. Also an attorney. She's appeared in *Slow Burn, Corrupting Cinderella, Strength From Loyalty, Tattered on My Sleeve, White Heat, and White Knuckles*. She's married to Empire city court judge, Damon Oak. Their story, *Objection*, will be available one day.

Tawny: Sway's ol' lady. The "Queen B" rules the downstate charter of the Lost Kings MC with long talons and a sharp tongue.

OTHER IMPORTANT RECURRING CHARACTERS

Liam Hollister: the former of Sheriff of Teller's hometown, he's now a member of the Empire Police Department. My stand alone, *Bullets and Bonfires* is his story.

Carter Clark: Charlotte's goofy, often inappropriate younger brother.

Mercy: Charlotte's best friend.

Jake: One of Wrath's business partners in Furious Fitness. His brother, Sully is friends with Liam. Jake has appeared off and on throughout the series since *Tattered on my Sleeve*. You also spend time with him in *Bullets and Bonfires*.

Sully: Has mostly just been mentioned as helping out at Wrath's gym and now that Furious is no more, Wrath's been working at the place Sully owns. He's a significant character in *Bullets and Bonfires* and may or may not, but probably will have his own book someday.

Remy Holt—Huh, who the fuck is that?

Griffin Royal—Who?

LOST KINGS MC TERMINOLOGY

Crystal Ball: The strip club owned by the Lost Kings MC and one of their legitimate businesses. They often refer to it as "CB."

Conference Center: The clubhouse of the Lost Kings MC. It was previously used as a high-end religious retreat and is sometimes still jokingly referred to as the "Conference Center" or "Hippie Compound."

Empire: The fictional city in upstate NY, run by the Lost Kings MC.

Furious Fitness: The gym Wrath owns. Often just referred to as "Furious." It burned down in *White Knuckles (Lost Kings MC #7)* and currently Wrath's in the process of rebuilding.

Green Street Crew: Street gang the Lost Kings do business with. Often referred to as "GSC." "Loco" is their leader and frequent nuisance to Rock.

LOKI: Short for Lost Kings.

OTHER MCS

Vipers MC: The former rival MC of the Lost Kings. Used to run Ironworks.

Wolf Knights MC: Rival and sometimes ally of the Lost Kings. Their president, Ulfric, appeared in *Slow Burn* and stepped down in *Between*

Embers (Lost Kings MC #5.5.) Merlin took over as President of the Wolf Knights. Their SAA, Whisper, was a partner in Wrath's gym. Actions taken by the Wolf Knights have had a serious impact on the Lost Kings in the past and their relationship is tenuous at the moment. We discovered in *Beyond Reckless (Lost Kings MC #8)* that Merlin is Charlotte's uncle. Keeper is their VP. Other members include Hudson and Tiki.

Devil Demons MC: Based in Western NY. We first "saw" them in *Corrupting Cinderella (Lost Lost Kings MC #2)*. We met their president, "Stump" in *Strength From Loyalty (Lost Kings MC #3)* and learned he played an important part of Trinity's past in *Tattered on my Sleeve (Lost Kings MC #4)*. We saw Stump and his son Chaser in *White Heat (Lost Kings MC #5)* and *Between Embers (Lost Kings MC #5.5)*. Chaser is actually the hero of a novella I wrote, *Kickstart my Heart*, which I plan to republish…one day.

South of Satan MC: A few members made a brief appearance in Beyond Reckless. We don't know much about them or what their intentions are.

OTHER MC TERMINOLOGY

*Most terminology was obtained through research. However, I have also used some artistic license in applying these terms to **my** romanticized, fictional version of an Outlaw Motorcycle Club.*

Cage – A car, truck, van, basically anything other than a motorcycle.

Church – Club meetings all full patch members must attend. Led by the president of the club, but officers will update the members on the areas they oversee.

Citizen – Anyone not a hardcore biker or belonging to an outlaw club. "Citizen Wife" would refer to a spouse kept entirely separate from the club.

Cut – Leather vest worn by outlaw bikers. Adorned with patches and artwork displaying the club's unique colors. The Lost Kings' colors are blue and gray. Their logo is a skull with a crown.

Colors – The "uniform" of an outlaw motorcycle gang. A leather vest, with the three-piece club patch on the back, and various other patches relating to their role in the club. Colors belong to the club and are held sacred by all members.

Dressers – Slang for a motorcycle "dressed up" with hard saddle bags and other accessories. It's designed for long-distance riding.

Fly Colors – To ride on a motorcycle wearing colors.

Mother Chapter – First chapter of the club.

Muffler Bunny – Club girl, who hangs around to provide sexual favors to members.

Nomad – A club member who does not belong to any specific charter, yet has privileges in all charters. Nomads go anywhere to take care of business, usually at the request of the club president.

Old Lady/Ol' Lady – Wife or steady girlfriend of a club member. Has nothing to do with her age.

Out Bad – The shorthand way of saying a club member has been kicked out of the club for some kind of betrayal. Someone who is "out bad" might be in hiding from the club.

Patched In – When a new member is approved for full membership.

Patch Holder – A member who has been vetted through performing duties for the club as a prospect or probate and has earned his three-piece patch.

Property Patch – When a member takes a woman as his Old Lady (wife status), he gives her a vest with a property patch. In my series, the vest has a "Property of Lost Kings MC" patch and the member's road name on the back. The officers also place their patches on the ol' lady's vest as a sign they have agreed to always have her back. Her man's patch or club symbol is placed over the heart.

Road Name – Nickname. Usually given by the other members.

RUB – Slang for Rich Urban Biker. A term generally used by real bikers to describe a person who rides an expensive motorcycle on weekends and never very far. A poser.

Run – A club sanctioned outing sometimes with other chapters and/or clubs. Can also refer to a club business run.

DEDICATION

Never expect loyalty from people who can't give you honesty.

CHAPTER ONE

Teller

"WOULD YOU PUT your damn phone away before you get us into an accident," Murphy scolds from the passenger seat of my truck.

"Shut up. The light's red. I'm worried about Charlotte. Haven't heard from her all day."

"You think hanging out with Alexa last weekend scared her away?"

I snort. Doubt it. Charlotte eased right into helping me care for Alexa. Been thinking all sorts of things that are way too soon to be thinking about ever since. "No," I finally answer.

"Well, I need your full attention tonight." He motions toward the green light and lets out an exasperated snort.

"You got it." He's right. Time to pull my head out of my ass now. Worry about Charlotte later. "She's probably just catching up on work from last week." While she never came right out and said it, I'm pretty sure she rearranged her schedule to help me out. Something I both appreciated and felt guilty about.

"Do you want my opinion?" Murphy asks.

"Not really."

He chuckles. "Tough. Brace yourself."

When I let out a short laugh, he continues, "You don't want to admit it, but you need a chick who sets boundaries."

"You think that's what she's doing?"

"I mean, she's a strong chick who isn't afraid to say no to you."

"And that's a good thing?"

"Yes."

It's true. She's sweet as hell, but she's got a fiery temper and not afraid to call me out when I'm being a dick. Even more, she listens and wants to know *why* I'm such a moody jerk.

"This is real. Otherwise, you're taking a huge risk for just a fuck."

I reach over and punch him. "She's not—"

"I didn't say she was."

"She's feisty when she wants to be."

"Yeah, I figured. That's why when you finally own her ass, it's—"

"Different." I understand what he's getting at. Bunnies are good for a quick release. For fun. But they can't keep my interest, and they don't give a shit about who I am beyond my place in the club.

"Better than anything you had before," he says with absolute authority.

"What would you know about it? You look at Heidi and she fuckin' jumps."

Should've thought that one through because I don't really want an answer.

Glancing over, I see he's wearing the smirk that suggests I'd rather not know what he's thinking. "Trust me, your sister has *no* problem expressing herself."

I snort and shake my head. An evil thought enters my brain and immediately leaves my mouth. "Fuck, she doesn't make you get on all fours and bark like a dog, does she?"

His laughter fills the truck cab and he punches my arm. "No, you creepy-ass perv. Where do you come up with this shit?"

This is too good not to keep poking at him. "Does she make you wear a bear costume?" I tap my finger against my cheek and pretend to consider it. "Because I can kind of see her doing that."

He's laughing so hard, I barely make out the, "You're such a dick," he sputters at me.

"What I was trying to explain—before you shared all the disgusting thoughts in your warped head," he says after he stops laughing, "is you still think of her as a bratty little kid. Not a woman who knows her own mind."

"No, I don't."

In a quieter voice, he adds, "I'm not taking advantage of her."

"Hey, I don't think that at all."

"Okay," he says, before turning to stare out the window. "I missed this."

"What?"

"Joking around with you." He runs his palms over his jeans a few times before continuing. "I'm so sorry I didn't go with you guys that day." His somber tone is weighed down with guilt and it brings me right back to the darkest parts of the last few months.

The darkness Charlotte's helped me crawl out of without even realizing it.

I swallow hard. I could've lost him too if he'd been there. "I'm not mad at you," I finally say.

"You asked me to go with you, and I should have. I knew—"

"I don't blame you or anything stupid like that." Never once have I thought Mariella's death was anyone else's fault but mine.

"Well, Heidi and me together hasn't helped. I don't—"

"I'm not mad at you about that either."

"You're not?" he asks, sounding genuinely surprised.

"She's my baby sister. I don't want her with anyone. And you're my best friend. It was a little weird for me."

"It's not about you," he says quietly.

"Yeah, I get that. It's not that I think you two shouldn't be together. I trust you to take care of her." He doesn't say anything, so I keep going. "I'm sorry I didn't take you seriously when you tried to tell me how you felt about her."

"You wanted her out of the life," he guesses. "Away from the MC."

"I used to feel that would be the best thing for her."

"I understand that," he says slowly. "But the club's her family too. Lost Kings run through her blood, same as ours. Why is that so bad?"

"You know the risks we take," I explain. "I'm driving you to an illegal, underground fight for fuck's sake."

"This is nothing new. She's aware of the risks." He holds up a hand, cutting off any protest from me. "Maybe not details, but she's not stupid."

"I know."

"I'll bust my ass to make her happy and give her whatever she wants. And at least I know if something ever happens to me, the club will take care of her."

I blow out a breath. "Yeah."

"Thanks for helping us go on that trip, by the way. We always talked about something like that. It was nice to finally be able to go."

"Always? You've been together for a few months."

He lets out another exasperated huff. "You realize, she was my friend first, right? We used to talk about road trips and all sorts of shit." He shakes his head and stares out the window. "We were planning to do a spring break run before she got pregnant."

"You what? Really?"

His voice takes on a sharper edge. "You seem to have this notion that she's with me by default or I'm with her out of some twisted obligation." I catch him smirking at me from the corner of my eye. "It's starting to hurt my feelings, bro."

I hesitate, because even though he's trying to make a joke, I think he meant what he said. "I don't think that, Blake."

"Sure, okay." He's quiet again for a few minutes. "I'm sorry I haven't been around more. All this stuff with the gym and the house and—"

"I'm happy for you, brother."

"That the gym I was about to buy into burned down?"

"No, you asshole. Come on, once everything's sorted out it's gonna be huge."

"Thanks." After a few minutes, he chuckles. "So, bear costumes, huh? What kind of fucked up shit are you into?"

His phone goes off and he checks the text. "That's a relief," he says. "Ruthless backed out."

"Who?"

"Remy Holt. I actually like the kid. Wasn't looking forward to kicking his ass in front of his whole crew."

"You going soft on me?"

"That's what she said."

Laughter busts out of me at the stupid joke. "I walked right into that."

"Yeah, you did."

"You nervous?" I ask.

"Nah."

"Who'd they replace him with?"

Another text comes in. "Don't recognize the name," he mumbles, tapping his phone. "Trying to look him up." After a few minutes, he gives up and sets the phone down. "Not much on him."

"Great. He's probably some big Russian dude built like a tank."

He holds out his arms, stretching to my side of the truck. "I ain't exactly small, bro."

Slapping his arm out of my way, I laugh. "I'm well aware."

We rag on each other all the way to the old warehouse where the fight's being held. "Why are these things always in abandoned warehouses?" I ask, turning off the truck.

"Because we have so many around here?" Murphy offers. "This isn't the same crowd that used to show up for Wrath's fights. Still illegal as fuck, but at least they have some rules. Guy who runs it is solid."

"If that's supposed to reassure me, it doesn't."

"Teller, look at me." I meet his steady green eyes, and there isn't even a hint of fear in them. "I got this."

"I know you do, brother."

We meet Ravage in the parking lot and he slaps Murphy on the back a few times. "Ready, killer?"

"Fuck yeah."

Murphy wasn't lying. While the set-up is similar, it's not the same bloodthirsty crowd I'm used to. The people in attendance are younger but seem to have a lot of cash to throw around.

We check Murphy in and he's ushered into the back to wait his turn. Ravage and I watch the group of fighters for a few seconds, neither of us comfortable leaving Murphy alone and unprotected.

Murphy flashes us a thumbs up and waves us away.

Ironically, the kid he's fighting is actually Russian. A tall lanky guy they call Frogfoot.

"Not exactly terrifying," I mutter to Ravage.

"I've seen him before," Ravage says, as we find a spot up front. "He's quick. Jumps around a lot. Like a fuckin' frog."

Ravage and I stand shoulder to shoulder right outside the ring. He keeps his arms folded over his chest and his eyes moving over the crowd. Our combined size is enough to keep people away from us. We're both ready to pounce should things get out of control.

I don't trust these people to keep the fight honest, no matter what Murphy said. And fuck, if anyone dares mess with my brother, I'll kill them myself.

Surveying the warehouse, I lean over to Ravage. "How many exits you see?"

He tilts his head toward the back corners. "Three closest ones. Three more up front, but the whole place has broken windows and cracks wide enough to slip through."

"Fantastic, hopefully it doesn't crumble down on top of us tonight."

He barks out a laugh. "You sound like Rock."

Before I can respond to that, a tall, built kid comes over, holding out his hand. "You Teller?"

"Yeah," I answer slowly.

"Griff Royal." We shake hands, and he doesn't engage in any macho-posturing-bullshit.

"Stonewall, right?" Ravage asks.

Griff nods. "I'm not going in the ring tonight, though." He faces me again. "My buddy Remy wanted to apologize for backing out last minute."

Kid doesn't look like a biker, but he shows respect like one, which is unusual.

"It's all good," I say. "Murphy's got a lot of respect for Remy. Said he wasn't looking forward to beating him on his home turf."

Griff throws back his head and laughs. "Sounds like Murphy."

"While you're here, is Remy aware some guy tried to bring his sister to one of our clubhouse parties?" I ask. "Murphy shut that down."

A dark look crosses Griff's face. "No. He's not. I'll handle it."

Maybe I should've kept that to myself.

"Anyway," Griff says, shaking off his tense expression. "They're both signed up for another fight in a couple months. Maybe they'll get matched up then."

We shake hands again, and he strides back into the crowd. I'm not sure who he is in this particular underground circle, but people sure as fuck move out of his way when they see him coming.

"Motherfucker," I grumble under my breath. Murphy said this was his last fight. He better pray Frogfoot doesn't rough him up too much, 'cause I'm gonna kick his fucking ass for lying to me.

Finally, Murphy struts out, all furrowed brows and single-minded focus. I don't wave or do anything stupid to distract him.

The hairs on the back of my neck rise as the fight starts. Frogfoot is aptly named and his quick jumping style lands him a few punches. One fist to Murphy's stomach and one to the face.

But that's it.

Murphy shakes it off and backs up a few steps before going after Frogfoot. Like a machine, he hammers a sequence of punches to his opponent's stomach, side, and finally his face.

The last one puts the kid down and he stays down.

The crowd erupts in an explosion of shouting and cheering, rushing toward the ring.

From where I'm standing, I'm able to see the kid I talked to earlier, Griff, hand Murphy a wad of cash. Then, Murphy's on the move, throwing on his sweatshirt and picking up his bag from the side of the ring. He moves past the girls who approach him without a second glance.

"Holy fuck. Nice work!" Ravage shouts.

"Turn your slips in?" Murphy asks us.

"Doing it on our way out." I glance back at the crowd. "You staying for any other fights?"

Murphy doesn't even hesitate. "Nah, I wanna get home."

We start moving toward the exit and I duck over to the window to collect our cash.

Outside, Ravage takes his share of the winnings and slaps us each on the shoulder. "See you back at the clubhouse?"

Murphy chuckles. "Yeah, I definitely need to stop there before I go home."

"Speaking of lying," I say on the way to the truck.

"What's that?" Murphy asks.

"Had a chat with your buddy Griff. Says you've got another fight lined up."

I let that hang in the air while we get in the truck and I start it up.

We're on the highway when Murphy finally answers my question.

"The fight's a couple months away. If this went well, I was going to drop it."

"Good."

He sits back and closes his eyes.

I glance over. "You all right?"

"Yeah." He lets out a sigh and keeps his eyes shut. "Just want to get home and see my girls."

"How you planning to explain your face?"

Murphy waves me off, then winces. "I'll clean up at the clubhouse."

Even though I'm mad at him, his silence bugs me. "How you feeling?"

"Rough." He sits up, shifting in his seat. "Been slacking in my workouts. Going from a week-long run straight to the ring wasn't my smartest idea."

"Ya think?"

By the time we get home, he's vibrating with energy again, bouncing around the yard, pretending to spar with Ravage. "I really think I have one more in me. You know? Especially if I train right."

"You won this one," I say, shaking my head. "Go out on top."

"Yeah, but—"

"Why don't you worry about recovering from this fight first." Because I'm a dick, I poke him in the side. "I think you might have a cracked rib."

"Ow, you fuck." He gives me a solid punch to the arm.

"Damn, brother. Thought you were all tapped out."

"Don't test me right now. I got enough adrenaline left in me to fuck you up before I pass out."

Ravage snorts and slaps Murphy's back. "Sex will help calm you down."

I throw a punch at Rav to shut him up. That's the last image I want in my head. "Knock it off, fucker."

Unfortunately for Murphy, my sister's waiting for him in the clubhouse. "Fuck," he mutters under his breath as soon as he sees her.

"Busted." I snicker, not at all embarrassed that I'm acting like a ten-year-old. I've known Blake since I *was* ten, so it's normal.

"Oh my God, Blake." Heidi rushes over to us, grabbing Murphy's arm. "What the hell happened?"

"Nothing. I'm fine."

"He won, lil' sis. That's all you need to know."

She glares at me and plants her fist on her hip. "You knew about this?"

"Club business," I growl at her. Anger screws up her face and I square my shoulders. "Don't you dare slap me. You got away with it once 'cause I was being an asshole. Don't try it again."

"Hey," Murphy snaps, slapping my arm. "Watch it."

"Where's Alexa?"

My sister has the nerve to roll her eyes at my question before pointing upstairs.

"Why you over here, beautiful?" Murphy asks.

She turns her glare on him. "I was all by myself over there." She bites her lip. "I came over to help Swan with a few things." Her voice turns hard again. "I didn't know you were off getting the crap beaten out of you."

He reaches out, taking Heidi's hands. "I'm fine. Come take care of me."

The two of them go back and forth in low voices for a few seconds. Heidi's still bitching at him when he turns, gives me a smirk, flips her over his shoulder, and carries her to the staircase.

"Put me down." She squeals and giggles the entire way up the stairs.

The sound of what I'm pretty sure is his hand cracking down on her ass a few times is enough to make me look around for the nearest trashcan to hurl into.

"Some love spanks'll be good for her." Ravage claps his hand on my shoulder. "They're probably going to—"

"Finish that sentence, and I'll kill you."

He raises his hands in the air in surrender but continues laughing at me.

"Asshole," I grumble.

"I wouldn't go upstairs," Z calls out. "You know they're going at it."

Christ, the second Murphy and Heidi got together, I should've asked to swap rooms with one of my brothers. Or moved to the other side of the damn mountain.

"Don't they have a room at Rock and Hope's to defile?" I join Z who holds out his hand for a slap. "Alexa's here, so they're probably spending the night, aren't they?" I ask, as I sit next to him and take the joint he offers.

"'Fraid so, brother."

"Fuck this." I really want to call Charlotte. "I'm beat. I'm going to risk it," I say to Z who laughs.

As I pass Murphy's room, it's surprisingly quiet. It better stay that way.

Inside my room, I drop down on my bed, remembering how good it felt to have Charlotte here with me.

Hoping she's still up, I give her a call.

She answers on the second ring.

"Hey, where you been? I've been worried about you." That's a more stalker-boyfriend type of greeting than I intended, but it's the truth.

"Work's keeping me busy," she answers in a flat tone.

"Did I wake you up?"

"Sort of."

"Sorry. I was going to ask to come see you."

"I don't...that's not a good idea."

"How's your trial or whatever you had going on?"

"It's been a rough week."

This whole conversation feels off, but I can't tell if it's fatigue or something else. "I'll let you go back to sleep. Call me tomorrow."

"I—I'm going to be busy."

This is not the way I thought this call would go at all. "All right. Love you, Sunshine."

11

It's quiet on her end. So quiet, I think she's hung up on me. Then there's a sigh or a sob. I can't tell and it drives me nuts.

"Charlotte, are you okay?"

She makes a hiccupping sound that definitely makes me think she's crying. "I love you too, Marcel. I hope you know that."

Before I have a chance to ask more questions, the line goes dead.

CHAPTER TWO

Charlotte

I'M SCARED SHITLESS.

My fear blocks me from processing the grief of losing my mother.

The fear of my uncle possibly hurting Marcel won't go away either.

The funeral home Chuck demanded I meet him at, is a pleasant enough old Victorian house, painted a cheerful yellow and white. From memory, I park in the back. My heels click over the uneven sidewalk as I circle the building, unsure of what to do next.

Memories of sitting on that front porch trying to keep Carter occupied during my father's wake roll over me. My breath catches and my heart thumps painfully.

I can't believe she's gone.

Approaching the front steps slowly, I'm assaulted by a thousand different memories of my dad's funeral. Of everyone in the club riding to the cemetery in honor of my dad.

Of my mother downing so much vodka to blot out her grief she could barely stand up at the funeral.

They're both gone now.

Carter's sitting in a white rocking chair on the front porch but stands when he sees me. "What's wrong?"

"What do you think?" My tone comes out much sharper than I

intended. His face falls, and I feel like absolute shit. "I'm sorry, Carter."

My brother's the sweetest, most forgiving person on the planet and allows me to crush him against me. "I'm so sorry I wasn't there, Carter," I whisper, hugging him even tighter.

His body shakes from the effort of holding back his tears. "I *was* there," he croaks out. "It didn't help."

"It's not your fault."

He nods against me. "Right."

I know my brother. He'll blame himself.

"Why are you out here?"

"Waiting for you." He lowers his voice. "Chuck's come unhinged. I didn't want to be near him."

"Yeah, tell me about it," I mutter.

He gives me a strange look but doesn't have a chance to question me.

The front door opens. "You two coming in or not?" Chuck shouts.

Carter puts his hand on my back and ushers me inside, keeping himself between Chuck and me, which I appreciate.

Why he bothered having us meet him here eludes me. Chuck's not interested in our input. He makes all the decisions concerning my mother and since I honestly have no idea what she wanted, I sit there mute and let him.

When it's finally over with, the arrangements made, the bills paid by Chuck, he walks us out to the front porch.

"You two want to come to the clubhouse?" He gives me a pointed look. "Just gettin' together with family."

I can't think of anything I want to do less.

"I'm exhausted." It sounds feeble even to my ears, but it's the truth.

Ignoring my brother, Chuck pulls me aside. "You remember what I said, right?"

"How you threatened my boyfriend? Yes, I remember."

His eyes turn cold. "It wasn't a threat. You don't want to push me on this one, Charlotte."

"I wouldn't dream of it."

He pats my cheek. "Good girl."

"Come home with me," I beg Carter once Chuck's gone. "You shouldn't be there alone."

"It's fine. I want to look through some things before Chuck gets his hands on the house."

I can't think of anything of value in that house that Mom didn't sell off a long time ago. "Like what?"

"Photo albums. Some pictures of Dad. Mom's journals. You know, before she lost her ever-loving mind." He flashes a pained smile. "The stuff Chuck will just toss in a dumpster."

"Carter." My heart's breaking and I have to pause to collect myself. "I don't want you doing it alone. Let me run home and change clothes."

"Bring pizza or something?"

"You got it."

Less than an hour later, I stumble into my apartment intent on getting in and out.

Marcel's waiting for me in the living room.

My heart clenches at the sight of him. For the briefest second I consider falling against him and sharing everything.

Christ, what if my uncle has someone watching my apartment?

"Where you been, Sunshine?" he asks, moving in to kiss me.

I duck out of his hold. "Why are you here?"

"You sounded really down last night." He steps back, frowning. "I missed you." His head tilts. "What's wrong."

What if Chuck's on his way over now?

"Nothing. I had a bad day and I want to chill out." At least that statement's true.

"Okay, so let's chill."

"By myself."

A flash of hurt crosses his face, but he squares his shoulders. "Can I do anything for you? You want to talk about it?"

The end of my nose tingles and tears sting my eyes. I don't deserve this sweet, caring man who doesn't realize every second he's with me puts him in danger.

"No, I don't want to talk about it. Can't I have one night without you in my face?" My voice cracks and I have to look away.

"Are you mental?" He rattles the key to my apartment in front of me. "You gave me this."

"Yeah, well, it didn't mean come on over whenever you feel like it."

"Charlotte," he says, using a more reasonable tone. "What's wrong with you?"

"Nothing. I told you. I want to be alone. I need some space." Part of me hates myself for giving into my uncle's demands. But I don't know what else to do. "You're suffocating me."

Blowing out a frustrated breath, he sets my key on the desk and opens the door. "Let me know when you're feeling a little less psycho."

As soon as he's gone, I want to run after him and spill everything. Beg him to forgive me, protect me, and figure out this mess.

But that's a selfish thing to ask when I know how much it will cost him. So instead, I put my back to the door and stare at the wall.

The week's events sucker punch me in the gut.

My mother's gone.

My uncle threatened me. Threatened the man I love.

My brother's traumatized.

And I just chased away the only person who could help me make sense of everything.

I can't tell Marcel the truth. It's safer for him to write me off as a crazy bitch.

The alternative is unacceptable—sparking a war between his club and my uncle's.

That's exactly what will happen if Marcel finds out my uncle threatened me. Put his hands on me. A man like Marcel won't let that sort of behavior stand. He'll go after Chuck. The Wolf Knights will retaliate and it will be a disaster. People will get hurt.

If I allow that to happen, no, if I *cause* that to happen, Marcel's club will never forgive him. His club's his whole life. His family. My uncle's club ruined my life once, I won't allow them to rip Marcel's life apart.

The numbness that followed me all day ebbs and I slide down to the floor. As I sit there in my darkening apartment, the tears finally fall.

CHAPTER THREE

Teller

"WHAT THE FUCKING fuck?" I mutter for maybe the millionth time since leaving Charlotte's place.

I wanted to stay, but I didn't know the words to break through her freak out.

Shit, maybe I don't know her as well as I thought I did.

For a brief, insane moment, I consider calling her brother to see if he knows what's going on with Charlotte, but then I lock that crazy down. One, I don't know how to reach him and two, I'm not asking her little brother for advice on how to date his sister.

I drag my sorry ass into the clubhouse, hoping no one's downstairs to annoy me.

No such luck.

"How's that pussy whip tastin'?" Z asks with a smirk as soon as he sees me.

Goddamn is he a dick lately.

"What's up, you lazy shit? Why aren't you down at Crystal Ball?"

Dressed in only a pair of loose running shorts, he's busy tying his sneakers while the dogs dance around him.

"I was there all damn morning," he answers without looking up.

When he's finished, he gives me a more serious appraisal as I drop down on the couch across from him.

"You look like shit. What's wrong?"

Before I have a chance to tell him to fuck off, the front door opens.

Z's eyes widen at the prospect of fresh meat to torment. "Speaking of whipped," he yells to Murphy.

Murphy raises an eyebrow and slows his steps. "What'd I walk into?"

"Zero's being a dick."

"So, the usual."

Z's devilish gaze swings between us and I brace myself for whatever obnoxious taunts are about to come out of his mouth.

"Either of you tired of banging the same chick yet?"

A growl works out of my throat. Don't care for Z talking about my sister or Charlotte that way. Even if I don't know where I stand with Charlotte. "Really, bro?"

"Let it go." Murphy slaps my arm. "He's just jealous."

"Please, if anyone's jealous." Z lifts his chin at us. "It'd be you two."

Murphy's already shaking his head. "Nope. Sorry. It's a helluva lot better when you actually give a shit about the person you're with."

Something dark passes over Z's face. I think Murphy hit a nerve. I kick back and wait to see if Murphy's going to keep pulling at that thread.

Even though I'd rather not hear anything remotely related to his relationship with my sister.

Z, on the other hand, has no problem bringing Heidi into the conversation. "You're just saying that because you're banging his sister."

Murphy takes a few steps away from me before answering. "No. I'm not going into *detail* because I'm banging his sister."

"Asshole," I growl, leaning over to throw a punch at him. He sidesteps me easily and my fist only grazes his thigh.

Because she has perfect timing, my sister opens the front door carrying Alexa.

"Better hop to it, pussy-whipped boy," Z whispers to Murphy.

Murphy leans down, getting right in Z's face. "Damn right. Tastes delicious. You should try it," he says before meeting Heidi at the door. "Hey, beautiful."

He spends way too long groping her before they join us. Z smirks at me the whole time.

"Hi, Uncle Z."

"Don't talk to him. He's being a dick today," I warn her.

"Stop it," Heidi scolds.

Z throws a shit-eating grin my way and holds his hands out for Alexa. "Come 'ere, princess."

"I'm serious, Heidi. Don't let his foul hands touch my niece."

She rolls her eyes before handing Alexa to him. "Where's Charlotte?" she asks.

Since *crazytown* doesn't seem like an appropriate answer, I lift my shoulders. Thankfully, she drops it in favor of answering some of Z's questions about Alexa.

I swear the gentle way he treats my niece is about his only redeeming quality lately.

He sets Alexa in his lap, and the dogs lick and sniff her tiny feet, making her giggle. It's a cute scene that almost makes me forget what a dick he was being five seconds ago.

"You tired of this joker here yet, Heidi?" he asks, jerking his thumb in Murphy's direction.

Almost.

Her eyes widen. I flex my fingers. Maybe a fist to Z's face will snap him out of his mood.

Unfazed by Z's teasing, Heidi leans over and kisses Murphy's cheek. "Never, ever."

"Aw, you two are so sweet, I'm about to throw up," Z cracks.

Heidi takes Alexa from his arms and pats his shoulder in a consoling way. "Don't be jealous, Uncle Z. You'll find someone *one* day," Heidi says with a knowing smirk of her own. Murphy and I crack up.

My sister isn't easily fooled by any of us. And while she may love and respect all of my brothers, she'll always take Murphy's and my side over anyone else.

"That's it." He stands and signals the dogs to follow him. "I've had enough abuse from you three. Taking the dogs for a run."

"Don't trip," I call out. Z answers with his middle finger.

"Does Charlotte have any friends you could set Z up with?" Heidi asks after he leaves.

I cock my head, amused that my sister's worried about playing matchmaker for Z, who can pick up any chick he wants whenever he wants. "Hell no. I'm not subjecting any of her friends to that deviant."

Murphy chuckles. "Been there done that. He already 'dated' Hope's friend and look how that worked out," he reminds us.

"Did they actually date?" Heidi asks.

"Who fucking knows."

Alexa sort of closes her eyes and makes a little grunting sound. Something I learned she does right before—

"Oh. Oh, wow. Someone needs her diaper changed." Heidi glances at the stairs. "I think I have stuff for her upstairs."

"Want me to—"

She cuts Murphy off before he can make the offer. "I got it. Keep my brother company."

"What a good dad," I tease after she leaves. "Offering to change diapers."

"I was going to go upstairs, grab the diapers and bring them down here," he clarifies.

"Asshole."

He chuckles then winces.

"How's your face?"

"Better than yours."

"Please, if you looked this good, you wouldn't need to cover your ugly mug with that big ol' beard."

"Not my fault you're not man enough to grow one." He waves his fat finger in my face. "Whatcha got going on there? Couple chin pubes finally come in?"

I slap his hand away. "Fuck off."

When he stops laughing, he levels a more serious look my way. "Seriously, you look tense. You still mad at me about the fight?"

"I wasn't mad. I was worried." I tilt my head toward the stairs. "She still mad?"

A slow grin spreads across his face.

"Never mind. I don't want to know," I grumble.

"You and Charlotte have a fight?"

Blake knows me well. We've been able to read each other since we were kids. Something that developed out of self-preservation from growing up in a rough neighborhood and perfected to survive in the early days of the MC.

"Not exactly. She kind of flipped her shit. Said I'm over at her place too much."

His brows furrow. "I always suspected you'd be a clinger if you found the right girl."

"Is that your official opinion, doc?"

He drops the attitude. "Sorry. You two seemed tight the other day."

"I thought so too."

Not exactly familiar with sitting around talking about our feelings, we're quiet for a few minutes. "You think her uncle got to her?" he asks.

"Maybe. Last time she got weird it was because he ran his mouth about me."

"Really?"

"Talked to him about it at the party. Told him to back off."

He runs his hand down his beard a few times, thinking it over. "Probably pissed him off more."

"Christ, she's thirty-fucking-years old. He should butt out."

"Always knew you liked the older broads."

"You better never say that to her. And a few months doesn't make her *older*, you cradle-robbing bastard."

He snorts. "Actually it does." Under his breath, he mutters, "And you're the numbers guy."

"Is this your idea of being helpful?"

Shaking his head, he sits up straighter. "What're you gonna do?"

"Give her a few days? Then talk to her."

He pats my arm. "That's my boy."

I raise a brow.

"You really love her, fight for her."

"Thanks."

His mouth curls into another smirk. "She's already way out of your league though, so don't wait too long."

CHAPTER FOUR

Teller

M Y PHONE VIBRATES over the nightstand, tugging me from another restless sleep. When it actually clatters to the floor, I come fully awake. Leaning over the side of the bed, I sweep my hand over the rug until I grab it. Not bothering to look at the number, I answer. "What?"

"Where are you?"

"Who the fuck is this?" I rasp.

"Carter."

That makes me sit up. A couple days ago his sister basically told me to fuck off, so why is he bothering me at—I catch a glimpse of the clock on my nightstand—eight in the morning? "What do you want?"

I'd already made up my mind that if I didn't hear from Charlotte by the weekend, I was showing up on her doorstep and we were talking whether she liked it or not. I never expected her brother to call me.

"Where are you?" he asks. His normally dickish attitude strained with anxiety.

I do a slow stretch before standing and padding into the bathroom to brush my teeth. "Home."

"Are you coming?"

"Coming where?"

He hesitates, and for a minute there's nothing but static on the line. "She didn't tell you, did she?"

"Tell me what?"

"Our mother died. The funeral is today."

I'm so stunned, I can't respond for second. "Jesus Christ. I'm sorry." The words come out fast as I rush to my closet and reach for a pair of gray pants and jam my legs into them.

"Is she okay? Are you okay?" I slip on a plain black T-shirt while I wait for his answer.

"No, it's been a rough couple days. She needs you."

I'm moving quicker than normal for this hour, grabbing my wallet and keys, shoving them in my pocket. "Did she ask you to call me?"

He hesitates, and I wonder if Charlotte told him about our fight. Her attempt to end things between us. No, her attempt to *incinerate* things between us.

"She told me you two broke up, but—"

Shit, it hurts hearing she already started scrubbing me out of her life. "When?"

"When what?"

"When did your mom…die?"

"Tuesday morning."

Charlotte's dramatic re-evaluation of our relationship still doesn't make a lot of sense. "Why didn't she tell me?"

"Our uncle's acting like an asshole. Maybe she was afraid you being there would cause trouble."

Merlin. Somehow any problems between Charlotte and I always come back to that asshole. I can see how in Charlotte's head her actions make sense. I also know there's probably more to the story.

No way in hell is a shady old fuck like Merlin keeping me away from my girl when she needs me. "What about you?"

"I know you won't do anything to upset her."

"I mean, how are *you* doing?"

He exhales a sad, humorless sigh. "I've been better. So are you coming?"

"I'm leaving right now," I say as I open the front door, jogging over the gravel to my truck. "Where is she?"

"We're at her apartment. How long do you think it'll take you to get here?"

"Give me a half hour."

"It'll take her that long to pick out a pair of shoes." He huffs out another sad laugh.

"Hang on, kid."

"Right now, I'm just worried about my sister."

"I'm on my way."

We hang up and I toss my phone onto the console.

Heidi comes walking out of the woods, carrying Alexa. *Shit.* I'm supposed to watch my niece today.

"Where are you..." The question dies on her lips when she sees my face.

Slamming the truck door shut, I walk around the front to meet her. I take Alexa into my arms and kiss her sweet, chubby cheeks before handing her back. "I can't watch her today."

Heidi blinks. I've never bailed on her before and I hate doing it now, but Charlotte needs me.

"What's wrong?"

"Charlotte's mom died." I brace myself for the questions coming.

"Oh my God. I'm so sorry. Is she okay? Can I do anything?"

"No. The funeral's today. I'm leaving now."

Suspicion is written all over Heidi's face, but she doesn't ask any of the questions I know she wants to. She reaches out and touches my arm. "Do you think Blake or someone should go with you, just in case?"

Meaning Murphy must have warned her there's trouble brewing between our clubs and she's worried about me going there alone.

"I think it'll be okay. Her brother will be there." She doesn't seem convinced. "Her uncle would have to be a real piece of shit to start something at a funeral."

She hesitates, her gaze darting back to the woods—toward Murphy—clearly debating whether she should go get him.

"Hey." I grip her arm so she faces me. "I'm not wearing my colors. I'll keep my mouth shut." Unless Merlin does something to upset Charlotte, then I might gut him—funeral or not. But that won't reassure Heidi so I don't say it.

"If you need something or Charlotte needs… Anything, just call. Promise?"

"I promise."

"Tell her I'm sorry."

"I will." I lean down and kiss her cheek, then Alexa's before getting in my truck.

Our whole exchange took maybe two minutes but I'm still antsy to get on the road. Charlotte needs me. I don't contemplate why she didn't call me herself. Or why she picked a fight the other night. It doesn't matter.

I make it there in twenty-five minutes and double park on the street in front of her house. I eat up the concrete running over the sidewalk and up her front stairs. Carter opens the door before I have a chance to knock.

"She's in the bedroom," he says, nodding at the hallway.

Yeah, Carter can be an annoying little shit, but his expression, hell, everything about him is so bleak, I reach out and squeeze his shoulder. "You all right?"

His surprised eyes meet mine. I'm guessing no one bothered to ask how he was doing. From what Charlotte told me, I know he feels responsible for his mother. Slowly he shakes his head. "I don't know what I am, man. But thank you for coming."

I nod and head to Charlotte's room where I find her sitting on the floor in front of her closet, black shoes scattered all around her. "Charlotte."

She turns at the sound of my voice, looking up at me with so much sadness filling her blue eyes. I can't stand it and I rush over, kneel down and pull her into my arms. At first she's stiff, but then she lets out a harsh sob, her hands digging into my arms holding onto me tight. "I'm here, Sunshine. I'm here," I whisper, running my hands over her back.

"How? Who?" Her gaze lifts to the doorway behind me. "Let me guess, my brother."

"I'm glad he told me. *You* should've told me. You know I'd be here for you no matter what."

She shakes her head. "You don't understand."

"No, I think I do. And fuck that, I'm here for *you*. Nothing else matters."

She sobs and shakes her head. "You shouldn't be here."

"Charlotte, I'm not leaving."

Finally, she seems to give up and gestures helplessly to the shoes surrounding her. "I don't even know what to wear. She always hated everything I wore. Either I dressed too stuck-up, preppy, or slutty. I never made her happy no matter what."

"I've never thought any of those things about you. It doesn't matter. Wear whatever you're comfortable in."

I stand and help her up off the floor. The long, black, shapeless dress she chose falls to her shins. She slips on a pair of black flats. "She would've hated these." This time there's a hint of fire in her words. Defiance in her eyes. There's the Charlotte I recognize.

"Come on." I offer my hand, and she takes it, following me out to the living room. She reaches out and hugs her brother with one arm, never letting go of my hand.

The two of them follow me outside. Carter looks helplessly up and down the street. "You'll ride with us."

He doesn't argue with me, just watches as I help his sister into the front seat of my truck.

"Where am I going?" I ask once we're on the road.

Carter directs me to a cemetery in Slater County while Charlotte stares out the window.

When we arrive, the parking lot is full of bikes and bikers. Most if not all, are wearing Wolf Knights cuts. Not that I expected any different. Except for my ink, I'm free from anything identifying me as a Lost King. Even so, enough of these guys know who I am. Ignoring everyone around us, I help Charlotte out of my truck and wrap an arm around her shoulders, making it clear who I'm here for. Carter takes his sister's hand and walks on her other side.

Tension in the air is so thick, I wish I knew what went down the last few days. I'm basically walking in blind. Merlin, the fuck, steps away from the gravesite, meeting us with a cold stare and a hand to my chest.

If we were anywhere else, I'd knock his fuckin' hand away and punch the ever-living-shit out of him.

His bloodshot eyes and raspy voice almost make me feel sorry for him. Until he says, "Family only."

"Knock it off," Carter grumbles.

Keeping my arm around Charlotte I step forward a little and push her behind me. "I'm here for *her*. That's it." In a lower voice, I add, "Don't turn this into something it doesn't need to be."

He cocks his head, regarding me with suspicion while Whisper and a couple other members take up positions behind their president. "Your prez know you're here?"

Charlotte's trembling body forces me to remain calm. "You know I ain't here for my club," I explain with as much respect as I'm able to muster. "I'm here for Charlotte and Carter. That's it."

Merlin's gaze flicks to his niece, observing the possessive way my arm's curled around her waist. He doesn't even acknowledge his nephew. "Thank you," he says without a drop of sincerity in his voice. He tilts his head, indicating we should move forward. A subtle way of communicating to his brothers that he's allowing me to be here.

Asshole.

Ignoring the bullshit, I lift my chin at Merlin. Whisper shakes my hand and we have a few quick words before I lead Charlotte to a chair up front. Carter stares at me for a second before taking the seat next to Charlotte. He hasn't said a word to anyone since we arrived. His family treats him like he doesn't even exist, which really pisses me off.

I've been to way too many funerals already in my life, but this is the first time attending one for someone I never even met. From the stuff Charlotte's told me it doesn't seem like a great loss.

I keep that thought to myself and don't let go of her hand.

Charlotte

AFTER THE SERVICE, Teller's speaking to Whisper when Chuck pulls me aside.

"I thought I told you not to bring him here," he says in a low voice full of barely concealed rage.

"I didn't. He found out—"

"How?"

No way am I throwing my brother under the bus. Not with the erratic way Chuck's been acting all week.

"Mercy called him."

"Can't that little bitch mind her own business?"

"Stop," I spit out through clenched teeth. "Just stop. Teller's not here to cause trouble. It has nothing to do with your club stuff," I say, waving my hand at his leather vest. "My life is my life. Your club is your club."

His demeanor undergoes a radical change. "You're right, Charlotte. You know, I still remember you as a little girl." He runs the back of his hand over my cheek, and I brace myself not to shy away or show fear. "You were always such a sweet, cute little thing." His gaze shifts to

Teller. "Known him for a long time. He's a dark fucker like the rest of us. Not the kind of guy I ever wanted you to end up with."

"Well, it's not really your decision to make." I'm still frightened and angry about the way he threatened me the other day. That he physically hurt me without a thought.

Maybe he really is having a hard time losing my mother. Their relationship was long, complicated, and frankly, I never wanted to know much about it after my dad died.

Sympathy for my uncle leads me to try to reason with him.

"Uncle Chuck, you only know one side of him." I gesture to the bikers surrounding us. "You show one side to the club and to outsiders, but at home it's different. Dad was the same way."

"Don't you dare compare him to my brother."

I blow out a frustrated breath. I knew he couldn't be reasoned with. "Whatever you know about Teller, isn't the way I know him. He's very good to me."

"You know he got his last girlfriend killed, right?" He waits as if I'll be shocked or outraged at the information.

Instead, I give him a solemn nod. "He told me what happened."

"Bet he gave you the nice, sanitized version of events."

That's probably true, but I'm confident that whatever Marcel kept to himself was to protect me, not him.

It's on the tip of my tongue to mention how sweet Teller treats his sister and his niece, but feeling protective of Heidi and Alexa, I snap my mouth shut. The less Chuck knows about Teller, the better. Fewer things he can try to use against him in the future. Because as I stare into his flat, lifeless eyes, blue like my father's but without the same warmth, I know he can't be reasoned with and he won't let this go.

Teller's familiar heat brushes my side and he slips an arm around my waist. "You okay?" he asks.

"I'm fine."

"We're going back to the clubhouse to reminisce. You're welcome to join us, Teller," Chuck says in an almost cordial way.

"Thank you."

I open my mouth to protest, but Carter walks up on my other side. Chuck reaches out, ruffling my brother's hair. Something he probably hasn't done since Carter was six.

"Coming back with us?"

Carter glances at me and shrugs. "Sure."

In what feels like a repeat of the conversation we had a couple weeks ago, once we're in Teller's truck, I plead with him not to go to the clubhouse. "Let's just go to my place. We don't need to do this."

"Charlotte, he wants to honor your mother. It'll be fine." He glances in the rearview mirror. "Carter's got my back, right?"

"Not sure how much good it'll do you," my brother mutters. "But yeah."

The clubhouse has even more bikers than at the funeral. Charters from out of state. Teller scans the parking lot, staring at some of the plates. "Was your dad ever an officer in the club?"

"No. At least I don't think so."

"Merlin and your mom?"

"Don't go there."

He nods and opens his door.

"What's that about?" Carter asks.

"I don't know."

"I don't like this, Char. I think we should go home."

"It'll be fine," I answer, even though I'm not so sure. Picking up my purse, I dig out the tiny can of pepper spray I carry and stick it in my pocket. I make sure I have my cell phone in the other pocket and am about to open my door when Teller opens it for me.

"Come on." His voice is grim but his expression is passive. He holds out his hand and I take it, stepping down from the truck.

Carter jumps out next to us.

"I really don't want to hear any stories about how much of a *party* girl Mom was," he grumbles.

For an after-funeral reception, the clubhouse is wilder than usual. Music and laughter drift into the parking lot. The smell of alcohol, weed, and sweat slaps me in the face when Marcel opens the door.

Anxiety swirls in my gut. While my mother probably would have loved this sort of celebration in her honor, it leaves a ball of ice in my stomach.

The three of us shove our way through dancing, half-naked bodies, seeking a familiar face.

I nudge Marcel when I spot Whisper in a corner, watching the party with a severe expression in place. He lifts his chin when he sees us and Teller navigates our way to the other side of the room.

"How are you, Char?" Whisper's deep voice carries easily over the noise around us. As SAA to the Wolf Knights, I know his job entails keeping the club members in line with either threats of violence or actual beatings.

"Looks like you have your work cut out for you tonight," I shout. He leans over so he can hear me and I repeat my lame attempt at conversation.

One corner of his mouth lifts. "Any excuse to get shitfaced."

You'd think I'd be offended, but I appreciate the honesty.

"How you doin', Teller?" Whisper asks.

"All right."

Whisper nods to the cluster of chairs behind him. "Why don't you three stay back here where I can keep my eye on you." It's more of an order than a suggestion.

Marcel doesn't engage in any I-can-handle-my-woman posturing. He thanks Whisper and moves forward. Carter stays behind to talk to Whisper.

"I'm going to get drinks," Teller says. "Stay here."

"Are you sure?"

He nods and kisses my cheek. "I'll be right back."

Wrinkling my nose at the small couch, I take a seat. I planned to burn this dress after today anyway.

I slip my phone out of my pocket and check for any important work emails. I answer what I can and figure the rest will be there when I go back to my office.

The cushions underneath me bounce and I assume it's either Marcel or Carter, so I turn with a smile on my face only to encounter Hudson's solemn expression.

"Meant to talk to you earlier, but your bodyguard never left your side."

My frantic gaze searches the crowded clubhouse for Marcel or my brother. I finally spot them at the bar.

Slipping my phone in my pocket, I paste on a smile. "What'd you need to talk about?"

His lips turn down as if he's disappointed in the question. "I wanted to tell you how sorry I was about your mom. I didn't know her as well as some of the older brothers." He waves his hand at the room. "But she was always real nice."

At least she was nice to someone.

And, *ewww*. Is that his polite way of letting me know he never nailed my mom?

My gaze drifts to the bar again and this time there's a ratty, half-naked club whore with her arm around Marcel's neck.

Hudson follows my gaze. "Ignore Mady. She's a cunt. Always looking for conflict where there doesn't need to be any," he informs me. "Her life's pretty boring outside the club."

Well, that was blunt.

Shaking his head, Marcel extracts himself from Mady's sloppy embrace, picks up his drinks and nudges Carter with his arm. Together, the two of them move through the crowd toward me.

"You serious about this clown, Charlotte?" Hudson asks.

Sick and tired of people questioning me, I open my mouth to tell him to fuck off.

34

"Relax, I'm joking." His gaze searches the room before returning to me. "Your uncle's bent about it though."

"So I gathered."

"You staying long?"

It almost feels like he's trying to warn me. "Probably not."

"That's good."

I want to ask him why, but he stands and disappears into the crowd the opposite direction from the way Teller's approaching.

I accept the drink Teller hands me and take a long sip before meeting his eyes. He doesn't even mention Hudson.

"Everything okay?"

"I want to leave soon."

"Whatever, whenever you want, Sunshine. Just say the word."

Carter joins us, red-faced and sweaty. "He's a good wingman, sis," he says, flopping into the chair next to me.

"Gross," I mutter, taking another sip.

"He doesn't need a wingman," Marcel says, which makes my brother chuckle.

"Girls here are only interested in me because of who I'm related to," Carter says.

Teller shrugs and I wonder what advice he'd give my brother if I wasn't sitting right next to him.

Their banter is a nice distraction from the reason we're all congregated here.

Unfortunately, Chuck has to interrupt us. Correction, my uncle and his VP, Keeper, invade our small circle.

"Long day," Keeper says, patting my knee. "You all right, sweetheart?"

Somehow I manage to answer without cringing away from his touch. "As okay as I can be."

"Well, least your ma and pop are together again. Dean loved that woman something awful. And she was never the same after he died."

Chuck's eyes narrow and I'm not sure if it's the mention of my dad or the reminder of both losses.

Marcel's arm tightens around my shoulder and I relax against him, feeling completely protected.

"Haven't seen much of you lately, Carter," Keeper says. "Still doing your art?"

He says *art* the same way I'd say *fucking goats*.

Carter mumbles, "Yes." Then he glances at my half-empty cup. "Let me go fill that up for you," he says, leaving so fast, he splashes a bit of my drink in my lap.

I glare at Keeper for chasing my brother away when Teller had finally pulled him out of his guilt-ridden shroud.

"Carter's a talented kid," Teller says, smoothing over the awkward moment. "I've been trying to talk him into doing an apprenticeship for tattooing. Got a buddy who'd love to get his hands on him."

Merlin snorts.

"Why? He a fag too?" Keeper asks.

Silence falls over our group. An empty void where my uncle doesn't bother to defend his only nephew. Nope. Club first. Fuck family. Chuck might as well tattoo *that* on his chest. Right underneath his cliché "No Regrets" tat.

Teller takes a long sip of his drink before responding to Keeper. "I don't want to fuck him, so I never asked. You want me to tell him you're interested next time I see him?"

Oh, Christ, nothing makes these knuckle-draggers need to prove their manhood more than implying they might be gay. Marcel neutralized the insult to my brother with a few simple words and his don't-give-a-shit attitude.

Uncle Chuck guffaws loud enough to draw Whisper's attention our way.

I'm surprised he's tolerating someone insulting his VP's manhood in the middle of his clubhouse.

Especially someone from another club.

CHAPTER FIVE

Charlotte

I NEED TO come clean with Marcel.

Today showed me how in deep we are with each other. My foolish attempt to chase him away, thinking it would keep him safe, seems stupid and pointless now.

He deserves to know everything. I trust this man more than I've ever trusted anyone in my life. It's both terrifying and comforting.

When we return to my apartment, Carter pulls me aside. "I'm going to crash at Bianca's tonight."

"Are you sure? You can stay here."

"Nah. I'll stop by in the morning though. We can do breakfast or something." He lifts his chin toward my apartment where Teller disappeared so I could have a moment alone with my brother. "He's a good guy, Charlotte. Don't let the shit with Uncle Chuck and his stupid club interfere."

"I'll try."

"If it comes down to Chuck or Teller. Choose Teller."

"I think I already have."

"Good." He leans in and kisses my cheek. "Love you."

"We're orphans for real," I say.

"We've been orphans for a long time, sis. It's just official now."

"True."

"Feels good, right?" he says sadly, walking away.

"Love you," I call out. He throws his hand up in an answering wave.

Marcel's in my kitchen when I finally enter my apartment. "Where'd Carter go?"

"To his friend's."

"He all right?"

I almost cry from his concern. Defending Carter earlier came from a genuine desire to protect my brother, not from some arrogant desire to cause trouble in my uncle's clubhouse. "I don't know."

After my father died, no one gave a shit about Carter. Instead, my uncle fed my brother bullshit stories about how Carter was now the man of the house. Later, he called my brother a sissy for not wanting to learn to ride. When he realized my brother had no interest in prospecting for the Wolf Knights, Carter was of no use and he full-out ignored him.

Somehow Marcel's accepted my brother into the small circle of people who matter to him. Because of me. Because he's just a decent guy. A man so loving and loyal I can't even comprehend it. Good to his core no matter what he thinks of himself. He stood up for my brother in a way, that as a woman connected to the Wolf Knights, I've never been able to. In a way that matters in their world. He didn't have to risk pissing Chuck and Keeper off, but he did it because he felt it was right.

"I'm sorry about the other day." I accept the mug of coffee he hands me and take a seat at my kitchen table.

"Were you worried about me going to your mom's funeral?" he asks gently.

Staring into my coffee cup, I nod.

"I wish you'd told me." He shifts, his chair scraping across the floor as he moves closer to me.

"I didn't know what to do."

"I understand." His gaze settles on my face. "Don't chase me away again."

It's both an order and a plea.

"I know how strong you are," he continues. "You don't need me. But I want to take care of you, Charlotte. Whenever something bad happens, I want to be by your side."

My eyes water. No one's taken care of me since my dad died. I took care of Carter. Took care of my mother until I had enough and left for college. Everything after, I dealt with on my own.

Marcel pulls me into his lap, and I curl my arms around him, resting my forehead against his. His leg shifts, adjusting me in his lap, reminding me of the awful stuff he's survived. "You're wrong. I do need you," I whisper. "How about we take care of each other?"

"That sounds good to me," he answers in a low, rumbling voice.

Tears sting my eyes. "I don't want to hurt you, Marcel. Or cause problems for your club."

"Charlotte." He uses two fingers to lift my chin and meets my eyes. "The only thing that could hurt me is being shut out of your life."

I sniffle and nod.

"No more."

My hands twist in the folds of my dress. "I need to take this off."

His face remains passive. We're still on shaky ground. And I still need to come completely clean with him. He gives me a nudge. "Go on. I'll clean up in here."

I don't bother shutting my bedroom door. All I want to do is peel this awful dress off and toss it in a bonfire.

It feels like a flannel pants kind of day. I add a T-shirt and go find Marcel.

He's in my living room, sitting on the corner of my couch. Legs crossed with his ankle resting on his knee. Tapping his fingers along the edge of his boot. "Hey." He smiles and holds his hand out. "Feel better?"

A warm wave of emotion rolls up my throat, prickling my eyes with tears. "No." I don't quite know how to accept the comfort he's offering, but I allow him to pull me into his arms and hold me while tears run down my cheeks. "I feel so guilty," I whisper.

"Why, Sunshine?"

The nickname makes me smile through my sorrow.

He uses his thumb to brush the tears off my cheek. "Talk to me."

I take a deep breath and slowly let it out. "I'm relieved that she's gone and I know that's awful. I loved her, but I hated her too."

While I gather my thoughts, he holds me, rubbing slow, comforting circles on my back.

"She always seemed to hate me, but it's not like she treated Carter any better. I always wondered why she even bothered having kids. My dad was the one who did stuff with us." I babble out all the thoughts and feelings that come to mind while Marcel listens. "When he died, it was awful."

"Did your uncle help you guys out?"

Nausea rolls through me and I sit up. "Yes and no. He gave her money. Fed her habits. Kept a roof over our heads, so I guess that's something."

Without the full story, I probably sound like an ingrate to him.

I close my eyes, debating whether to share my darkest pain. If he ditches me because of my emotional baggage, better he do it now.

Before I fall any more in love with him.

Teller

CHARLOTTE LOOKS SO lost. I keep touching her, trying to reassure her I'm here and I'm not going anywhere. My hand curls around her neck, my thumb brushing her soft skin. Under my fingers, her pulse beats wildly, even though on the outside she seems calm.

"What's wrong?"

She shakes her head. "Nothing. After my dad died, Chuck was in and out of prison."

"Club still take care of your mom?"

"Ulfric made sure we were okay. He was more like an uncle to me than Chuck ever was. He tried to get my mom sober, but it never stuck."

"Yeah, I know how that goes."

She takes a few deep breaths. Trying to center herself? Calm down? I can't tell. "What's going on in your head? Your pulse is out of control."

Her eyes widen and she leans into my touch, rubbing her cheek against my hand. "It's nothing. I was such a stupid kid. I bought all the lies and crap the club preached. How innocent my uncle was. That he got railroaded by the system. The usual outlaw garbage."

She meets my eyes for a second and her gaze darts away. As if she thinks I'm insulted or will disagree. "Go on."

"So, my brilliant plan was to become a lawyer. Then I'd work for the club and keep them out of trouble." She squeezes her eyes shut and her cheeks redden. "It sounds *so* stupid now."

"It sounds like a girl who lost her dad young and wanted to hang on to what little family she had left."

Slowly, she opens her eyes. Her head tilts as if she never considered that was her motivation.

"So that's why you went to law school? You don't practice criminal law though."

I thought it was a casual observation, but something about my words causes her mood to shift. Her jaw tightens. She slides off my lap and puts her back to the arm of the couch so she's facing me and tucks one leg underneath her. "I planned to concentrate in criminal law. After Chuck's last stint in prison, he was a different man. Harder, meaner, but he also tried to do more for Carter and me. Took more of an interest in our lives."

The way she says it is almost creepy and a sick feeling settles in my gut.

"He promised to pay for law school if I worked for the club after graduation."

"Lot of money."

"You're not kidding," she mumbles.

"So what changed your mind?"

"I used to go to the clubhouse all the time when I was a kid. It wasn't like it is now. Or at least it wasn't when they had family days. But, we'd go there for barbeques in the summer, Easter egg hunts." She swallows hard. "Christmas."

"Yeah, the few times I was there when Ulfric was running things, it was a lot different. Tamer."

"Right. I was never afraid there. My dad had been a member. My uncle was a member, who would dare touch me?"

The sick feeling twists into a ball of dread in my stomach. "What happened?"

"Winter break my second year of law school, I went to the clubhouse. They were supposed to have a party for members' kids. Santa, Mrs. Clause, reindeer, all that Christmas crap. I said I'd help out."

"Carter come with you?"

"No. He had the flu. My mother was already at the clubhouse. I shouldn't have left Carter alone, but I'd already promised, so—"

In the short time, we've been together, it's obvious Charlotte is a woman who keeps her word. "You felt obligated."

"Yes." She swallows hard and tucks a piece of hair behind her ear. "This is so stupid," she mutters.

"No, it's not. Keep going." We're close to something, and I don't want her to back out. I want her to understand she can trust me with everything.

"After the families left, the 'real' party began. I guess there was another MC visiting from out of state."

"Who?" Her eyes widen at my sharp tone, and I work to calm myself. "Do you remember the name?"

"No."

"How—"

"Let me finish."

I snap my mouth shut and wait for her to go on. "I remember Chuck telling me I was old enough to stick around for a club party if I wanted to. My mother agreed. I was stupid and curious, so I stayed."

"And?"

Her cheeks turn pink. "I don't remember much after that. Which is both a blessing and a curse."

"Why?"

She stares at me for a few long seconds before continuing. "I woke up the next morning in one of the clubhouse bedrooms. Half-naked and hurting."

"Fuck." I stand and walk to the other side of the room, pacing for a few seconds, trying not to explode. When I finally stop, she's watching me with fear dancing in her eyes. "I'm sorry," I say, trying like hell to calm down.

After I sit back down next to her, she picks up the story.

"I didn't feel right. I was sick to my stomach. My head felt like it was going to split in two. I'd never lost a big chunk of time like that before."

"You didn't do the drunk-girl, college experience?" I say, trying to inject some humor before she exposes more of what I suspect is an awful story.

"No. I told you. I tried to fit in when I went to college. But not with that crowd. I worked hard because I wanted to earn at least a partial scholarship to law school. I had a steady boyfriend for a few years too, so I didn't bother going out much."

The boyfriend part is new to me, and I want to punch myself for actually being jealous of some guy she was involved with years ago.

"Same thing in law school. The drink 'til you puke thing never appealed to me."

"Go on."

"I hurt." She squeezes her legs together and the blotchy patches on her face and neck go from pink to red. "Down there. Bad. There was blood on me and I knew it wasn't my period."

A strangled noise works out of my throat and I sit forward. "Did you go to the doctor?"

She nods. "I went to the hospital." For a brief second, she meets my eyes. "More than one person raped me while I was unconscious. They found trace amounts of Rohypnol in my blood."

"Tell me you prosecuted these fuckers."

Her head tilts as if she feels sorry for me for being naive.

"I thought *my uncle* would take care of it for me. That's how *the club* works, right? Someone hurt a member of his family, I figured he'd want to handle it. It wasn't in my nature to go to the cops."

Knowing how my own club operates, that makes sense. I've personally dealt with at least three fuckers who hurt a woman I cared about. No cop or court was going to do what needed to be done, so we handled those situations ourselves.

Is that wrong?

It's wrong to hurt a woman. These guys would do it again and again without remorse. So, no, I didn't think it was wrong.

"I understand. Believe me."

"You rescued Mariella," she says. "A girl you barely knew."

"Right."

"And you took care of the ones who hurt her...who killed her, didn't you?"

"Damn fucking right." No point denying it. She might as well know who I am and what I'm capable of now.

"Well, my uncle didn't have your zeal or compassion."

My stomach drops. "What do you mean?" I ask in a low voice.

"He said 'my behavior' insulted him in his own clubhouse."

"What?" Even as a fucking kid I was able to sense something off about my mother's boyfriend and did everything I could to protect my sister. A grown fucking man blamed his niece for what happened under his roof? When he should've protected her? I can't fucking wrap my head around it.

Charlotte

AFTER MY FAMILY shut me down, ignored what happened to me, and expected me to do the same, I wanted to keep that pain locked down. I never tried to talk about it with anyone I cared about again.

Until now.

Until Marcel.

The weight of his gaze rests on me. His anger, his compassion, all of it flickers over his face, but he remains calm. Silent.

"Go on," he finally says.

"That's it. There's nothing else to tell."

"Merlin did nothing?"

"He didn't want to bring attention to my fuck-up." My hands ball up into fists in my lap. "He said, since I couldn't remember what happened, maybe I enjoyed it. Or even initiated it."

"Initiated it?"

I shrug. "He said to get over it and move on with my life. Maybe be more careful next time."

"What a fucking piece of shit." He stands and paces. "Does Carter know?"

"I never told him. He was still in high school. But I think he always suspected something. You've seen how impulsive he can be. I didn't want him doing something stupid and getting hurt."

And I was ashamed. I couldn't burden my little brother with something so ugly. But I leave that part out.

"What about your mother? Did you tell her?"

"Yes," I whisper. "She said 'what did you expect?' And—" I swallow hard and force out the final knife my mother lodged in my heart that day "—maybe if I wasn't so uptight a guy wouldn't have to drug me to fuck me."

"Jesus Christ." His mouth opens as if he has more to say, but instead, he shakes his head. "She blamed *you*."

"I know that sounds unbelievable, that no mother would say that to her daughter—"

He shakes his head. "No, it really doesn't."

The honesty between us is too much. Too brutal, and I turn away.

"I felt completely helpless. This horrible thing had happened and no one believed me. No one cared. I only remembered these tiny, horrifying fragments of that night and couldn't talk to anyone about it."

"What'd you do?"

"I stayed far away from the club. Told Chuck not to bother paying my tuition anymore. That I didn't need his assistance and I wouldn't be working for the club. Ever."

"You said that to him?"

"Damn right I did. Told him I'd pay him back every penny once I had a job and he agreed."

"I'm surprised he let you go that easy."

"I always assumed he felt guilty."

Teller snorts.

"Anyway, I went back to school furious. Switched my concentration to family law. Dropped and added classes the first day of the semester. Then I shoved it out of my mind. Buried myself in school work."

"How long'd that last?"

"Not long. By summer I started unraveling. I had more and more flashbacks and nightmares. I didn't know if they were actual memories or my mind filling in the blanks, but I started drinking to block it all out."

"That why you don't drink much now?"

"Pretty much." I hesitate, unsure if I want to continue revealing so much. "I hated myself. I couldn't stand being in my own body. I didn't know who had been inside it. What they had done. I felt contaminated," I whisper.

He nods, and the simple gesture gives me the courage to continue.

"I started having random hook-ups. It gave me a sense of control. I chose who I wanted. Did what I wanted. Remembered every detail the next day."

His jaw works but the words he comes up with surprise me. "I understand."

"Can you? There's not even a small part of you that's bothered?"

"Fuck no," he answers immediately. "I'm the last person…No, I'm not bothered."

"I almost didn't go back to school. But then, it felt too much like letting Chuck and my mother win if I dropped out."

"You pulled it together?"

"Sort of. My third year was rough. Christmas was horrible. Every jolly Santa I saw triggered me into a fucking panic attack."

"Christ." He runs his hand over the back of his neck a few times before facing me. His wild and haunted eyes hold me hostage, and I steel myself for the question he's about to ask.

"Do I? Have I ever done anything to…trigger you?"

The word rolls off his tongue unnaturally as if he's never used the word *trigger* in this context. Hell, I'm sure he hasn't.

I reach out and take his hand, needing the connection as much as I think he does. "No. Never," I answer honestly. "Please, don't see me any differently."

He stares at me for a moment. "I see you, Charlotte and I love everything I see." My eyes water and he squeezes my hand. "Go on."

"I finally stopped cycling in and out of these unhealthy hook-ups and found a therapist. I stopped dating altogether and concentrated on working through everything, but my grades went to shit. I buckled down to study for the bar exam and managed to pass. Chuck had the nerve to come to my graduation and pretend that he was proud of me. Bragged to all his bros about helping me out. I wanted to kill him."

Maybe I should have left that last part out. Marcel looks ready to kill someone.

"Since my grades were so bad my last year, I had trouble finding a job. I was so happy when I finally did so I could start paying my uncle back."

Marcel's jaw tightens, but he doesn't say anything.

"That's it. I'm sorry I didn't tell you sooner."

He works his hand over his chin and seems to be struggling for what to say. "When you were ready, you told me. Nothing you said changes how I feel about you. If anything, I...thank you for trusting me."

"I trust you more than I've ever trusted anyone in my life." I swallow hard, thinking about the way my uncle's acted over the last few weeks. "I wanted you to understand why if it comes down to my family or you, I choose *you*." Christ, that sounded heavy. "Well, and Carter told me to pick you," I say to lighten things up.

A smile breaks the serious expression he's been wearing. "Did he now?"

"Yup, right before he left."

"See, I knew I liked that kid for a reason."

"Thank you for always being so good to him. For sticking up for him."

"He's important to you, he's important to me. I don't *dislike* him. He could use a good ass-kicking once in a while, though."

I can't help laughing.

"Come here," he says, curling his hand around the back of my neck. He pulls me closer until I'm kneeling next to him on the couch. "You need to understand something. I'm here for you. I'm on *your* side. Always."

"No one...I've never really felt that before. No one has ever been there just for *me*."

He heaves in a deep breath and lets it out slowly. "I've done so many things wrong, Charlotte. Hurt people I care about. Let them down. I don't deserve to have you in my life. I'm scared I'll fail you too."

He thinks he's hard, that he'll end up hurting me eventually.

But he's the kindest man I've ever known.

Teller

"ANYTHING ELSE, SUNSHINE?" I ask after a few minutes.

She sits up, teeth biting her bottom lip but doesn't answer.

"Your meltdown the other day. It was more than just your mom." I'm guessing here, but I think I'm right.

Her gaze slides to the floor.

"Charlotte, look at me. Did something else happen?"

Finally, she slowly nods. "Chuck threatened me. Told me not to bring you to the funeral."

"Motherfucker." That dirty piece of shit is definitely going to ground. Taking him out requires time and planning though.

And permission from my club.

Unless Merlin comes at me first. Then I'm within my rights to shoot him, gut him, beat him to death. Whatever.

Tonight, I'm not leaving Charlotte's side.

"I panicked. I knew if I told you, you'd go after him. I was afraid it would start trouble between your club and his. I didn't want to be responsible for that."

I graze her chin with my fingers and tip her head back so she meets my eyes. "Please hear me when I say this, Charlotte. If I told any one of my brothers even half of this story, they'd be picking up a shovel to help me bury your uncle's body."

"But—"

"No. Don't ever hide something because you're worried about that. I'll protect you. No matter what. Merlin can come at me all he wants. I'll fuckin' kill him."

"You won't…you won't tell your club this will you?"

Eventually I'll have to spill at least some of this to the club. First, they need to understand why she can be trusted. Second, I'll need a good reason to call for a vote to put Merlin down.

Oh, yeah. Murder's on my mind.

I answer her as truthfully as I can. "Not unless I have to."

Charlotte's a smart woman who understands how things work in our world and what my answer means.

CHAPTER SIX

Charlotte

MARCEL AND I talk for hours. Well, mostly I talk, and he listens. Completely worn out, I end up falling asleep on the couch. At some point during the night, Marcel carries me to bed. He curls his body around mine, and that's the last thing I remember.

Opening the door to all that past pain leaves me feeling like a deflated balloon. Familiar waves of self-loathing crawl over my skin the next morning. The feeling that I'm forever tainted no matter what I do or how many children I help. Something I thought I'd left far behind.

Tears prick my eyes even though my therapist warned me this could happen. Might happen if I ever found myself in a serious relationship.

"What's wrong?" Marcel rasps from beside me.

"Nothing." I turn to face him and goddamn is he beautiful. "Thank you for staying last night."

"You say that as if you think I'm ever gonna leave."

When I don't respond quick enough, he sits up. "Charlotte?"

"I love you," I whisper.

He gives me a lopsided smile. "I love you too." He leans down to kiss me, and I wrap my arms around his neck, keeping him close.

Nose to nose, our eyes meet and I almost cry with relief at the desire shimmering in the teal blue depths.

Still, he seems cautious.

Slow and gentle our lips meet.

"Marcel?"

"What do you need?"

I need you to still want me.

"You."

"I'm right here."

I shift, arching my back and he finally seems to get it. He slides his hand up and under my shirt, kissing my skin as he bares it. "Where do you need me?"

"Inside me."

A low growl works out of his throat as he strips my shirt off the rest of the way and wrestles my flannel pants down my legs. I'm just as frantic, pushing his boxers over his hips.

His eyes burn with a need as urgent as mine. The hard press of his body settles against me.

Eager for him, I wrap my legs around his waist.

He stops to give me a maddeningly slow kiss. I moan and arch my back, hungry for more. I trail my fingers down his chest and stroke his cock.

His eyes open, staring down at me.

Guiding him to me, I rub the hot head of his cock through my wetness.

Our eyes lock. "Take me," he urges.

I run my hand over him again, and he flexes his hips, pushing himself into me with agonizing slowness.

"Finally," I breathe out.

He chuckles against my neck. "Impatient this morning?"

I tilt my hips, inviting him deeper. "Harder."

Instead of harder, he pulls out, and I moan. "Nooo. What are you doing?"

"Shh." He trails kisses down my neck over my breasts, down my stomach. "Should've done this first," he murmurs against my skin.

Finally he settles between my legs. "Open for me."

He waits patiently and hums his approval when I dig my heels into the mattress and lift my hips.

The worshipful way he stares at all of me.

It's everything.

His thumbs rub against the edge of my inner thighs, driving my need higher. He skims his fingers down over my lips and I gasp.

Over and over he strokes, kisses, massages, licks my most intimate places.

He explores me with his tongue, placing his palms on my inner thighs and pushing them farther apart.

Needing to hold on to something, I dig my fingers into my pillow.

My head thrashes from side to side. "Holy…oh my God." I come so hard I can't catch my breath.

His eyes find mine and he nuzzles his face against my core. "Love your pussy, Sunshine. Love your taste and how you feel wrapped around my cock." He trails kisses higher, his tongue tracing a path over the crease of my thighs. His big hands grip my hips, kneading and claiming. "Love your legs. Especially wrapped around me."

His hands sweep over my stomach. He glances up, eyes full of heat. "Love your belly that's going to carry our kids one day."

I gasp at the words…at the idea of a future with him and how right it feels. He doesn't stop to elaborate. His hands brush over my ribs to cup both breasts. "Definitely love how perfectly these fit my hands."

My laughter turns into a contented sigh as he settles over my body, easing himself back inside me.

I'm on fire. Beyond thought.

In seconds, with a few simple touches and words, he's obliterated every single one of my fears.

His arms wrap around me, holding me tight, his face buried against my neck as he thrusts harder. Completely full and surrounded by his love, I slowly come undone. Wave after wave of bliss flow over me.

"Harder," I whisper.

He grabs my hands, pushing them over my head, pinning me down. Pounding into me. "Like that? Is that what you need?"

"Yes."

His breathing turns ragged. Our sweaty bodies slap together. My body pulses with pleasure.

"Charlotte." He groans, jerking into me. "Fuck." He releases my hands, and grabs my hips, squeezing and holding until his entire body stills.

He rolls to the side, pulling me with him, so I'm draped over his chest. Utterly boneless and content, I lay half on top of him, stroking my fingers over his hot, damp skin. He turns, watching me with affection and reverence in his eyes.

Under his gaze, I feel naked. Stripped bare. He knows everything about me now and still loves me. I can see it. Feel it.

"I love you," he says as if he'd read my mind.

"Love you too."

I do. I love Marcel beyond all reason. Trust him with everything.

He intertwines our fingers, lifting and kissing the back of my hand.

On the nightstand, his phone buzzes. He curses and twists to grab it.

"Shit," he says, reading the text and setting the phone back down.

"Everything okay?" He hesitates to answer me and I think I know what's coming. "Club business?"

"All the guys are back and Rock wants us to sit down."

I brush my fingers over his cheek, trailing over his lips. "I'm okay. Really." I don't ever want him to feel like he has to make a choice between his club and me.

Not because I think I'll lose, but because I don't want him to.

I pat his chest and sit up. "Carter's supposed to come over for breakfast. I'll be fine."

The fact that my brother will be over later seems to help him make his decision.

"Shower with me first," he says, tugging me out of bed.

"Well, I can't say no to that." I pull out of his hold and dash into the living room. He follows me and runs his hands over my ass while I'm bending over, searching through my desk. I find the key and hold it out to him.

"This belongs to you."

He accepts it with a smile that turns serious. "You're not getting it back this time."

Teller

THANK FUCK FOR the long drive to the clubhouse. It gives me time to think about how to handle this situation.

Bikes are lined up along the stone wall when I pull into the parking lot.

Everyone's home.

In the living room, brothers are clustered around Rock and Wrath.

"Teller!" Rock calls out when he sees me. He gives me a side hug. "Where you been, knucklehead?"

"Charlotte's," I answer, not caring if the guys razz me for being whipped.

Rock nods as if he's pleased to hear it.

"Where's Hope?"

"At the house. She'll be over in a little bit."

He gives Wrath the signal to herd everyone into the war room and I follow him inside.

I haven't been a total slacker while they were gone. I've got numbers that make everyone's eyes bug out. Like a little bitch, I also tattle on Murphy by adding his winnings from the fight to the club's pot.

Wrath shakes his head but surprisingly stays quiet.

Rock's more vocal. Staring Murphy down, he asks, "You get this out of your system, now?"

"Think so."

This time, Wrath shoots a glare at Murphy. "Watch your tone."

Z reports that he tracked down the two thieves and they won't be an issue anymore. No one asks for further details.

"Malik stop in to see you?" Rock asks.

"Yeah, dude's got a big fucking chip on his shoulder, but he could be useful to the club if he can lock down that attitude."

"Okay, keep me updated."

We run through a few more matters and before Rock ends the meeting I raise my hand.

"I might have an issue I need the club's help with."

Wrath groans. "Don't tell me, Merlin's already busting a gasket over your girl?"

I snap my fingers and point at him. "Got it in one try."

"Jesus Christ," Z grumbles.

"What are you asking the club to do?" Rock asks.

"I'm not sure yet."

"What happened?" Rock asks. "Start there."

"Her mom died."

Most of my brothers offer some sort of condolence, not realizing what a bitch her mother was.

"Merlin ordered or threatened her not to take me to the funeral."

"Let me guess," Rock says. "You went anyway."

"I didn't know he had a problem until afterward. Her brother's the one who asked me to come."

Wrath raises an eyebrow, but I'm not in the mood to get into details.

"That's why you were having issues?" Murphy asks.

So much for not getting into details.

"Yes. Once I got there and made it clear to Merlin I was only there for Charlotte and Carter, he seemed to step back. Invited us to the clubhouse afterward, but I don't think he's suddenly going to be okay."

"Carter's her brother?" Z asks.

"Yeah."

"You went to their clubhouse unprotected and alone?" Wrath asks.

"I wasn't wearing colors or anything. I laid low."

"Bro, that's beyond fuckin' stupid," Dex says. "What if he and his crew jumped you?"

"I didn't know he had an issue with me at the time."

"Your girl didn't mention it before you went in?" Wrath asks in a low voice that snaps my attention to him. "You're not the least bit concerned about that?"

"Why?"

"You need me to spell it out for you, little brother?"

"Fuck you. Don't patronize me."

"Well." His lips curl into a half-smirk. "At least she's teaching you some big words."

"Come on, bro. That ain't necessary," Murphy says.

Considering I've been such a dick to him lately, I'm surprised Murphy's sticking up for me against Wrath.

"She *did* try to talk me out of going back to the clubhouse. I didn't know why at the time and I thought he'd take it as disrespect if we didn't show up."

"He say anything to you?"

"I got into it a little with Keeper when he said some shit about Carter."

Wrath smirks. "You and your big mouth. Can't help yourself, can you?"

Since Wrath seems to be amused, I don't take offense. I sit back, tapping my pen against the edge of the table. "Pickin' on Carter's like kicking a fucking puppy. I wasn't gonna sit there and let them talk shit about him without saying something."

Rock nods in approval before glancing around the room. "Right now, Merlin's issue seems to be with her. He hasn't threatened you, right?"

"No. I thought we had an understanding." I take a deep breath. "I'm asking the club to protect her if things get any worse."

"You sayin' you're taking Merlin's niece as your ol' lady?" Ravage's tone conveys every bit of his shock.

"Yes." As soon as I say it, I know it's true. Of course I am. I stare at my hands for a few beats before continuing. "She didn't tell me right away because she was afraid I'd have words with Merlin and she didn't want to start any trouble between our clubs."

"So she led you into a dangerous situation to protect the club?" Wrath asks. "How thoughtful."

"Do you have to be such a dick?"

"Simmer down, Both of you," Rock barks. He turns to me. "Keep us updated on the situation. If it gets worse, we'll discuss it again."

He's not bringing it up for a vote. Not yet. I can live with that. They don't have enough information yet.

Rock dismisses everyone but asks me to stay.

"You all right with this?" he asks after the door shuts behind Murphy.

"I understand."

Rock tilts his head, studying me for a moment before answering. "You're sure about her?"

"More than ever, Prez."

He sighs and runs a hand over his head. "I know there have been times when I was hard on you."

"No—"

"Let me finish," he growls, cutting me off. "You've always been a good kid, Marcel. What were you, twelve? When I caught you trying to sneak into the garage?"

"Yeah, something like that." That has to be one of the most humiliating days of my life.

"You impressed the hell out of me."

This is news to me. And I know for sure Rock isn't easily impressed by anyone.

A couple questions land on my tongue, but I wait for him to continue.

"You were already an adult. Had a lot of responsibility. You never complained though. Always did what needed to be done."

"Had no choice."

"Sure you did." He keeps his steady gray eyes focused on me. "You reminded me a lot of myself. Still do. If I'm hard on you, it's just because I didn't want you making the same mistakes I did." Finally, he glances away and I feel like I can take a breath.

"You think I'm making a mistake with Charlotte?" I ask.

"Not at all. She understands the life. Doesn't put up with your shit."

"You think that's a good thing?" I joke.

"Yes. It's also what you need to keep you level."

"Hope doesn't give you shit."

He snorts and shakes his head. "Here? No. Home—"

"Trin doesn't—"

He points at the door. "You *do* remember her volunteering to let Ransom grab her and arguing with Wrath about it? Trin picks her battles carefully. But don't ever think she's a pushover. It takes a strong woman to put up with this life." His mouth curves into a smirk. "You know damn well Heidi gives Murphy hell when he needs it."

Now it's my turn to snort.

"Charlotte messed up with Trinity. Not gonna lie, Wrath won't forgive that anytime soon. You wouldn't either if the roles were reversed. But she owned up. Apologized. Tried to make it right as soon as possible. She's not a coward."

"She did feel bad about it. Still does."

"I know. That's why I think she'll make it here. She's tough, but she has a heart."

"She really does."

"The right woman." His mouth curls into a smile. "Even if she's full of flaws will make you a stronger man."

"You think Charlotte's the right one?"

"Don't know. Doesn't really matter what I think. You're smiling more than scowling these days. I know that."

After some of the things Charlotte told me, I'm questioning myself. Rock's shrewd gaze travels over me.

"Anything else?"

"She...shit, I feel like an asshole even talking about this."

"It's what I'm here for," Rock says.

"You're the only one I trust not to make a joke out of it. Or to slip up and say something to her." I also know Rock won't treat her any differently if I tell him this. And it's been bugging me.

Rock waits patiently for me to continue.

"She likes it...rougher than I'm used to."

He raises an eyebrow.

"Rougher than I'm used to handling a girl."

He nods slowly without commenting right away. "You talk with her about it?"

"No. I think she just expects—"

"You to do it because you're a big, rough guy?"

"Maybe."

He sighs and glances at the door. "I saw so much shit in the early days of the club that I always wanted to make it clear to you two that you don't hurt women."

Yes, Murphy and I had lots of those talks with Rock.

"But you're smart enough to know the difference between hurting someone and giving your woman what she asks for."

"Yeah, I get that."

"Does it bother *you*?"

"No. Fuck. I feel like it should, but—"

He holds up a hand. "Got it."

Jesus, I feel like a teenager having a talk with my dad. Except I'm not a teenager and my dad was long gone by the time I was old enough for *the talk* normal kids have with their parents. Watching, learning, experimenting at the clubhouse is where it's all come from.

"It's more than that. She likes…" Shit, this has been bothering me for a while now. "Something Mariella told me Ransom used to do all the time. To terrorize her." The brutal stories of that fucker choking her until she passed out while he raped her have never left me.

"Figured you had your reasons for taking him out the way you did."

I flash a grim smile. Rock's seen me at my very worst and stood right by my side. All my brothers have at one time or another, but Ransom's death was the only one I ever enjoyed. I'm not proud of that, but the fucker had every bit of pain coming his way.

"If it bothers you, talk to her. Maybe don't mention Mariella," he suggests. "Whatever you do, don't ever make her feel bad about it, though."

"I don't…at least I don't think I have."

"If she needs something you don't think you can give her, that's fine. There's nothing wrong with being honest with yourself. But, don't you dare shame her about it."

"I wouldn't."

He nods as if he really didn't think I would.

I crack a smile. "Bet you didn't expect to have the birds and bees talk with me when I was almost thirty."

"Fuck, you make me feel old." He jerks his thumb toward the rest of the clubhouse. "Murphy and Heidi are killing me as it is. He tries to get Alexa to call me grandpa one more time, I might gut him."

I can't help laughing. Rock even laughs with me.

"I got Jasper and a bigger crew up here while they were away. Made a lot of progress on the house. So, they should be out of your hair soon,

I hope."

He waves his hand in the air. "I'm kidding. It's fine having them there." He gives me a more pointed look. "Murphy done with this fighting bullshit?"

"I think so."

He slaps the table. "Anything else?"

"No, just Merlin's a bigger dick than I ever realized," I say.

"Figured there was more to the story." He levels me with a stern glare. "You'll tell the club when it's right."

It's both an observation and an order.

I'm still hoping I can diffuse things before they get out of control.

Except, Merlin's a loose cannon, so keeping this from turning bloody might not be up to me.

CHAPTER SEVEN

Charlotte

After Marcel leaves, I look for my phone to text my brother.
I can't find it anywhere.

Not in the shitty black dress I was wearing. Not in my purse.

Nowhere.

Did I lose it at the clubhouse?

I know I had it with me yesterday. In fact, it's the last time I remember having it at all.

Shit.

I scribble a quick note for my brother and head down to the last place on earth I feel like visiting right now.

When I arrive, the back door of the clubhouse sits ajar. I open it in increments before peeking inside. It's dark and shadowy except for light spilling out of their chapel. I had hoped the only person I'd run into might be a random club girl cleaning up after the guys.

Skirting the chapel door, I stop at the bar and do a quick search of the shelves behind it to see if someone turned in my phone.

Nothing.

Next, I hit the couch we'd been sitting on. My whole body cringes as I shove my hand between the cushions. Good God only knows what I'll encounter. A lot of crumbs. Something sticky. Something sharp.

Something I'm pretty-sure-but-don't-want-to-verify is a used condom.

"Blech," I mutter, wiping my hands on my jeans.

"You need to remind her who her family is, Prez." That sounds like Keeper's voice. Intrigued, I move closer to the door.

"Don't tell me how to handle my family," Chuck snaps.

"All he's saying is you need to reel her in closer, not piss her off." I can't identify that voice, but it has to be another member.

"Fuck their grow op. Ironworks is more valuable to us," someone else says.

"That's what we want a piece of." I recognize that voice—Hudson. "I don't think Charlotte can help us on that one. We should leave her out of it."

"Aw, that's precious. You still sweet on lil' Charlotte?" Keeper taunts. "Pissed she's gettin' it regularly from a King?"

"Fuck you."

"Watch how you address your VP," Keeper warns.

"Start acting like a fucking VP then," Tiki says, which makes me laugh. Tiki's older than dirt and been a member forever. VP or not, Keeper won't give him lip.

"Fucking bullshit, them cutting us out of Ironworks after all the times we've helped them out over the years," Uncle Chuck grumbles.

A ball of ice settles in my gut.

I've known all along my uncle would try to exploit my relationship with Marcel and I'd been fully prepared to tell him to fuck himself when the time came. The fact that the whole club seems to be discussing it at the table is worse than I anticipated.

"I might be more cautious, brother." That grave tone can only belong to Whisper.

"'Bout what?" my uncle snaps.

Whisper's voice lowers, and I have to creep closer to the door to hear him. "Teller's not someone you want to mess with."

"I'm not scared of that dumb fuck."

My blood boils hearing him speak that way about Marcel.

"He earned that treasurer patch when he was nineteen. You think a club with the resources they have would vote in a moron to handle their money?"

"What'd you hear from Loco?" Chuck asks, ignoring Whisper's logic.

"Nothing," someone answers. "That fucker's been sucking down Lost Kings Kool-Aid for too long."

"Sucking Rock's dick is more like it," Chuck jokes. "You put some pressure on him?"

"With what leverage? He won't budge. Seems convinced Rock's crew has his back."

A few moments of silence pass before my uncle speaks. "How can you work with Wrath for years and be so useless?" That question has to be directed at Whisper.

"We never talked MC business at the gym."

Chuck grumbles something that I can't catch.

"I'm inclined to agree with your SAA. Loco's scared shitless of Teller," someone else cautions.

"Loco's afraid of someone?"

"Said Teller's a crazy motherfucker. I'm guessing it has something to do with the Vipers disappearing."

"You think Rock's crew was part of that?"

"Without a doubt."

My uncle's quiet for a second.

"All the more reason to have Charlotte find out what she can." That sounds like Keeper. "If she's gonna keep spreading her legs for him, let's use it to our advantage, Prez."

Fuck you, Keeper.

"Did they go in wearing colors?" Chuck asks. "So that crazy asshole understood who he's dealing with?"

"Fuck no. That'd be suicide stepping on Lost Kings' territory—"

"Kings don't run Ironworks yet as far as I'm concerned. These fools want to patch-over, they need to fucking earn it. Have them go back and make it clear the threat to his business is very real."

"Merlin—"

"Get it done." He mumbles a bunch of curses. "What?" he snaps.

"While they're working that angle, let's see what Charlotte can find out for us," Keeper suggests, and it's ticking me off that he keeps bringing me into this bumbling plan.

"Char ain't gonna spy on her lil' boyfriend," my uncle spits out and I bet it's pissing him off to admit in front of his bros that he can't control his niece. I'd laugh if I wasn't approaching pee-my-pants level of fear.

"Don't need her to," someone says. "We got this."

"You drop a bug in it?"

"It ain't the eighties, Prez. All I needed to do was upload an app."

"Whatever." My uncle doesn't have a sense of humor when it comes to people making him look stupid, so whoever that was clearly doesn't fear him all that much.

"Prez, with all due respect, this is a bad idea," Whisper cautions.

"You spent too many years working with Wrath. Forgot who your brothers are."

"I ain't forgot shit."

"Ulfric never shoulda allowed you to be in business with him. Our clubs shouldn't be mixing money."

"Fuck you. That *mixing* brought a lot of money into this club."

"Yeah, and turned you into Wrath's bitch."

"I ain't no one's bitch. I'm urging you to reconsider this plan. Teller isn't stupid. You saw how protective he was of her at the funeral. He figures out you bugged his girl's phone, it's gonna start a world of trouble we don't need right now."

"I got a right to keep tabs on my niece," he says in that sanctimonious tone that sets my teeth on edge. "I want to make sure she's being treated right. Fuck only knows what goes on in their clubhouse."

Oh, please.

Whisper's loud sigh seems to say the same thing. "Teller won't buy that for a hot minute."

"How's that asshole gonna figure it out?"

"Well, for one, they ain't gonna let her near their clubhouse without Z checking her for shit just like that."

"Bullshit."

The room's dead silent for a few minutes. A chair creaks. There's the harsh thump of something slamming against the table.

"Fine. I gave my opinion. We're still allowed to do that, right, Prez?" Whisper says. I can vividly picture the sneer he's probably wearing.

In the silence, I imagine the two of them staring each other down. "We finally got peace in this area. Got our own setup with the Devil Demons—which the Lost Kings helped us set up, I'll remind you. We're earning well. Keeping clean. I don't think stirring up a war over a few miles of shitty Ironworks territory is worth it, but that's on you, brother," Whisper finishes. He's not quite challenging Uncle Chuck, but he's coming awfully close.

I'm pretty sure in a fight to the death, Whisper would win, and I'd stand on the sidelines with my pom-poms cheering him on.

"Thanks so much for your permission," my uncle says, each word dripping with anger.

There's another creak and the door swings all the way open. I jump, ramrod straight, trying like hell to seem casual and disinterested.

"Oh, hey, Uncle Whisper, is Uncle Chuck around?" I ask, sounding way too sunny and eager.

He stares at me for a few seconds. Trying to gauge how much I overheard.

"Hey, Char. How you been?"

"Good. Except, I think I lost my cell phone last night."

"Sure. We always find a few every weekend." He lifts his chin at me.

"How's that boyfriend of yours treatin' you?"

"Teller?" My voice squeaks. Maybe if I sound like he's not all that important to me, they'll lose interest. "Fine, I guess."

One corner of his mouth twitches as if he knows I'm full of shit. "Check with your uncle. He might have seen it," he says smoothly. If there's one thing these assholes know how to do, it's lie with ease. And while he might have just challenged my uncle at the table, outside the chapel he'll protect and stand by his club no matter what. "He's in there if you want to talk to him."

Before I can answer, he reaches back and knocks on the door. "Mer, your niece is here to see you."

"Come in," my uncle calls out. As if he's some sought-after CEO instead of a shifty-ass criminal.

Merlin's at the table with Hudson, Keeper, Tiki, two other members whose names I don't remember, and one guy who isn't wearing a cut.

"Hey, Uncle Chuck. I think I left my cell phone here last night." The more I think about it, the more likely it seems one of these assholes lifted my cell phone from me. I've never lost it before.

My gaze strays to Hudson, who had the perfect opportunity. He won't meet my eyes, which makes me think I'm on the right track.

Asshole.

"Oh," Chuck says in a bored tone. "Someone turned a phone in." He holds up my phone. "This it?"

"Yup." I snatch it out of his hand, afraid to touch it, knowing they defiled it somehow. "Thank you so much, Uncle Chuck," I gush in the most syrupy tone I can muster up.

"How you doing, princess?"

Barf.

"Still sleepin' with the enemy, Charlotte?" Keeper asks, earning a glare from my uncle.

I raise an eyebrow. "Excuse me?"

He ignores my icy tone. "If you're datin' bikers now, we got plenty of eligible Knights. You shouldn't be with a King."

"Uh, I'm not with him because he's in an MC." I'm with him despite his MC ties—I keep that to myself though. No reason to go scorched earth on the insults yet.

Chuck seems ready to blow. God forbid he can't keep control over a situation.

"You need anything, let me know, Char."

"Will do."

He nods, dismissing me and I've never been so happy to get the hell away from him.

In my car, I take several deep breaths. My phone sits on the passenger seat taunting me. I have no idea if they're listening right now. If they're recording everything or if it's triggered by my voice. How am I going to explain this to Marcel without tipping off my uncle?

That's right. I plan to tell him everything as soon as I can.

It's not even a question.

I already know where my loyalties lie and they're not with the Wolf Knights.

I WENT STRAIGHT to Charlotte's house after my talk with Rock. I'm waiting on her front steps when she pops out of the alleyway.

I stand and meet her on the sidewalk, grabbing her by the hips and kissing her hard.

She pulls away before I'm finished with her. "Hey, Teller," she says with an edge to her voice. Strained.

Something's wrong. She rarely uses my road name when it's just the two of us.

"What's up?" I lean in to brush another kiss over her lips, but she jerks her head back. "What's—"

She stops me by pressing two fingers against my lips and shaking her head. Intrigued and only mildly alarmed I follow her inside.

"What's—"

She cuts me off again, pressing me up against the door. Holding me there with a hand to my chest, she leans over and grabs a small pad of paper and a pen.

Christ, it's distracting when she leans over, pushing her ass into my crotch while she writes something down. My hands curve around her hips and I grind myself against her.

Ignoring my not-at-all smooth moves, she turns and thrusts the paper in my face.

My uncle bugged my phone.

I snap the paper out of her hand and read it again. Yeah, it doesn't say anything different or provide more detail.

Plucking the pen out of her hand, I scribble down: *How?*

She lifts her shoulders.

"You want me to order a pizza, babe?" I ask.

Another shoulder lift. This time she adds a *what the fuck* face.

"I'll go down the street and grab it, okay?"

"Uh, sure."

Stay here. I write down.

Shit. I want to tell my club about this as much as I want Wrath to punch me in the balls while saying "I told you so" a couple dozen times.

Z's the one who takes care of our tech stuff and I think he'll go easier on me, so that's who I dial.

"'Sup, brother?" he answers on the second ring.

"I need you."

All ease vanishes from his voice. "What's wrong?"

"Charlotte…it will be easier to explain it to you in person."

"Is she okay?"

"Yeah, but I'm at her place. Can you come here?"

"Sure. I'm at CB now. Give me a few minutes."

It occurs to me after we hang up that I didn't give him Charlotte's address, but I'm not all that surprised when Z shows up half an hour later all on his own.

He slips his bike into a small space in front of Charlotte's. She joins us outside. Her fearful eyes meet mine, and I kiss her cheek to reassure her. "It's okay. Z knows more about this stuff than I do."

"What's going on?" he asks as he approaches, taking the two of us in slowly. "Hey, Charlotte," he says, giving her a friendly chin lift.

"Charlotte thinks her uncle bugged her phone. Can you take a look at it?"

It takes a lot to ruffle Z, so he barely skips a beat. "Where is it?"

"Inside."

"Why do you think he bugged it?"

She hesitates. "I lost my phone and went to look for it at the clubhouse. While I was searching, I overheard some things."

Z watches her with narrowed eyes in a way I don't particularly care for.

"Can you be more specific?"

"Not out here, bro," I mutter, slapping his arm.

Charlotte motions for us to follow her inside. The three of us pretty much fill up her living room. Z checks the place out. Not in a judgmental way.

Well, he's not judging *her*. It's more of a why-you-letting-your-girl-live-here once over.

He holds out his hand, and Charlotte slips him the phone. Without speaking, he flicks it on and wanders over to the couch, dropping down, completely absorbed in searching for the app. After a few seconds, he motions me closer. "What are we doing?"

"Don't know."

"I think we should feed them some false information and see what happens."

"All right."

Z stares at me for a few more seconds. "What do *you* want to do?"

He's asking if I plan to report this to the club. I definitely *should.* This isn't a secret I should ask Z to keep. "Can we keep this between us for now?"

"Yeah, brother. I won't say anything. But think on it."

And by *think on it* he means *come clean with the club soon.* "I will," I promise.

He lifts his chin and addresses Charlotte. "You mind getting a new phone?"

"No. Of course not. Did you find it?"

"Yeah. It's off right now, but I'll need to examine it more to make sure they didn't tamper with anything else."

"Okay."

I'm proud of the way my girl doesn't argue with Z or even question him. "I use that phone for work, though. If I go get a new phone set up can you forward the calls to it?"

"Absolutely."

She grabs her keys but hesitates by the front door. I should go with her, but I need to talk to Z.

I approach her slowly and take her arm, leading her outside. "You okay running to the store yourself?"

"Yes. Of course." Her gaze darts to her front door. "Is he going to tell the rest of your club?"

"Not yet."

She bites her bottom lip. "I hate causing trouble for you."

I lean in and press a kiss to her forehead. "What did I tell you?"

She nods and gives me a quick kiss. "I'll be back in a few minutes."

I watch her leave before going back inside.

"Where you at with her?" Z asks as soon as I shut the front door.

"You heard me this morning. I'm *with* her."

He watches me closely for a few beats. "I don't see anything else on here. Clumsy attempt to bug her. I'm not sure if they're really that stupid and lazy or they're trying to throw us off of something bigger."

"Great."

He stands and motions me closer. "Hear me out before you get all pissed off."

Naturally that raises my hackles. "I'm listening."

"Let me place a few cameras."

"Are you fucking serious? First thing she did was tell me. And you want—"

"Ease up, bro. Think about it. Is she trying to gain your trust by telling you about this, only to fuck you over harder later?"

"No."

"Then you've got nothing to worry about."

"It's a shitty fucking thing to do."

He humors my attitude because we both know I'm going to agree to whatever he suggests. Especially since he's sticking his neck out by not taking this to the club right away. I trust Charlotte and I want my club to trust her too.

Z tries a different tactic to convince me. "Think of it as a security measure. This place is nowhere for a girl to be living on her own."

"Fuck off with your fake-ass concern."

Despite some dickish behavior lately, Z's normally pretty chill and easy-going. It takes a lot to push him to Wrath levels of scary. Instead of getting pissed-off, he seems to find my outburst amusing. "We both know you're going to say yes. Why you makin' my life harder?"

"You're a dick."

"I know, brother."

"Where?"

Rather than rubbing my nose in my reluctant agreement to his plan, he opens the door and points to a heating grate opposite the entrance. "View of the front door." He steps inside and points to another grate in her living room. "That'll give me a straight shot down the hall into the kitchen." He points to a spot in the opposite corner. "Front door from the inside. That's it. Not trying to be a fuckin' creeper, sticking them in her bedroom or bathroom. Just want to get a sense of whether Merlin or any of his crew stop by on a regular basis."

"I've stopped over unannounced a bunch of times and only people I've ever run into are her brother or her best friend, Mercy."

"She hot?"

"Shut up."

"You sure the brother has nothing to do with the club?"

I snort because maybe it's time for Z to meet Carter. "Yeah. His uncle's a dick and treats him like he doesn't even exist. He's got no love for the club."

Z lifts his hand, absently stroking his fingers over his chin. "He ride?"

"No."

"Doesn't matter. He still might be able to help us out."

Not wanting to encourage that line of thinking, I ignore the comment. "When?"

"Whenever you say. You got a key?"

"Yeah."

He nods as if he's proud we're at the key-exchanging stage in our relationship. "She work nine to five?"

"Longer usually."

He makes a face as if he doesn't approve. And good God, if we're all cavemen, Z's the cave-*maniest* of us all.

"Is she taking time off or going back to work tomorrow?"

"She's supposed to meet up with her friend in the morning."

"All right. Good. So tomorrow, we'll set it up."

Still pissed, I grumble, "Thanks for including me in your B&E."

"Want me to ask Rock instead?"

"Fuck no."

"Then shut your mouth."

"Asshole."

He follows me into the kitchen and I pull two beers out of the fridge, handing one to him and we both sit at the table.

"You seem at home here," he observes.

I shrug.

"This where you've been spending all your time?"

"Where else?"

"Seems you'd find her a better place."

I pick at the label on the bottle before answering. "I don't think she'd appreciate me telling her where to live."

"This keeps getting serious, you movin' in here?"

"As long as I'm with her, it really doesn't matter."

His eyes widen. "Bro, her whole apartment could fit in your bedroom at the clubhouse."

"Yeah, I don't think Wrath's gonna be okay with her living at the clubhouse."

"He'll come around." He sits back and watches me for a few seconds. "How bad you think this is gonna get with Merlin?"

At the moment, my opinion of Merlin couldn't be lower. But I try not to let what he did to Charlotte bleed into my opinion on a club issue. "Not sure. He's an asshole. I know that. Been after her from the jump to either get info on the club or drop me. Keeps trying to scare her away by telling her I'm dangerous," I explain.

"Is it like a daddy's girl kinda thing? He doesn't want to see his niece with anyone? Or specific to you?"

It's pretty fucking obvious Merlin doesn't give a single fuck about Charlotte's well-being. "It's about me being from another club. He doesn't give an actual fuck about her."

The front door opens and slams shut. "I don't think I've ever been in and out of there so fast," Charlotte says in a rush as she hurries into the kitchen. "Hey, guys."

She automatically hands Z her phone, and he wanders back out to the living room to do whatever he's going to do.

I stand and pull her into my arms. "I'm sorry, Charlotte."

She wraps her arms around my waist and rests her chin on my chest, staring up at me. "I'm the one who's sorry for having such an asshole for an uncle." Her teeth sink into her bottom lip and her gaze shifts to the hallway. "I need to tell you some of the stuff I overheard. Z should hear it too."

My jaw clenches. What the hell did her uncle say?

"What's that, sweetheart?" Z asks, strolling into the kitchen and setting her new phone on the table.

He shrugs off the glare I throw him for the 'sweetheart' and focuses his gaze on Charlotte.

She pulls away from me, and gestures for us to sit at the table. "Do you need anything?" she asks Z.

He taps the side of his beer bottle. "All set. Thank you."

I pull out the chair next to me and she takes it. "Okay. So when I got there they were discussing my relationship with Teller, obviously." She rolls her eyes, making Z laugh.

Reaching over, I place my hand over hers.

"My uncle was certain he could get information from me about your club." She turns to me. "Whisper stuck up for you. Said you weren't dumb enough to share stuff with me."

"Go on," Z says, sitting up.

"Chuck—Merlin—wanted to know if they squeezed any information out of someone named Loco? About Ironworks. They said they couldn't because he's too loyal to Rock."

"That's how they said it?" Z asks.

She blushes and looks away. "Not exactly." She gives us the exact words, and Z chuckles.

"Rock will love that."

"Who else was there, Charlotte?" I ask.

"Besides Whisper and Chuck?" She pauses to think about it. "Keeper, Tiki, Hudson, a couple guys whose names I don't remember and one I didn't recognize at all."

"Not a full club meeting," Z says.

"Interesting."

"Supposedly this Loco guy is scared shitless of you," she says, raising an eyebrow at me.

Z bursts out laughing. A small smile tugs at the corner of my mouth. That's not a story Charlotte needs to hear.

"That's it. Oh, he gave Whisper shit for being in business with Wrath. Seemed disappointed he didn't have any information about whatever your club's into. Whisper said MC business was never brought into the gym."

"Whisper stood up to Merlin?" Z asks.

"He was pretty pissed that my uncle's trying to stir up trouble for no reason and cautioned them not to bug my phone." She nods at Z. "He warned them you'd search me for something like that."

Z snorts but doesn't deny it.

"It was so much to take in, and I was scared shitless the whole time." Charlotte taps her finger against her chin as if she's trying to remember another nugget of information. "Oh! Jesus. This was the most important part." She shakes her head as if she's frustrated with herself and I put my arm around her shoulders.

"You're doing fine."

Z glances at me and nods as if he's impressed.

"Whoever went to speak to Loco is from another club and they're trying to patch over to the Wolf Knights. Chuck's using that as some sort of test. Told them to go back and this time wear their colors in Ironworks so Loco takes it more seriously."

"Jesus Christ." I lift my gaze to Z. "Has to be South of Satan MC. That's why he's been cozying up to them."

"That's what I figured too. I think that's everything," she says. "If I think of anything else, I'll tell Marcel."

Z stares at her for a second before nodding. "Thank you, Charlotte. I'm sorry you're getting dragged into stuff that has nothing to do with you."

To say I'm shocked doesn't begin to cover it. Z doesn't apologize often or for much. He must actually like Charlotte.

She leans against my side, resting her head on my shoulder. "I tried to warn him my uncle would be an asshole."

That pulls a chuckle from Z. He stands and slaps my shoulder. "Yeah, when he wants something, nothing stands in his way."

Charlotte peeks up at me, her eyes full of so much heat, I'm close to kicking Z's ass out the door.

"All right," Z says. "I'm out. You staying here tonight?" he asks me.

I nod without taking my eyes off Charlotte, and Z slaps my shoulder again. "Walk me outside."

"Yeah, okay." I lean over and kiss Charlotte's cheek. "Be right back."

"Jesus Christ, you're fucking whipped." Z laughs and smacks my chest as we land on the sidewalk outside.

I don't bother defending myself because I'm okay with it.

"All right," he says in a more serious tone. "I'm taking her phone, so her place should be fine." He stares at the building a little longer and I hope that means since Charlotte came clean, he's willing to call off the whole "lets spy on Charlotte" escapade.

"Meet you here around ten?"

My face must show my disappointment.

"Listen, if it makes you feel better, I trust her. She did good remembering all that shit and it's obvious she's on your side."

"Thanks."

"Don't thank me yet. We're still setting those cameras up."

"I figured."

He steps closer and lowers his voice. "Honestly, I'm concerned. I don't like that he's willing to use her to get to us or that he's clashing with Whisper. Friction like that in a club can end up blowing shit over

78

all of us."

No kidding. We've lived through that before. "If he's really trying to patch over SOS, we're in trouble."

"Yeah, that could squeeze us right out of Ironworks." Z glances up and down the empty street before continuing his thought. "Empire's not an issue. We have enough connections to hold this territory."

"But we'd have another Viper's situation."

"Yeah, but worse because this time we wouldn't have Wolf Knights on our side."

"Fuck. Merlin's such a greedy dick."

"Sounds like Whisper agrees. That's good. He's been a member long enough that he's gotta have some sway with the others."

"Jesus, Rock's gonna kill me."

Z raises an eyebrow. "This ain't your fault, bro. Sounds like he's been putting this in motion for a while now." He glances at Charlotte's brownstone. "Shit, if you two hadn't hooked up, we might not have realized the extent of this until it was too late."

Logically, I know he's right, but I'm not ready to pat myself on the back just yet.

Z's not finished talking me into placing the cameras. "What if they try to bug her apartment next? Think of it as a way to keep her safe."

Reluctantly, I agree, even though when Charlotte finds out we've been spying on her, it could ruin everything we have.

"It's not her fault." It's a lame response, but it's all I got.

Z isn't unsympathetic, but we both know whose fault it is doesn't matter. He gives me a quick hug. "Call me if anything else comes up."

Charlotte's in the living room when I re-enter her place.

"What's the verdict?" she asks as soon as I close the door behind me.

I'm going to spy on you.

"Nothing. Z appreciated the details. You helped us out a lot."

"Good. That's what I...Marcel, I meant what I said. I choose you."

I close the distance between us and sit next to her, pulling her into my lap. "Yeah?"

I don't deserve her words, but I need to hear them again.

Her uncertain eyes meet mine briefly. "There's no choice. It's always going to be you." A soft smile curves her lips and she peeks up at me through her lashes. "I told you I'm Team Teller and I meant it."

I want so much to be worthy of her loyalty.

CHAPTER EIGHT

Teller

KNOWING I PLAN to betray Charlotte's trust first thing in the morning brought on a wicked case of insomnia. Having her curled up against me all night only made it worse.

I'm up early, fixing breakfast for her when she sneaks up behind me, wrapping her arms around my middle and pressing her warm body against my back. "I love finding you here in the morning," she says, her voice rough with sleep.

Glancing over my shoulder, I answer. "You sure?"

"Absolutely."

Still keeping one arm around me, she moves to my side and inspects the eggs and toast I prepared. "Are you trying to make me fatter?"

Reaching under her shorts, I grab a healthy handful of her bare ass and squeeze. "Yes."

She squeals and slaps my hand away, so I shove the shorts down past her ass cheeks and lay a few smacks on each one. "Now, stop talking trash about my girlfriend and eat your breakfast."

Slowly she turns her head and stares at me with wide eyes.

"Problem?" I ask, crossing my arms over my chest, barely keeping the smirk off my face.

Her mouth twists, and it's hard to tell if she wants to jump me or knee me in the balls.

"Keep looking at me like that, and you'll be eating breakfast with my dick in you."

She doesn't respond to that either.

My gaze travels down her body, taking in her rapid breathing and hard nipples.

"That's it." Is the only warning she gets before I advance. Taking her by the hips, I lift her and set her on the counter. I strip her shorts off the rest of the way and yank my cock out.

Instead of words, she uses her legs to show me what she wants, hooking them around me and pulling me closer. I fist my cock, dragging it against her pussy. Leaning in, I cup the back of her head, gently tugging her hair. "You're soaking wet. Should I put my hand on your ass every morning?"

She tilts her head and watches me from the corner of her eye like she's embarrassed or it's too much. My lips drag over her neck, and I grip her hair tighter. "Tell me."

Again, she responds with her body. This time wrapping her hand around my cock and guiding me to her. Grabbing her ass, I drag her to the edge of the counter and slam into her.

Finally, a sound leaves her lips. A soft grunt.

"That what you wanted?"

Her head falls back, and she closes her eyes.

"No, Sunshine." I gather her hair again and pull. "Eyes open."

When her gaze fixes on me, I drop my hands to the straps of her tank top, sliding them down her arms and pushing it down so she's bare from the waist up. All perfect creamy skin flushed red from her chest to her cheeks.

I lean down to kiss her, holding her in my arms while I thrust in and out with increasing speed.

More soft little noises escape her mouth, hot breath drifting over my skin. She tips her head back, exposing her neck. "What? You have to tell me what you want, Charlotte."

"Please." Her voice is nothing more than a ragged whisper. "I'm so close."

My hand moves between us, finding her clit and I drag my thumb in circles around it.

"Oh. Not. Yes." Nothing she says makes any sense.

I take my other hand and grip her jaw, tilting her head so I can taste her skin.

"Yes, yes." She squirms closer and fuck, I swear, I need three more hands to handle this hot as fuck woman.

"Put your hand on your clit," I growl against her ear, wrapping my arm around her.

Using my palm as a barrier to protect her windpipe, I gently squeeze the sides of her neck in pulses. Once. Twice.

Her whole body tightens. Bare inside her I feel every little flutter and squeeze. Her loud cries fill the room, and I have to take several deep breaths because I'm not ready to come yet.

"Look at me," I demand.

Her eyes are hazy and unfocused when she meets mine, but she smiles.

For a second I stop my frantic thrusting and squeeze the sides of her neck again. "You need to get fucked harder?"

"Yes," she breathes out.

"Say it."

"Fuck me harder."

I slam my hips into her and run my hands over her head, stopping to cup her cheeks and stare into her eyes. "That's my girl. All you had to do was ask."

She's too blissed out to laugh and knowing I did that to her sends a blast of heat down my spine. "If you want to come again, do it soon," I warn her.

She reaches up, wrapping her arms around my neck. Her fingers trail over my scalp leaving me with a shivery sensation. "Fuck. Charlotte."

Our mouths meet, lips and tongues sliding against each other, sloppy and frenzied. My hips jerk, coming so hard my vision blurs.

Both of us breathing hard, we pull back a few inches and stare at each other. I brush her hair off her sweaty forehead.

"You're legit gonna kill me, Sunshine."

"Thank you." Her voice is solemn when I was going for silly after so much intensity.

"For what?"

She shakes her head and drops her gaze. "For always knowing what I need."

I tip her head back. "I'm not a mind reader though. I need you to talk to me so I don't hurt you." Again, I try for levity and raise my arms flexing my muscles. "I'm a big brute, you know."

That finally gets a laugh out of her. She presses her palm to my chest and slides off the counter. "No, you're not. I trust you. You're...the sweetest, best...I love you."

I'm hot all over from her sweet words. I pull her into my arms and kiss the top of her forehead. "Your breakfast's cold by now."

"That's okay. I'm full of *you*."

I snort, and she giggles against me, then backs away. "Wow, we're a mess."

"Go grab a shower. I'll clean up and make something else for you."

Charlotte

MERCY JUMPS UP as soon as she sees me enter the restaurant. "Oh my God, come here," she says, holding out her arms. "I'm so sorry."

"Thank you."

We take our seats, and the waiter hurries over to pour me a glass of water. After he leaves we study our menus without speaking.

"Do you know what you want?" she asks after a few minutes.

"Honestly, I'm not hungry."

"Do you want to go somewhere else?"

"No."

She ends up ordering breakfast while I suck down multiple cups of coffee.

"I wish you'd let me come to the funeral," Mercy says.

God, that's probably the one thing that could've made the funeral even worse. Exposing my best friend to my degenerate family. "Trust me, you didn't want to be there. Hell, *I* didn't want to be there."

"Did your uncle at least treat Carter okay?"

I snort out a laugh. "He was a monumental asshole as usual." My lips curl into a smirk. "Marcel handled it."

She raises an eyebrow. "Mr. Bad Boy?"

"Stop calling him that."

"Sorry, I didn't realize it was that serious."

I nod, staring into my coffee. "He's it, Mercy." I give her a brief explanation of what went down at the funeral but leave out the parts about my uncle threatening Teller and spying on me.

"Wow. Your uncle's needed someone to put him in his place for years." She taps her spoon against her glass a few times. "I guess Marcel's not so bad after all."

"Even Carter approves."

She throws her head back and laughs. "Now *that's* saying something. He's never liked any of your boyfriends."

"Nope."

"Is he handling things okay? I know your mom had…issues, but he lived with her after all."

"It's been difficult."

She finishes and signals the waiter for our check. "So, my plan was movies and then eating an obscene amount of ice cream. Why don't we stop by and see if Carter wants to join us?"

"I'd like that."

The first thing she does when she sees Carter is throw her arms around him. "How are you, lil' bro?"

"Jeez, it only took my mom dying to get a full body hug from you, Mercy?" Carter says.

She pushes him away. "Don't make me regret it." She cocks her head. "I thought Charlotte said you had a girlfriend?"

He closes and locks the front door and follows us to Mercy's car. "Stop telling people Bianca's my girlfriend, would ya."

"What else should I call a girl you spend so much time with?"

"As platonic as it gets."

"Carter, do you bat for the other team?" Mercy asks sweetly. "Is that what you're trying to tell us?"

"Considering I've been trying to get in your pants since I was twelve, no."

I jam my fingers in my ears. "La, la, la, la, I did *not* just hear that."

Mercy laughs, not at all offended by my brother's candor. "Sorry, buddy. I still like my men a little more seasoned."

"That's all right. Wait until you get to cougar age and want some young man meat. I'm going to tell you tough shit."

"If I never hear my brother refer to himself as 'young man meat' again, it'll be too soon."

We banter back and forth like that all the way to the mall.

Carter ends up falling asleep in the middle of the movie. I don't have the heart to wake him, because if I had to guess, this is the first time he's slept since he found mom's body.

"Have a good nap, little buddy?" Mercy asks after the movie.

"Actually, yeah."

"Why don't you come home with me," I suggest on our way to drop him off at home. "I hate the thought of you staying in the house all alone."

"No offense, but I don't think I can tolerate listening to you and Teller going at it all night."

Mercy cracks up.

"We *can* control ourselves, you know." Except for fucking on the kitchen counter like we did this morning.

"Oh my God, look at her face, Carter. She's turning red. Are you picturing the sex God with the platinum tongue trying to convince you with his magic peen?"

"Sweet Jesus, would you let me out of the car before I hurl?" Carter groans.

Teller

CHARLOTTE'S SO LATE leaving the apartment she misses Z by only a couple minutes.

"Ready?" he asks.

"Oh yeah. Can't wait to spy on my girlfriend. Highlight of my fucking day."

He sets a hand on my shoulder. "It sucks. But you know it needs to be done." Z's words are sincere, so I can't even be mad at him.

After dropping his bag on the kitchen table, he pulls out what he needs. "Going to check for any other bugs first." He glances around. "She got a computer?"

"She takes her laptop to work with her."

"All right. Another time."

Great, something to look forward to.

I let him work as he scans her Wi-Fi first for any wireless cameras in the area. He pulls out his laptop and plugs it directly into Charlotte's router. "Nothing," he mutters.

"Good."

Ignoring me, he continues his search. When he's finished, he returns to the kitchen. "Help me set these up."

The heating grate in the entryway to her building turns out to be a real bitch to get loose. We end up scratching up the plate in the process. "No one's gonna notice unless they look too close," Z says.

"Be more careful inside her place."

The second and third cameras go in much easier. Z grabs my phone and sets it up so I can monitor the feeds. He also maintains access to it, which I can't say I'm thrilled about. "You have it backing up somewhere?"

"Yeah. Learned my lesson with Furious." All the surveillance video was backed up at the gym, so when Ransom burned it down, we had nothing.

"You can access it anytime you want this way." He shows me a few things I'm probably never going to remember then hands my phone back to me.

"I'll probably fast forward through the footage once a night or so to see if there's anything there."

"Fine."

Z doesn't make any of the obvious jokes one might make in this situation. About how I can be sure Charlotte's not cheating on me or how he can't wait to see her dance around in her underwear. "Thanks for not being a dick."

In a rare moment of seriousness, he says, "I don't exactly enjoy this, you know. But at least when you tell the club, they'll know you were being proactive."

"At least there's that," I answer dryly.

"And if Wrath kicks my ass for not bringing it to the table right away, you're covering Crystal Ball for me for a least a month."

Finally, something to laugh about. "Only if he doesn't kill me first."

CHAPTER NINE

Teller

STILL TORQUED FROM bugging my girlfriend's apartment, I need to do something constructive.

And if it sparks off trouble, I really don't give a fuck.

My first stop's the bank.

My next stop is the Wolf Knights MC clubhouse.

In the past, Whisper's talked enough about the club for me to know Merlin spends most of his days here.

On a weekday afternoon, the parking lot's deserted except for two trucks and three Harleys.

I knock at the back door all polite-like.

The door swings open and the brunette who tried to climb me like a fucking tree the last time I was here greets me. Her lips curl into a smirk that looks more deranged than seductive.

"Hello, Mr. Goody-Two-Shoes Biker." She sets one hand on her hip, drawing my attention to her nearly non-existent leather shorts. "Change your mind?"

"No," I answer with what little patience I have. "I need to speak to Merlin."

She gives me a once over—more business than personal this time—then opens the door wider.

"He's in his office," she says, pointing to a partially open door a few feet away. I follow her the short distance, almost knocking her over when she stops dead in front of me. "Merlin? There's someone here to see you."

"Teller?" Merlin stands. "Thanks, Mady," he says, dismissing the girl. "What's on your mind?" he asks, coming closer. His steps are short, almost hesitant.

Aw, is he scared of me?

He should be.

He glances at Whisper and Hudson who both shrug.

Whisper watches me with narrowed eyes. Even if he and Merlin aren't gettin' along right now, doesn't mean he's going to back me if this goes badly.

"Need to have a word with you," I explain.

Merlin gives me an indifferent shrug. "So, speak."

"It's a personal matter."

That finally prompts him to order Whisper and Hudson to leave the office.

"You got something to tell me about my niece?" he asks once they're gone.

"You could say that." I pull the thick envelope of cash out of my pocket and hold it out in front of me. "This is to pay off the rest of Charlotte's debt."

He frowns and snaps the envelope out of my hand. "She told you?"

"Yeah, she told me the *whole story*."

Merlin raises his chin, shooting a cold glare at me. "I suggest you adjust your tone when you address me."

I stare back, harder and colder until Merlin flinches and gives in. "I don't know what she told you—"

"Yes, you do." I lower my voice and take a step closer. "Your niece. Your own flesh and blood. What the fuck's wrong with you?"

He flinches again but tries to appear indifferent. "You know how it is."

"No, I really don't. Explain to me how you let your niece get raped in your clubhouse and refused to find the fucker and gut him."

I swear he pales as he steps back.

"Mind your own business."

"Charlotte *is* my business." I watch him carefully for a few seconds, thinking over what I'm about to say. "She's my old lady now. *Mine.* Get used to it."

His expression locks into cold, hard anger, fists balling up at his sides. Unfortunately for him, it doesn't intimidate me one bit. "You need to drop this. It doesn't concern you."

"You're dead wrong. Everything about her is my concern."

"Christ, Teller, it was fucking years ago."

"Why don't we find someone to rape *you* and in seven years let me know how you're feeling about it."

That only seems to make him angrier. "Find it hard to believe your club's willing to back you up."

"That's my problem."

"She's disloyal anyway."

"*She's* disloyal? Why the fuck *should* she be loyal to you?"

"I'm her fuckin' uncle, that's why!" he shouts. "Her father was my little brother."

"Yeah, bet he'd be real grateful to know how you took care of his girl."

"You don't know what the fuck you're talking about."

"Was she drugged and raped in this clubhouse or not?"

He clamps his lips shut, so I fire off another question. "Did she come to you for help and you blew her off or not?"

Ignoring both questions, he asks, "You tell Rock, her crazy, drug-addled version of what happened?"

I don't even bother responding to his attempt to discredit Charlotte. "This ain't about either of our clubs, and you know it."

He steps closer and lifts his hand. I think he's planning to poke me in the chest, but he takes one look at the glacial expression I'm wearing and stops. "You wanna take her on so bad? She's all yours. Have fun explaining why her brother's homeless."

"What's Carter got to do with this?"

"I'm fucking sick and tired of carrying that kid, and now that Cindy's gone, I don't have to. He can get the fuck out of that house."

"His *mother's* house. Because he was taking care of her," I remind him.

"Guess you don't know everything. It's *my* house. I let her live there because I knew she couldn't fuckin' keep a roof over her head otherwise and I promised my brother I'd do that."

"You're gonna kick your own nephew out of his house? Right after his mom died?"

"He's a fuckin' pussy who's never gonna be useful to anyone."

While Carter might not be MC material, he's a good kid. Hearing Merlin run him down makes me want to punch him in the mouth even more than I already did.

"You do what you gotta do, Merlin." I step back. "Tell me something, do you know who hurt Charlotte that night?"

He shakes his head, refusing to look me in the eye. "No. Don't believe the way she told it either," he says with zero conviction. "Never did."

"Yeah, well I do." I step closer getting up in his face. "You wanna know why Loco's so fuckin' afraid of me, Merlin?" I taunt in a voice just above a whisper. "I know that's been driving you crazy."

His jaw clenches, neck seizing with tension. "He's fuckin' nuts, that's why."

"He ain't that crazy. No, he saw what happened to a certain snake who hurt a woman I cared about." I pause and glance down at my hands. "Well, what was left of him."

"That why Charlotte's so bent on suckin' your dick? 'Cause you promised to get justice for her or some bullshit?"

I'm so done with this asshole and issue my final warning. "One way or another, I'm going to find out who hurt her. You better fuckin' pray that you didn't have anything to do with it."

Merlin's face darkens. "Don't you fuckin' threaten me."

"It's not a threat. I protect what's mine."

He stalks over to the closed office door and throws it open. "I think we're done here."

"Yeah. We are."

ONCE I'M IN my truck, I head straight to Charlotte's to give her a head's up about all the shit that's about to go down.

I don't make it that far. I'm crossing the Empire City line when my phone rings. I press the button on my steering wheel and the call comes over Bluetooth. Charlotte's anxious voice fills the truck. "Marcel, where are you?"

"On my way to your place. What's wrong?" I'm not sure why I ask, I can guess what's coming.

"My brother called. He said Chuck stopped by and told him he has twenty-four hours to get his shit and get out of Mom's house. Said to ask *you* why."

"Fuck." That fucker moved faster than I expected.

"I'll explain when I get there."

"Marcel," she says, drawing out my name. "What did you do?"

I take the exit that leads me into downtown Empire. "I'm almost there, Charlotte."

"Park in back. I left my car on the street."

"Thanks, Sunshine."

Her soft laughter soothes me.

Fifteen minutes later, I'm about to knock on her door, when she throws it open.

"What's going on?"

No way am I starting this conversation without kissing her first. I wrap my arms around her, pulling her against my chest. "First, kiss me."

She tips her head back, a hint of a smile playing over her lips. Her arms wind around my neck and I lean down, pressing my lips to hers, taking time to taste her, tell her with my body how much I missed her.

Before I explain I'm the reason her brother's now homeless.

Painfully conscious of the cameras in her apartment, a knot of guilt tightens my stomach.

A soft sigh eases out of her when we part. She rubs the back of her hand over my cheek. "What happened?"

"I paid off your loan to Merlin."

All softness vanishes. "Oh, Jesus Christ. I told you to let it go."

"Fuck that shit."

"I'm not some…gold digger who expects you to pay my bills."

"Trust me, I know you're not. It's not about that and you know it."

"Fine, how'd my brother get dragged into this?"

"Your uncle said some shit and I made it clear that you're my old lady. Let him know how I felt about the way he treated you."

She exhales a heavy sigh. "Marcel—"

"Someone needed to stand up for you, Charlotte. Even if it's too many years too late."

"Thank you," she says, her voice a rough whisper.

"He said if I was taking on responsibility for you, I could have Carter too."

"Shit." She bites her lip. "He wasn't planning to stay there much longer, but still."

"I'm sorry. I swear I never thought he'd get caught up in this. All I could think about was paying your uncle off."

"You really didn't have to do that, but thank you."

"I'll help Carter out any way I can."

"He's going to stay here for a few days. It'll be okay." She looks up at me again. "Your old lady, huh? There's a title I never thought I'd want."

I fit my hands over her hips. "But now you do?"

"Maybe."

"What can I do to convince you?"

"Kiss me?"

Holding her face in my hands so she knows there's no escaping, I kiss her with everything I'm feeling.

The whole time aware Z could be watching us.

CHAPTER TEN

Charlotte

MARCEL'S NO COWARD. As soon as my brother crashed his way into my apartment, Marcel explained what went down with Uncle Chuck.

Well, respecting my need for privacy, he gave my brother an edited version of what led to the impromptu eviction.

"Whatever, dude, it's cool. I didn't want to be there anyway."

"We can take my truck over tomorrow morning and get whatever else you need. I'll rent you a storage unit or something until you find a new place."

Carter doesn't argue. He seems too shocked.

"This is my fault, Carter. I'll fix it," Marcel promises.

It takes my brother a few minutes to come up with a simple, "Thanks."

Later that night, my tiny apartment's feeling more cramped than usual as I settle down and try to sleep.

Marcel pulls me into his arms, the hard length of him pressing into my back. "You smell so good," he says, nuzzling my neck.

"My brother's like five feet away."

"I think he knows we fuck."

I jab my elbow in his ribs. "Not funny."

He chuckles, jostling my body. "Can you be quiet for once?" he asks, lifting my T-shirt and grazing my hip with his rough fingers. "Hmm?"

"Guys," Carter calls out. "Just so you know. I can hear like every word you're saying. Teller, if you could not violate my sister tonight, that would be awesome."

I can't help bursting into giggles. Marcel rolls to his back, also laughing. "We need to stay at the clubhouse."

"That works for me," Carter yells.

"Shut up and go to sleep," I shout back.

The next morning's a little less awkward.

"Thanks for controlling yourselves last night," Carter says when he sees Marcel.

Marcel glares at him and scrubs his hands over his face before accepting a cup of coffee from me. He leans in and presses a kiss to my cheek, then joins my brother at the table.

"Sleep okay?" he asks Carter.

"Once I was sure you weren't going to maul each other, I slept like a baby."

"Christ," Teller mutters. "This is what I get for giving my sister such a hard time."

I laugh and pat his shoulder. "From what she's told me, you have *years* of big brother karma to work off."

"By the way." Carter points his fork at Marcel. "You could put a shirt on at the breakfast table."

Marcel slaps my brother's hand away. "Be happy I bothered with pants."

"*Eww.*"

Marcel sits back and chuckles, then winks at me.

"Talk about bad karma," Carter grumbles. "I got shot down by Mercy yesterday, evicted, and now tormented by my sister's platinum-tongued sex God."

"Shut up," I snap.

"Is that what you call me?" Marcel asks, sticking out his tongue and wiggling it at me.

"No. That's what Mercy calls you," Carter says.

"Both of you need to stop talking so I can eat my breakfast." I set a plate in front of Marcel and one on the table for me. As soon as I take my chair, Marcel grabs one of the legs and slides it closer, wrapping his arm around my shoulders.

"Now, why does your friend call me that, Sunshine?" he asks in a low voice.

"What did I tell you about fishing for compliments?"

They finally, mercifully shut up so we can eat in peace.

Checking the time, Marcel nods at Carter. "Hurry up. I want to get over to the house early and start loading up my truck."

Carter's fork clatters to the table, bit of scrambled egg flying every-where. "You're really going to help me do that?"

"Yeah. Unlike you, I don't just run my mouth to hear myself talk."

I SPEND THE rest of the morning helping Carter move the few things he actually wants to keep out of his mother's house and into a storage unit. The whole time we were at the house, Carter kept checking the road as if he was afraid Merlin would show up any second.

He didn't.

I get a text from Rock as I'm dropping Carter off at the apartment.

We have a situation.

That's code for "get your ass to the clubhouse now."

On my way.

Did Merlin contact Rock and tell him about our little chat? It'd be a bitch move on Merlin's part, but not exactly surprising.

"You're not coming in?" Carter asks.

"Can't. I need to get home."

The kid almost seems disappointed. "Thanks a lot for helping me. I really appreciate it."

"Least I could do after getting you kicked out."

"It's not your fault our uncle's an asshole."

He gives me a quick fist-bump, and I head to the clubhouse.

Murphy meets me in the garage.

"What's going on?"

"Something went down at Loco's."

"Why's that an emergency for us?" I guess it's not so unusual for us to help Loco out, but it doesn't normally require all of us sitting down at the table.

"Rock will explain it. I'll see you inside."

Z rides into the parking lot, and I wait for him. "Fun times," he greets me.

I hold up my hands before he says anything else. "I'm spilling everything today, right after Rock tells us what this is about."

"Thanks, brother." He cocks his head and flashes a slight smirk. "So, who's the little dude staying at her place?"

I shove him sideways. "You asshole."

He grins even wider. "Ease up, I was fast forwarding through and saw someone that wasn't you or her. I assume it's her little brother?"

"That would be Carter."

Z and I are the last ones to the table, which is unfortunate because Rock's in a foul mood. Not a good omen considering what I have to share with my brothers today.

He doesn't wait for everyone to settle down, he just jumps right into the problem.

"Loco called. He got paid a visit by two wanna-be bikers asking a lot of questions about us." His pissed-off glare lands on me.

"I can shed some light on that."

Everyone at the table focuses their attention on me, which I gotta say isn't real comforting at the moment.

I sit up, elbows on the table, clasping my hands in front of me.

Nothing less than the whole story will work here.

"Merlin's been trying to dig up information on what we're doing in Ironworks. He seems to still think it's in play."

"No shit," Wrath says.

"Fuck him," someone else adds.

"Well, when Loco didn't break, he tried to bug Charlotte's phone."

"When exactly was this?" Rock asks.

I swallow hard under the weight of his penetrating stare. "Day after the funeral. She lost her cell phone. Went back to get it and overheard some stuff."

At this point, the only sound in the room is the air moving in and out of our lungs.

Z raises his hand, taking some of the heat off me. "He brought me in right away."

Here's where letting Z know about the bugging will save my skin.

Wrath nods, but Rock doesn't seem as forgiving. "That so?"

"Yes, Prez." Z sits up, carefree attitude disappearing. He and Rock go way back and are tight, but in this room, Rock's the president. Everyone knows their place. "They're fucking stupid though. Put some two-bit app on her phone. Even if she hadn't overheard them, she probably would've noticed it."

"They place something less obvious somewhere else?" Wrath asks.

"Not that I could find. I went through the phone thoroughly. Just to be sure, I had her buy a new one. Did a full sweep of her apartment and found nothing else."

"And?" Rock prompts, knowing there's more to the story.

"Teller and I placed a few select cameras at her apartment."

Shit, I feel like an asshole when he says it. Not that my brothers will judge me or care. It only helps my case.

Finally, Rock lightens up and sits back. "She know about them?"

"No."

One corner of his mouth lifts in a wry, but not unkind way. "Good luck with that."

"What else?" Wrath asks.

"Well, it's South of Satan MC who went to visit Loco. Merlin ordered them to go back, this time wearing colors."

"Fuck me," Dex mutters.

Z lists the rest of the information Charlotte gave us one by one.

"Aw, Christ. Guess I gotta stop wanting to punch Loco every time I see him," Rock jokes.

"You think she was telling the truth?" Wrath asks Z, completely ignoring me.

"I do. She was real eager. Concerned with giving us everything. Didn't try asking questions about what she heard, just told us straight."

Murphy raises his hand. "From what I know about Charlotte, I believe her too."

"Big surprise," Bricks mutters.

"Knock it off," Z says. "I don't think I need to break this down for you like you're a five-year-old. SOS patching over to the Wolf Knights is a huge problem for us."

Wrath seems to be deep in thought, drumming his fingers on the table. "Whisper's never gonna go for that. He's been talking about wanting to move his club in a *less* risky direction."

"Whisper went toe-to-toe with him, from what Charlotte overheard."

"That's not good either," Rock says, echoing the concerns Z laid out the other day. He pulls out a burner phone and sets it on the table. "Christ, I guess I need to warn Loco he might be getting another visit."

As Rock says it, his phone blows up.

"Yeah?" Rock answers.

"Rock!" Loco's voice comes through the speaker phone loud and clear and crazy as ever. "I bagged some big game for you today. Need you and a few of your boys to swing by and take a look."

While I know Loco's always paranoid about our phones being tapped by law enforcement, his "code" sounds ridiculous and isn't that hard to crack.

"Was just about to call you. We'll be there in an hour."

Rock hangs up and shoots a glare my way. "You'll be joining us." He points in the direction of the garage. "Take the van in case we're bringing bodies back with us."

"Got it," I answer, not about to argue with Rock over anything at the moment.

"You gonna call their prez?" Wrath asks.

"What would you like me to do, look him up in the Outlaw yellow pages?" Rock shoots back. "Let's go see what we're dealing with first, then I'll decide how to handle it."

He runs down a short list of who he wants headed to Ironworks and gives instructions to everyone staying behind.

"Move," he orders.

"Prez, I'm gonna ride with Teller if that's okay," Murphy asks.

"No. I'm riding with him." He gives me a hard look. "I need more information out of him."

Super.

Murphy's not about to argue with Rock, so he heads into the garage with the rest of the guys.

Wrath and Z ride ahead of us, while Murphy and Dex take up the back.

Rock keeps me in suspense while I navigate to the main highway.

"There's more to your story, isn't there?" Rock finally asks.

"Yes."

"We'll deal with this first, and then we're going back to the table.

Today."

"Okay."

"You stick with me when we get to Loco's."

Loco meets us on the sidewalk out front. "Damn, forgot when all your boys are ridin' the whole neighborhood hears you coming." He holds out his hand and Rock takes it, pulling him in for a quick bro-hug. Something that seems to throw Loco off and make him happy at the same time.

"Thanks for calling."

"Who else am I supposed to call when a couple bikers try to rough up my girls?"

"Good point."

He leads us inside through a door under the front stairs.

"Never used this entrance before," Z cracks.

Loco turns and warns Wrath to watch his head. "Supposed to be a basement apartment, but I've found other uses for it," Loco explains.

I can only imagine what those other uses might be.

Inside it's dark and the faint stench of mildew clings to the air.

Behind us, there's a *thunk* and a string of curses from Wrath.

"Told you to watch your head," Loco says without a trace of humor.

Malik's perched on a small metal folding chair outside a closed door. He stands as soon as he sees us.

"How're our guests?" Loco asks.

"Quiet since our talk." Malik's gaze sweeps over us and he nods at Z and Dex.

"This fucker moved like lightning," Loco says, demonstrating some crazy move while Malik shakes his head. "Lucky you were here to take them down."

Rock turns and jerks his head at Z, Murphy, and Dex, indicating they should stay outside. Wrath and I follow him inside with Malik and Loco at our backs.

The two SOS members I met at the Wolf Knight's picnic are sitting on the concrete floor back to back, bound and gagged.

"I know it's not very original," Loco says almost as an apology. "I went for easy over artistic."

None of us bother to decode that.

"Oh!" Loco says, running out of the room.

Rock raises an eyebrow and Malik shrugs. "It's easier not to ask questions."

Loco returns with two South of Satan leather cuts.

"Well," Rock says, drawing the word out for maximum humiliation. "What kind of biker lets some gangster jerk his colors? You two even put up a fight?"

The fact that they're both still breathing tells me all I need to know about their dedication to their club. Only way someone takes my colors is over my dead body.

"I'll leave you boys be," Loco says. "Let me know when you're done so I can hose down the floor."

The younger kid, Sticks, if I remember correctly, starts squirming, trying to break free.

Rock tilts his head, indicating he wants me to move in and help with the persuasion part of the interrogation.

"All right. Here's what we know," Rock says. "You're working with the Wolf Knights to move into our territory."

Sticks drops his gaze and shakes his head.

"Don't fucking lie or this is gonna be an uncomfortable afternoon for you."

I crouch down and take their gags off. "Sticks, right?"

He nods while keeping his eyes trained on Rock.

"Who's your buddy?"

"Thumbs."

"Shut up," the other one hisses.

"Here's how this is gonna go," Rock says. "First one who tells me what I want to know, avoids getting a beat down from Teller."

Rock's a man of his word. First one to squeal will probably get hammered by Wrath or Rock.

"Yeah, you'll just have that one do it." Thumbs sneers and jerks his chin at Wrath.

"Now you're taking the fun out of it," Wrath says.

"How long you been a member, Sticks?" Rock asks.

He eyes Wrath wearily before answering. "Got patched-in this year."

"Their vetting process obviously needs improvements," Wrath mutters.

"This patch-over to the Wolf Knights. That something your whole club's voted on? Or is it just you two geniuses?"

Neither of them answer.

Rock nods at me and since Thumbs rubbed me the wrong way the second he opened his mouth, I slam my fist into his face.

His head snaps back, hitting Sticks. Blood trickles from his nose and he glares at me. "That the best you got?"

"Just warming up."

"My dad's planning to challenge our president in the next election!" Sticks shouts.

"Well, that explains how you got patched-in," Wrath says. "Daddy bought your way into the club?"

Thumbs starts laughing.

My boot lands on his leg. "What's so funny, jackass?"

"Guess he's not as dumb as he looks. Got it on the first try. Sticks ain't never been club material."

"Hate to break it to you, Thumbs, but neither are you."

Rock throws out his arm, keeping Wrath back.

"How many in your club are involved in this plan?"

"My father, uncle, and a couple other older members," Sticks answers.

"Jesus, selling out your blood *and* your club in the same breath," Wrath says. "I'm feeling a lot less concerned about these fools moving

105

into Ironworks."

Thumbs finally perks up and seems to realize one way or another this isn't going to end well for him. "If I tell you what you want to know, will you let me go instead of turning me over to my president?" he asks.

"Now you wanna bargain," Rock says. "How long has this been going on?"

"We were gonna patch over to the Vipers until your club took them out."

"So you went to the Wolf Knights?"

"Merlin came to us once you froze them out of Ironworks."

"Just Merlin?"

"He said he hadn't convinced the rest of the club yet."

Rock turns to Wrath. "Good to know."

"Guarantee Whisper was a hold out. He woulda recognized these punks for what they were right away."

"All right, let's fill in some details. You been messing with Loco's business. What else?"

"Dad's setting up a meth lab on the outskirts of Ironworks. We were trying to work out distribution through the Wolf Knight's network."

Wrath snorts. "They don't have a network. They do business with Stump's club and us."

"Maybe the Demons are branching out?" Rock suggests. "We'll deal with that later."

Rock gives the signal, and I haul Thumbs to his feet. Because there's no honor in beating a defenseless man, I untie Thumbs' hands, then plant my fists in his face and gut.

Since I'm still keyed up from not punching Merlin in his smug face yesterday and not fucking my girlfriend last night, beating the shit out of this little bitch is good tension relief.

He throws a few weak punches that only fire me up more.

Rock pulls me off Thumbs a few minutes later.

"I still need to call his president."

Thumbs spits at both of us and Rock punches him in the throat, knocking him to the ground.

Wrath pulls a cell phone from Sticks' pocket and flicks through it. "Who's your president?"

He groans and sits up. "Trip."

Wrath opens the door and calls Malik over. "Are you free to drive them out to the Ironworks line and drop 'em off for their prez to pick up?"

"What's wrong? You don't want 'em ridin' bitch with you?"

Wrath rolls his eyes, and it's probably a good thing we warned him ahead of time about Malik's cheery personality.

"Didn't you tell my brother you wanted to prospect for us?"

"Yeah."

"Then be glad I didn't ask you to lick my boots before loading them up."

I lean against the door and cross my arms over my chest. This should be good.

"You need help, Dex can go with you."

Dex's startled expression clearly says *what now?*

"Who the fuck you think carried their asses down here? I don't need Dexter looking over my shoulder."

"Great. You're big, can carry shit, and run your mouth. You want a cookie?" Wrath sneers.

"See," Loco says, strolling into the room. "Told you they'd get along great. It's like I got my very own *Wrath* salt and pepper shakers."

Wrath answers that absurdity with an angry growl and stalks back into the room.

Z steps up to deal with Loco and Malik, and I return to see what Rock needs.

"Give me your word this ends now," Rock says into the phone. "We roughed 'em up and we're keeping their cuts, but our guy's gonna dump 'em off at the border for you to pick up and deal with however you see fit."

I raise an eyebrow at Wrath who shrugs.

When Rock finishes, he doesn't even look at the two guys before walking out to talk to Loco.

"This should be handled. Their prez isn't too happy with them, but if you notice anything unusual, let me know."

"You got it. Glad I could help."

Rock holds out his hand. "Thanks for all your help, Loco. Appreciate that we can always count on you."

Behind them, Wrath wipes away a fake tear. I roll my eyes at him and he laughs.

Outside on the sidewalk, Rock pulls us in. "We still have business to discuss," he says, shooting me a look. "No detours. I want everyone back at the table."

My blood quickens.

In about half an hour, I have to decide how much of my girl's secret I need to share with my club in order to keep her safe.

CHAPTER ELEVEN

Teller

"WELL, THAT WAS a whole lot of fuckery," Rock grumbles as we trudge into the clubhouse. "Everyone at the table. Now."

As soon as everyone's seated, I focus my attention on Wrath. "Now, are you satisfied that we can trust Charlotte? Everything she said panned out."

Not used to the disrespectful tone, he takes a second before answering me. "Am I happy she came to you right away? Yeah. Do I *trust* her completely now? Absolutely not."

I stand, placing my hands on the table. "You motherfucker—"

Z's hands clamp down on my shoulders, pushing me back in my seat. I'd been so pissed I didn't notice him get out of his chair and move behind me.

Around the table, my brothers shift and murmur.

"Simmer down," Rock says, slapping the table.

Wrath—fucker that he is—sits back, folding his arms over his chest. His way of letting me know my outburst didn't faze him.

"Teller," Dex snaps. And Dex isn't one to usually snap. "Think about it for one second. If she's so quick to betray her club. Her blood. How can we ever trust her to be loyal to us?"

Nods and murmurs of agreement go around the table.

"Exactly." Wrath sits forward. "Despite what you think, I'm not trying to be an asshole here."

I slide my gaze over to Rock, who tilts his head, subtly asking if I get it.

Shit.

I just witnessed first hand a guy give up his club and his blood without hesitation. I understand where he's coming from.

Looking Wrath straight in the eye, I apologize. I'm still pissed. But I owe him that respect. "She has her reasons."

Wrath pins me with a help-me-to-help-you stare. "What are they?"

"It's...her story. And it's ugly."

Rock and Wrath share a look. "You gotta give us something, Teller," Rock says in the most mellow tone I've heard him use all day. "You know this."

"I...fuck." Everyone at the table has their eyes trained my way. Am I willing to do this? I'm so fucking torn between my feelings for Charlotte and my loyalty to my club.

"Rock, you know better than anyone how bad blood can fuck you over." I look around the table. "We saw it today. But almost every one of us has experienced in in one way or another. That's what binds us to the club and each other, isn't it? We'd bleed for each other."

"If you're wrong about Charlotte, you willing to bleed for it?" Wrath asks.

"Yes," I answer without thinking.

Silence.

If I'm wrong about Charlotte, I'll most likely get my ass kicked out of the club in a painful way. Considering my knowledge of the club's activities and my years of access to sensitive financials, I might not make it out at all.

"Give us something," Wrath says.

Ultimately, sharing this helps both Charlotte and my club. I just hope Charlotte sees it that way when she finds out I betrayed her.

Clasping my hands together in my lap, I stare at them for a few minutes. Remembering Charlotte's racing pulse and trembling body when she told me her story.

She didn't make it up.

"Her second year of law school, she went to a Wolf Knight Christmas party that was only supposed to be for family. They had another club there."

Rock shifts and sits forward, anticipating where I'm going with this.

"Which club?" Rock asks.

"She doesn't know or she doesn't remember. I'll get to why in a minute."

"Go on," Z encourages.

"One minute she was getting ready to go home. Next thing, she woke up in a bedroom half-dressed and…hurt."

"They roofied her," Sparky says.

"Someone did."

"In her uncle's club?" Wrath's tone is full of disgust. "Jesus Christ."

Fuck this hurts so bad. "It's fuzzy for her. She only remembers bits and pieces that don't make sense."

Knowing my girl went through this and no one was there for her, makes me feel powerless. Even though it happened before we even met.

Never again.

"Anyway, she went to the hospital. It was…bad." I can't lay out every single ugly detail for the club.

"She press charges?" Wrath asks.

I sneer at the question. "No. She went to her uncle thinking he'd handle it. Find out who it was and take care of it." I pin him with a serious stare. "The way this club would handle that situation."

"Right on," Stash mutters.

"And?" Rock asks.

"He refused." I swallow hard because this is the part that wrecked me the most. "Basically told her she probably enjoyed it. To stop making a big deal out of nothing."

"Son of a bitch." Murphy's fist knocks against the side of my chair.

"Ulfric had to be in charge then," Rock says. "He wouldn't have allowed that bullshit."

"It was the holidays. He was away, and Merlin refused to bring it to him when he got back. I'm sure he felt it would make him look bad in front of his brothers."

Rock shoots a glare Wrath's way. "Who else they do business with?"

"Fuck if I know. Stump's crew, but—"

"No," Rock cuts him off. "He wouldn't tolerate that either." He glances back to me. "Go on."

"That's it. Her mother didn't want to hear about it. Merlin's been giving her cash since her ol' man died, so she wasn't going to risk losing that." At least that's the only explanation I can come up with for her mother's shitty behavior.

I have to stop for a second. "Charlotte realized all their family-first stuff was nothing but bullshit. She may be outspoken now, but she grew up around the club. When he shut her down, she gave up." My lips twitch into a half-smile, thinking of Charlotte's brave 'fuck you' to the club that betrayed her.

"What?" Z asks.

"She couldn't push it any further, but she went back to school the next semester and changed her concentration."

"So?" Wrath asks.

I shake my head, but the smile stays on my lips. I really have it bad for this woman. "You don't get it, Charlotte went to law school to be a criminal attorney. She wanted to *help* her club. Believed the we're-an-innocent-club-of-Harley-enthusiasts-persecuted-by-the-cops bullshit. That was her way to contribute to the club."

"Fuck," Murphy says.

"Yeah, so after they betrayed her, she switched from criminal law to family law. Decided she'd rather help children than criminals."

I meet Wrath's stare. "Do you get it now? They weren't loyal to her, why the fuck should she be loyal to them?"

"If it's true, yes."

I don't even get the fuck you out of my mouth before he turns to Rock. "Is that something Hope can confirm for us?"

"Confirm what?" I snap.

Again, Z puts his hand on my shoulder, and I love my brother, but he's in danger of having his fingers broken if he tries to calm me down one more time.

"Teller," Z says in a reasonable tone. "All he's saying is that if she really did switch majors, it would make her story more solid and we'd feel better about trusting her."

"Yeah, but you better never piss her off, T, or she'll be ratting us out," Ravage says. He's laughing as he says it, but I don't find it one bit funny.

"Don't be a dick," Wrath snaps. "What he's talking about goes way beyond a stupid fight."

"Fuck you, Ravage," I snap, leaning over the table so I can stare him down. "She has plenty of information on the Wolf Knights. Coulda gone to the Slater County DA at any time and dropped that knowledge, but she never has."

"Good point," Wrath says. "If she was vindictive, she could've gone to the police or another MC a lot sooner."

"Sorry," Rav mumbles.

I fall back in my chair. "She split from them. Soon as she got a job, she started paying her uncle back. That fucker had the nerve to take her money after what he did."

Rock raises an eyebrow.

"After she confided this to me, and then with him bugging her phone. I went and paid that debt off," I explain. "Which made him kick her brother out of the house."

"Shit, little brother, you got yourself your very own Jerry Springer show," Dex jokes.

"What a fucking dick," Bricks murmurs.

Wrath's fingers drum against the table while he thinks everything through. "Let's see if Hope can confirm it. Where is she?"

"Probably right outside. We all know she can't stand to be away from her man for too long," Ravage says.

As wound up as I am, even I laugh.

"Ask her to come in," Rock orders Birch since he's closest to the door.

"How is she supposed to confirm it?" Stash asks.

"We'll see," Z says.

"Gee, Prez, feels like we've been having the women at the table an awful lot lately," Bricks jokes.

Rock's not in a joking mood. "This isn't exactly dinner table conversation. Keep in mind, we've asked our women to do an awful lot to help us out lately."

"I know. I know." Bricks holds up his hands. "Just kidding."

Rock's harsh expression transforms the second Hope enters the room. Birch holds the door open for her, then follows her inside.

"Hey, Baby Doll," Rock greets her.

Her gaze darts around the table, a shaky smile flickering over her lips. "What's up?"

Z stands, pointing to his chair. "Here, take my chair, Hope."

Rock nods at him and Hope rounds the table, sitting next to me. Z takes up a position behind Wrath.

Under the weight of all our attention, Hope fidgets and shifts in her chair. "Is everything okay?"

Rock covers her hands with one of his own. "Everything's fine. We need you to help us out with something."

"Of course." Her nervous expression settles into something more fierce and eager. Hope may not have understood the club when she and Rock started dating, but after the things we've gone through the last few years, there's no question of her commitment or loyalty to us.

It was Wrath who objected the loudest to Hope in the beginning. So, I have faith he'll come around on Charlotte. Eventually.

Wrath leans forward. "What was your major in law school?"

She scrunches up her nose. "You don't really declare a 'major' in law school. At least not at my school."

Wrath gives me a pointed look that Hope doesn't miss. "Is this about Charlotte?" she asks.

"No," Wrath answers.

Hope squints, clearly unconvinced. "You can concentrate in an area of law though. It's optional."

"Like what?" Z asks.

"Um, estate planning, that's what Adam's concentration was," she says, reminding me of her friend who handled my grandmother's estate. "I concentrated in family law. There's criminal law, civil litigation. That's just the few I can come up with off the top of my head."

"Okay." Z paces behind Wrath's chair. "Would that be on a transcript?"

"Yes. There will be a notation and you receive a separate certificate."

"What if you switched concentrations?" Wrath asks.

"I don't think there would be a notation about the switch." She seems to consider a few possibilities before continuing. "You could probably tell from the classes the person took. With a few exceptions, second year you can pick most of your course list. So that's when you might choose your area of concentration."

"Okay," Rock says. "So, if someone was going to, say, concentrate in criminal defense work, they'd start taking those classes second year?"

"Well, yes. But you're also required to take evidence and criminal procedure second year because they're such a big part of the bar exam."

"There any other classes you'd take for a criminal—"

"Sure," Hope says, cutting him off, her body vibrating with excitement. She rattles off a list of classes. "Then you have to do a clinical for practical experience. Like the P.D.'s office or the D.A. Depending on what experience you wanted."

Wrath leans over, snatching a piece of paper from the middle of the table, and scribbles a few notes.

"What'd you do, Hope?" Z asks.

Her cheeks flush. "Well, I wasn't sure what I wanted to do. My second year I took a wide range of courses. Evidence and criminal procedure were my favorite so I took advanced classes in those. Completed my clinical in family court."

"So, the criminal classes were a waste then?" Z asks.

She wrinkles her nose again like the question offends her. "Not at all. Family and criminal law overlap in some areas and the same rules of evidence still apply."

Z nods slowly, taking in her words.

"I could probably be more helpful if you told me *why* you're asking," she suggests, glancing at me, and then Wrath, Z, and finally Rock.

Hope's not stupid. Even though our faces give nothing away, she continues. "Charlotte graduated a few years after me, but—"

"That's not necessary, Hope," Rock says.

"Well, from the few times Charlotte and I have gone up against each other, I can tell you she's a skilled negotiator and knows the rules of evidence better than some judges do," she grumbles the last part which makes Rock chuckle and pat her hand.

Warmth spreads through my chest. Hope's not fooled by our blank faces. She knows what's going down, and she's sticking up for Charlotte.

"Thanks, Baby Doll," Rock says, eye-fucking her as if the entire club isn't at the table.

Hope tilts her head, staring at Rock with so much heat the uncomfortable level ratchets up another hundred degrees. "Am I dismissed now, Mr. President?" she asks in a husky voice.

"Don't start," Wrath warns.

Rock shoots a glare at him, but Hope's eyes never leave her husband.

"We're good, Hope. Thank you," Z says.

Before leaving, she reaches under the table and squeezes my hand. Not out in the open where the guys can see and rib me for it as soon as she's out the door. A quick reassurance and it means more to me than I even understand.

"Dick," Rock says after she leaves, leaning over to punch Wrath's arm.

Wrath attempts to dodge the blow, laughing the whole time.

"What?" Stash asks, which makes Dex and Z crack up.

"You never noticed?" Wrath asks. "When she calls him 'Mr. President?'" he forces out a poor imitation of a breathy-voiced Hope. "It's like her fucking mating call."

"Shut up," Rock snaps.

"When she calls him, *Rochlan*, in that voice you better watch out," Wrath snickers and ducks out of range of Rock's fist.

"No one needed to know that," Murphy moans.

"Assholes," Rock mutters. But the corners of his mouth are slightly tilted up, so I don't think he's all that mad.

Sure. If I said something like that about Hope, Rock would have his boot on my neck by now. Wrath says it, and it's funny.

"So? Does she pass?" I ask Wrath.

"Depends. Can we verify any of the stuff Hope said?"

Z takes his seat again. "Yeah. Easy. I'll hack into the school records and grab her transcripts. Take a look." He glances at Rock. "Have Hope look 'em over?"

Rock's shoulders lift. "Rather not."

At the end of the table, Sparky bursts out laughing. "I can't believe we're talking about Charlotte's transcripts. Like she's applying for a fucking job or something."

Wrath pins me with a stern stare. "She is. Teller's ol' lady."

CHAPTER TWELVE

Teller

I STUCK AROUND after church and drank one too many with my brothers. Our way of patching things up after a heated afternoon at the table.

"She's not like any other woman I've been with, ya know?" My words slither out slurred. Or maybe my ears are slurring. Don't know.

"Let me give you a tip," Wrath says, leaning in like he's about to toss some serious knowledge my way. "Don't say that to her. Ever."

"Why? It's a compliment."

"Doesn't matter. No woman wants to think you're comparing her to someone else you fucked."

"She knows I've—"

Z decides to add his two cents. "Take a few seconds and picture her with someone else."

Drunk as I am, my blood shoots to boil. Wrath points a big finger in my face. "See."

"Chicks feel the same way," Dex adds.

I paste on a cocky smirk. "I'm the best she's ever had."

Wrath snorts. "Yeah, that's great. Still, I'm warning you. You're inviting a shit storm of trouble if you say that to her."

Murphy's been quiet through this whole exchange. "Got anything to add, Mr. Perfect?" I ask.

He seems startled by the question. "Why the hell would you ask *me?*"

"Because you were a bigger whore than I ever was."

"Fuck you." He shoves me backward. "That's not even true."

"I think you're equally whore-iffic," Sparky says, laughing at his ridiculous joke.

Talking about Charlotte is making me miss Charlotte.

Earlier she said she and Carter were watching movies and eating pizza and I figured I should give them some brother-sister time without being in the way.

Since I'm in no condition to drive anyway, I stumble over to the bar.

Swan peers up at me, a slight curve to her pink lips.

"Haven't seen much of you lately."

"How you been, Swan." I definitely slur her name.

Without asking what I want, she plunks a glass in front of me and raises an eyebrow. "Jack and Coke?"

I nod and signal for her to stop at one finger of Jack. Her smile fades and she meets my eyes. "You seem happier lately."

"You think so?"

"Well." One corner of her mouth quirks up. "You're taking less Jack in your Coke these days." She takes in the way I'm slumped over the bar. "Or at least you *were.*"

"Yeah."

She touches my hand briefly. "Good. Where's your girl tonight?"

The fact that Swan doesn't seem to know about Charlotte and Trinity's spat, means Trinity hasn't told anyone. Something I'll have to thank her for later.

"Home."

I stumble back to the couch, throwing myself down and closing my eyes.

"Welterweight!" Wrath shouts in my ear. Fucker can outdrink every single one of us.

Someone—probably Sparky—sparks a lighter near my head and the sweetly distinct scent of marijuana fills my nose. "Wakey-wakey time to bakey."

Yup, definitely Sparky.

"Get that out of my face," I mumble.

The couch dips next to me. "You need a ride downtown?" Murphy asks.

I crack open one eye. "Why're you still here instead of home with the wifey?"

He rolls his eyes. "Because *you're* here for once. I didn't think you'd get shitfaced off two beers and pass out like a little bitch."

"It was more like ten cocktails," Sparky adds helpfully.

"I'm good," I say to Murphy, ignoring Sparky. "I'm staying."

"How's PT going?"

"Think I'm as good as I'm gonna get. Before you ask, yes, Violet cleared me to ride again."

Murphy wraps his arm around my neck in a light chokehold, pulling me closer. "What the fuck!? Why didn't you say so sooner?"

"Brother, if you don't let go, I'm gonna puke on you."

He releases me and shoves me back.

"Fuck," I grumble. I wait for my head to stop spinning before continuing. "She said it could help strengthen my knee and thigh more," I explain, running a hand over my leg.

"That's good." He grins at me. "Tomorrow?"

"I'll see how I feel."

"Weather's supposed to be clear the next two days."

"Don't badger me." I glance around. Sparky's baked and I doubt any of our conversation penetrated his stoner bubble. "Don't tell anyone else, okay?"

"Whatever you want."

I must drift out again, because the next time I open my eyes, Wrath's sitting next to me with Trinity in his lap. "Where'd you come from?"

"Well, hello sleepyhead," she says.

Wrath glances over. "I'm calling you *lightweight* from now on."

I crook my finger at Trinity and she leans down toward me. "What?" she whispers.

"Thank you for not…saying anything about what happened. With Charlotte."

She seems surprised. "It's done and over with, Teller. Charlotte and I talked it out. We're fine."

"I really like her a lot."

"I can tell," she says in a teasing voice. Her features smooth into a more serious expression. "She really likes you too."

"I'm gonna patch her and marry her."

Her lips curve up. "Well, she's certainly got pluck. I'll be proud to call her a sister."

It's probably just the alcohol tightening my throat, making it impossible to form a response.

Charlotte

"WHAT, NO DICKNOTIZER tonight?" Mercy teases as she sets a box of pizza on my kitchen table.

"You have *got* to stop with that."

Carter scowls in Mercy's direction. "Yeah, vulnerable ears in the room, you know."

She ruffles his hair. "Don't be jealous because your sister's getting it regularly."

"Do you actually hear the words that come out of your mouth?" Carter mumbles around a mouthful of pizza.

Her phone goes off and she ignores it, plopping into a chair and taking a slice of pizza instead. When it rings a second time, I raise an eyebrow.

"It's my dad. He wants me to get to know this big, surly fireman, but every time I try talking to him, I just want to punch him in the mouth."

"Sounds like love." I snicker behind my napkin and she throws a piece of crust at me.

"Shut up."

"Wait, is your dad trying to whore you out for votes?" Carter asks.

Not offended at all, Mercy shrugs. "Pretty much."

Carter wrinkles his nose. "Jeez, and I thought our biker family was fucked up."

"Politicians are just a different shade of criminal," Mercy says.

This conversation's making me uncomfortable for reasons I don't fully understand, so I get up and throw out my paper plate and start cleaning up the table.

I really miss Marcel.

Then, I'm mentally kicking my own ass, because dammit, I'm an independent woman who can spend a night with family and friends instead of my boyfriend.

"Earth to Charlotte. What movie do you want to watch?"

"Uh, pick out whatever you want. I'll be right back."

Weak. Fuck, I can't go more than a few hours without hearing his voice. I mentally berate myself the whole time I'm dialing his number and waiting for him to pick up the call.

He answers by slurring my name as a greeting.

"'Sup?"

"Are you drunk?"

"*Yesh.*"

I've never seen Marcel anything other than in complete control, and it's cute listening to him slur his way through our conversation.

"How was your day?"

"Action-packed," he says, then laughs.

"Is that code for club business?"

"Kinda. Hang on a second, I want to go upstairs so I can hear you better."

"Oh. Is there a party?"

"When isn't there?"

A few minutes later, it's quieter on his end. "That's better. What are you wearing?"

I can't help it, the corny question makes me laugh.

"Never mind. I'm gonna picture you in that pink-nipple-unicorn tank top."

More laughter spills out of me.

"I love your laugh, Sunshine."

"I miss you."

"Fuck. Murphy offered to drive me down there, but I thought you were doing family night with Carter."

"I am. He's out in the living room with Mercy."

"Oh. And you called me?"

"Told you I missed you."

"That's nice. I like that, Charlotte," he says, sleepiness creeping into his voice.

"Are you falling asleep on me?" I ask.

"Yes, but keep talking to me. Love the sound of your voice."

So, I keep talking until I'm pretty sure he's out.

"Love you, Marcel," I whisper before hanging up, missing him more than ever.

CHAPTER THIRTEEN

Teller

THE NEXT MORNING, Murphy—persistent little asshole that he is—bangs on my door. Early.

"You're lucky I was up."

I woke up about an hour ago with my phone plastered to my face and a wicked headache, wondering what stupid shit came out of my mouth last night. Advil cured my headache, but I'd have to wait until later to find out who I managed to piss off with my drunk ass.

"You look better than I expected after last night. He steps back. "How you feeling?"

"Surprisingly okay." I glance down at my hands, which ache. My knuckles are banged up, reminding me of all the shit that went down yesterday.

Murphy grinds his fist against his palm. A sure sign he's got something on his mind. "What?"

"No one's really up yet if you wanted to fire up The Ol' Judge without an audience."

"You're not gonna let this go, are you?"

The corner of his mouth twists into a cocky smirk. "No." A little more serious, he adds, "Just to the park and back."

"Let's do it."

We meet out front a few minutes later and he nods at my leathers.

The only reason my accident didn't turn more of my skin into road hamburger was because I'd been well-covered and even though it's a short ride and I'm sweating my balls off, I'm not taking any chances.

He waves his hand at the bike I've had since I was a teenager. "You gonna ditch this rat bike and buy something new?"

"Not yet."

I wait for him to say something about how there's no spot for Charlotte on the back, but he doesn't mention it.

"Everything's solid," Murphy assures me as I stare at both of our bikes. "Went through T-CLOCS this morning. But you can do it."

"No. I trust you."

It's not the tires, controls, lights or anything else making me hesitate. It's me.

Fuck.

Mounting the bike is easier than I expected. My leg doesn't protest the movement that still comes naturally. I straddle my ride and get reacquainted with my old, familiar friend. I go through checking the foot pegs, the turn signals, and adjust my mirror before turning it over.

"Park and back?" Murphy shouts over the combined rumbling of our idling engines.

My fear gives way to tingling anticipation.

As much fun as Murphy and I have had over the years partying, fucking, hustling, and fighting, one thing we bonded over early on in our friendship was our love of riding.

Even before we patched into the club, we loved to be on the open highway on the machines that we built and worked on during our off-hours. Together, we've ridden thousands and thousands of miles. We know each other's riding habits and can communicate with the rev of our engines.

I'm back in my element colors flying, wind in my face.

In some ways, not being able to get out on the open road has been worse than my injuries. The last few months, I tried to convince myself

I'd be okay if I couldn't ride again.

Fuck, I missed this. Experiencing every detail of my surroundings. The scent of earth and pine trees as we pass the gate and turn onto the main road.

Almost every day I drive a portion of this back-country road, but without my big, soundproof cage surrounding me, I'm free to notice all the things I've been missing.

A whiff of fresh cut grass, followed by cow manure hits my face and then it's gone. As we climb the mountain road that leads to Fletcher Park, the temperature drops at least five degrees.

The wind moving around me, my bike rumbling under me, my fear, the exhilaration, all of it melds together. My body and my senses are engaged, working together in a rhythm that both soothes and makes me hyper-aware of everything.

I'm alive.

We slow as we enter the park and pull into the overlook lot. I shut the bike down and pull off my helmet.

"How'd it feel?" Murphy shouts.

One thing became clear on the short ride up here.

I've never feared dying.

Not living has always been my biggest fear.

CHAPTER FOURTEEN

Charlotte

"CARTER'S STAYING AT his friend's house," I explain to Marcel over the phone. "My place is all clear."

"Why don't you come up here tonight?"

"Yeah?" I tease. "You want me up there?"

He lowers his voice until it's a sexy rumble over the phone. "You know I do."

I can't erase the smile from my face after we hang up.

He called earlier to tell me he'd finally gotten on his bike. Alexa's happy squeals in the background intensified the ache in my chest. Old Charlotte would be horrified to know how much I've come to love being with this man.

How much I miss him when we're apart.

I need to change out of my ratty lounge-around-the-house clothes, but I also want to finish what I was doing before Marcel called.

Since it'll take him awhile to get here from the clubhouse, I have plenty of time to do both.

The scent of lemons fills the kitchen as I slice through one after another. My metal citrus squeezy device isn't meant for this kind of abuse. "I really need a friggin' juicer," I mutter. Or I should just buy lemonade. I'm not sure why I got it in my head that making it myself was better.

A knock at my front door startles me so bad I almost slice my finger off.

That was quick.

"Marcel, where's your key?" I yell as I run to the door.

It's not Marcel.

"Hey, girlie. How you been?" Uncle Chuck says, using his bigger size to muscle his way into my apartment.

"Uh, come on in."

For a second, I stare at the entryway and consider running.

Outside. Where it's safe.

Come on. I'm being ridiculous.

I shut the door and turn to face Chuck. "What brings you by?"

"Need to talk to you."

"Okay," I answer, striding back to the kitchen.

Chuck follows. "So, you and your boyfriend are tight, huh?"

"Yes."

"Been telling him stories?"

Frankly, I'm surprised it took him so long to stop by and complain about the visit Marcel paid him. My fear seems to have ebbed away. A dangerous glibness taking its place. "Only true ones," I say over my shoulder.

I turn and he's practically on top of me. "Back up."

My attempt to assert myself seems to amuse him. His mouth slides into a half-smile that looks evil as hell.

He stares at me with too much intensity to be harmless. "Why would you tell him? No man wants a woman with your history."

My cheeks heat. "My *history*? You mean the history of how my own uncle set me up to get raped?" It's only a guess, but nothing about that night and the aftermath has ever made sense to me.

A flicker of something I can't identify passes over his face. "Most of the shitty things you think about me are probably true, Char. But that?"

Anguish or maybe regret turns his last words into a rough whisper.

"Well, the alternative is you allowed it to happen or lost control of the situation." I inject more venom in my voice. "Otherwise, how do you explain a big, powerful officer of an MC not keeping his own niece safe under his roof?"

His nostrils flare, but I'm not done. All the anger I convinced myself I'd let go of years ago rushes back with furious intensity.

"How *dare* you try to assert yourself in my life now. All because your overinflated ego can't stand me being with a man you don't approve of."

His lips twitch with rage. "You don't want to keep trying to unravel this, Char."

Anger shoots through my veins, making me reckless. "*Stop* trying to tell me how to feel about what happened. Every time you and Mom did that it was like being raped all over again."

He winces, but I keep going. "Who did it, Chuck? You must have some idea. Was it someone from the visiting club? One of your own? You? What'd you do? Offer me up as some party favor to one of your bros?"

Chuck snaps. Before I process what's happening, he backhands me across the face.

The blow knocks me off balance, and my side slams into the counter, knocking the breath out of me. The tang of blood fills my mouth.

Tears spring to my eyes.

"What the fuck?" I scream, hoping my neighbors are home and call the police.

Before it's too late.

"You smart-mouthed little bitch. You never listened or did what you were told. Even when you were a kid. My brother thought it was funny. His little princess mouthing off. He thought it would keep you out of the life."

I jolt with shock at the mention of my father. "What're you talking about?"

"I tried warning him if you didn't know your place it would only make things harder on you. People in our world see a mouthy little cunt and want to break her."

"Know my place? I don't *want* a place in your world."

"Then what the fuck are you doing with Teller?" he shouts in my face.

"He's nothing like you!" I yell back.

"You're fooling yourself, girl." He tilts his head, a sly smile forming on his lips. "Did he tell you how he got the last girl he was with killed?"

"Actually, yes."

His eyes widen. Clearly, he hadn't expected that answer, but he recovers fast. "I'm sure he didn't tell you the whole story. Only the parts that make him look good."

That's how little my uncle knows about Teller.

"Why'd you have to tell him all that? Were you thinking he'd restore your honor or just trying to make me look bad, Char?"

The wild anger pulsing through him scares the shit out of me. My hand slides over the counter, searching for the knife I'd been cutting lemons with.

Just in case.

My fingers curl around the blade, slicing through my skin. Lemon juice burns as it seeps into the wound. I whimper, but Chuck's too focused on my face to notice. He seems to think my pained cry is out of fear and twists his lips into a smirk.

He pushes me against the counter, into the corner where I'm trapped by his heavy body.

I might not remember what had happened to me years ago, but my body remembers and recoils in fear.

An image or maybe a memory dances at the edges of my brain.

He claps his heavy hands over my shoulders and shakes me. "Bad things happen to good people every fucking day. Why couldn't you leave it alone? Bury it and move the fuck on?"

"I did. I tried," I whisper. "You don't understand."

"Teller won't let this go. You know that, right? That what you wanted? Your man to come play big badass protector for you? Show me up in my own clubhouse? Thinkin' he's so much better than me, because he woulda handled it differently when he doesn't know shit."

"Not everything's about *you.* He had a right to know."

He sneers. "Why? You got some sort of disease? He's probably full of them."

Bile and shame rise in my throat, burning like acid. "You're disgusting," I spit out.

He presses in even closer. "And you're pathetic. Still complaining all these years later because some guy wanted to fuck your uptight ass so bad he had to knock you out to do it."

My stomach lurches and ice crackles through my veins. It's almost word for word what my mother's reaction had been. And no matter how much time goes by, my family's dismissal of what was done to me never stops hurting.

"*That's* why I told him," I spit out.

"What?"

"That's why I told him," I repeat, finding the strength to raise my voice. "So that when the day came he and his club would understand *why* I'd turn my back on my own family. Why you have never earned my loyalty or respect. And why you never will."

Like a rattlesnake, he strikes fast, slapping my other cheek. Pain explodes through my skull, but I don't have time to shout or fight back. "I don't have to *earn* your respect after everything I've done for you. You *give* it."

I close my eyes and shake my head. "Never."

The knife.

My fingers tighten around the handle.

"You won't survive in his club either. Always thinking you're too good to follow the rules."

"What rules? The rules where if I don't spy on people you bug my phone?"

That finally gives him pause. "I knew you overheard something the other day. And here I thought Keeper was just too stupid to load the app right on your phone."

"You don't have a shred of remorse for anything you do, do you?"

He moves in closer and afraid he's going to hit me again, the hand holding the knife swings wildly. The blade catches him between the ribs, but he keeps coming, forcing it in deeper.

Stunned, I release the knife.

His eyes go wide and he staggers back, falling to the ground. He grips the knife handle, blood pouring from the wound.

"I wouldn't," I rasp. "You pull it free, you'll probably bleed out."

He stares at me as if he never expected me to be capable of violence.

Never expected me to fight back.

Without taking my eyes off him, I pat the counter, searching for my phone and call 911.

But someone's already banging at my door.

I stagger to the living room and throw the door open.

One of Empire's finest stands there. "Miss are you okay? We had a call—"

My mouth moves, but no sound comes out. He takes in my wild eyes and roughed-up appearance and pushes into my apartment.

His gaze lands on my uncle slumped on the floor, blood pooling around him. The officer, who I now recognize as Marcel's friend, rushes into the kitchen, calling for an ambulance and backup.

I drop onto the couch trying to make sense of the last fifteen minutes.

My uncle losing his damn mind.

And I defended myself.

In the kitchen, Chuck feebly answers a few questions before passing out.

Another officer arrives and another. Then an ambulance.

"Miss," the first officer says. "Officer Hollister," he introduces himself, sitting across from me on my coffee table. "Can you tell me what happened?"

He looks at me more closely. "You're Teller's girl, right?"

"I'm a lawyer," I whisper.

Teller

ON MY WAY to Charlotte's my phone rings. Z's voice blasts over the Bluetooth when I answer.

"Where are you?" he shouts.

"On my way to Charlotte's. Why?"

"Get over there now."

"What's going on?"

The call drops as I enter downtown Empire. Lark Street's crowded with several cop cars. Lights flashing. An ambulance.

There's no time to call Z back.

An officer's blocking traffic from the section of the street that includes Charlotte's apartment.

"Fuck this."

I jerk the wheel, jumping the curb to make the sharp turn down the alleyway behind Charlotte's apartment. Throwing the truck in park, somewhat near Charlotte's car, I grab my keys and run through the alleyway to her brownstone.

"No. No. No." The chanting's coming from my mouth.

With each slap of my foot against the pavement, a question explodes in my head. Why didn't I stay here with her last night? Why wasn't I here earlier? Why'd I choose today to go for a fucking joyride? What the fuck happened? Is Charlotte okay?

Please let Charlotte be okay.

All my worst fears are confirmed when I burst out of the alleyway. The cops are clustered around the front steps to Charlotte's apartment, blocking anyone from getting too close to her building.

An Empire cop comes dangerously close to my fist in his face when he stops me with a hand to my chest. "You can't go up there."

"Like fuck I can't. My girlfriend—"

"Let him up," someone calls down. I lift my head and my cop-buddy Liam's staring down at me from the top step.

Pushing the other officer out of my way, I leap up the steps. "Where's Charlotte?"

Outside, the ambulance takes off, lights and sirens blaring.

"Liam, where is she?"

"Inside." He holds up a hand but doesn't touch me. "You need to get her a lawyer."

"What? Why? She *is* a lawyer."

"She said that."

"Is she okay?"

He nods. "Do you know a Charles Clark?"

Not recognizing the name at first, I shake my head, then stop myself. "Yeah, Chuck. Her uncle."

"What's their relationship like?"

"He's an asshole. Been up in her business since we started seeing each other."

Liam angles his body, pushing me closer to the stairway and drops his voice. "He suffered a pretty bad knife wound. Before he passed out, he said she did it."

"Is she okay?"

"She's hurt. She says he attacked her first and she stabbed him by accident."

"You questioned her while she's hurt?"

"Come on Marcel, I'm not a total asshole. EMS treated her. She refused to go anywhere or to call a lawyer. Once we got *him* out of here, I was going to call you."

Yeah, Liam probably assumed it was club-related, and I'd kill Merlin for hurting Charlotte.

He's not totally wrong.

"Where is she?"

"You can't talk to her."

"Is she under arrest?"

"Not yet."

"Liam, give me five minutes with her. I can clear this all up for you."

He stands back and cocks his head. "Something I need to know?"

"Let me talk to her first."

He looks away, out the front door. "Go ahead."

I rush past him into the apartment, barely noticing all the people crowded in the kitchen. My gaze narrows on Charlotte sitting on the couch.

"Marcel!"

I wrap her up in my arms. "Are you okay?"

She sits back and rage wells up inside when I see her split lip and reddened cheek.

"What happened?"

"Chuck. I thought it was you. He came in. We argued." She shakes her head. "It got out of control so fast."

I take several deep breaths, beating back the fury threatening to consume me.

Later. I'll kill him later.

"Marcel, I think they're going to arrest me."

Cupping her chin, I lean down, my lips close to her ear. "I need to tell you something. Please hear me out."

She turns, frantic eyes searching mine. "What?"

Keeping my voice low, I hold her wrists in my hand, careful not to disturb her bandaged fingers. "I'm gonna get you out of this. But you're going to be pissed when I tell you how."

She swallows and in an extremely patient way says, "Marcel. I love you. But I'm about to be arrested for attempted murder." She leans in lowering her voice to an urgent, but exasperated tone. "So, if you can get me out of that, I don't really fucking care how you do it!"

"Shh. Play along and pretend you knew about this the whole time."

She grits her teeth. "Knew about *what*?"

"After your uncle bugged your phone, Z and I placed some cameras in your apartment. He wanted to be sure we could trust you. And I knew it would help me prove to the club you can be trusted."

She laughs.

And laughs.

Nutty, breath-stealing laughter.

Christ, maybe her mind finally broke under the stress of all this crazy shit.

Breathing hard, she shakes her head and gives me a crooked not-quite-all-there smile. "Where?" she finally asks.

I point to the hallway. "One out there." I point out the other two in the living room.

"The bedroom?"

"No."

"Bathroom?"

"Fuck, no."

She tilts her head. The shock seems to have worn off. "You did it to make sure you could trust me?"

I cup her face in my hands. "No. *I* already trust you, Sunshine."

She exhales a heavy sigh and shakes her head. "Shit. I can't even be pissed, you sneaky bastard."

"I'm sorry. I hated doing it."

"Well, it looks like it's going to be the thing that saves my bacon." She nods at the door. "Call your buddy in."

CHAPTER FIFTEEN

Charlotte

"EXPLAIN TO ME again why you set up hidden cameras in your apartment, Miss Clark?" Officer Hollister asks in a bored, disbelieving tone.

"Chuck's been erratic since my mother died. I didn't trust him. In the past, he's had people spy on me. I was afraid he or someone working for him might try to break into my apartment." I point to the front windows of my apartment that extend from ceiling to floor and shrug. "It was a precautionary measure."

"A proper deadbolt or locks on the window might have been a cheaper choice," he says dryly. "But continue."

He slides his patient, professional cop stare from me to Marcel, where it turns into more of an I-know-you're-both-full-of-shit glare. "I suppose you installed the cameras with your girlfriend's permission?"

"A buddy of mine did. But I helped him." Marcel rubs his hand over my back. "Chuck hasn't been thrilled about us dating. Wanted to make sure she was safe."

"Uh-huh." Liam grunts. "Right." He jots down a few notes and glances up again at Marcel. "This buddy have a name? One of your *brothers*, I'm guessing?"

"Angus Frazier," Marcel supplies and I realize I had no idea what Z's real name was.

Liam ducks his head, speaking into the radio at his shoulder. "Who's the guy out front?"

He listens to the low static that I can't make out at all.

"Send him in."

Z's filling up my doorway a few seconds later.

"Have a seat, Mr. Frazier," Officer Hollister says, nodding to one of my kitchen chairs that had been dragged into the living room earlier.

Before sitting, Z observes the scene around him. How close Teller and I are sitting. The injuries on my face and hands. I narrow my eyes and glare at him a little. In response, his mouth gives the barest hint of a twist.

"What can I help you with, officer?" Z asks in a disinterested tone.

"You place some equipment in Miss Clark's apartment recently?"

Z doesn't skip a beat. "Yup."

"At her request?"

"Yup."

"The purpose?"

"A safety precaution."

He asks Z more technical details. While Officer Hollister was able to view the video of my uncle bursting into my apartment and our argument leading up to the stabbing on Marcel's phone, the police want to have their own copy to examine. Z makes arrangements to provide it to them.

Officer Hollister stands. "Miss Clark, you're not under arrest, but I'm going to caution you not to leave the area. Officially this is still under investigation."

Marcel's arm tightens around me. "I'm bringing her to my place, but it's still in Empire County."

"That's fine."

Marcel stands and shakes the officer's hand. "Thank you."

Officer Hollister jerks his head toward the door. "Let's talk."

Marcel leans down and kisses my cheek. "I'll be right back." He and Z share a look and a nod before Marcel follows his friend out the door.

Z sits up. "You okay, Charlotte?" The concern in his voice seems genuine. I don't detect a hint of remorse for spying on me though.

"As good as one can be after getting attacked *and* finding out my boyfriend and his buddy invaded my privacy."

There's that twist to his mouth again, like either he can't believe a female has the nerve to speak to him that way or he finds me entertaining.

"And if you say you did it for my own good, I'm going to kick you out of my apartment."

His mouth stretches into a wide grin. "Not for your good." He jerks his chin toward the door. "For his."

I cross my arms over my chest and wince at the pain in my hand. "What else do you want me to do to prove myself?"

Z seems to understand that by *you*, I mean the *club*. He leans forward, elbows on his knees. "Just keep doing what you're doing."

"Were you this suspicious of Hope and Trinity?"

He takes the nosy question in stride. "Trinity? No. She'd been with the club a long time. Girl's loyal to her core. Hope wasn't as much of an issue of loyalty as it was understanding."

"You didn't want her to inadvertently bring unwanted attention to the club," I say.

"Right." He touches his chest. "Personally, I like you. I think if you were a rat, you would've sold out your uncle's club a long time ago."

"Never occurred to me, honestly. I don't know what they're into. Never wanted to know."

"That's good. A good ol' lady doesn't ask questions."

I roll my eyes, and he laughs. "Hope's a lawyer. She never asks questions?"

"Don't know what she and Rock talk about in private. But in front of us? No."

"What are they talking about?" I gesture toward the door.

Without looking away, he answers, "Probably warning Teller not to retaliate against Merlin and let the police handle it."

My hand flies to my mouth. "Oh, shit. I hadn't thought of that."

His lips quirk. "A little naive for a lawyer who grew up around bikers, no?"

"Forgive me, I did take a few knocks to the head."

He doesn't laugh at my sarcastic tone. In fact, the humor drains from his expression, leaving one pissed off biker across from me. "Don't worry. He's definitely going to pay for that."

"Well, I did jam a knife into him."

Our conversation ends when Teller steps back into the apartment, closing the door behind him with a quiet click. Z raises his eyebrows and Teller subtly inclines his head. I watch the unspoken exchange, trying to determine what they're planning.

"What did he say?" I blurt out.

"Merlin's in surgery. Once he's stable, he'll be discharged from the hospital straight to Empire County Jail." Teller's gaze falls on me. "Liam's leaning toward self-defense. But it's not totally up to him. You might have to give another statement."

"I should probably have an attorney..." Mentally, I run over the criminal attorneys I know. Good God, I don't want to have to call David and ask him to help me.

"Hope can do it," Z suggests.

"Or I know someone if she can't, or you don't want to involve one of your friends," Teller adds.

"Thanks."

Teller sits next to me, taking my uninjured hand in his. "Tell me what happened now."

"What?" I gasp in fake shock. "Your video didn't have sound?"

Z chuckles. "No."

A key scrapes in the door and Z reacts as if we're under attack. "Relax. It's probably my brother."

"Hey, Charlotte—" Carter stops dead in his tracks. "What the hell?"

In all the craziness, I never called Carter to tell him what happened.

Carter eyes Z warily then Teller. "Hey, Teller. What's going on?"

"Relax, kid," Tellers says, introducing him to Z.

Z sits up and shakes Carter's hand.

"Jesus, Char. What happened?"

I glance at Teller and I think he understands I only want to tell Carter a portion of what happened.

I recite a carefully edited version of events, leaving out my rape seven years ago and the cameras.

"What the fuck? He must be taking Mom's death harder than we thought," Carter says when I finish.

Is *that* what brought on his sudden bout of craziness? Or something else?

Clearly uncomfortable around Z and Teller, my brother stands and paces. "So this was all about you and Teller dating?" He stops and glares at Teller. "I warned you something like this would happen. You swore you'd protect her!" he shouts.

Shocked at my brother's outburst, I open my mouth to defend Teller but he squeezes my hand and answers the accusation.

"I know, Carter. I should've seen this coming after the other day. I'm sorry," Teller says.

"Carter, I'm fine."

"There's more to this you're not telling me, isn't there?"

I duck my head. "No."

"Charlotte." The anguish in his voice makes me lift my head and meet his eyes. "What if someone else in the club comes after you?"

"I'm going to stay at Teller's place tonight."

His wary gaze shifts to Z and back to my face. "Are you sure that's a good idea?"

Teller seems to understand what my brother's afraid of better than I do. "Z's here to protect her, not hurt her, Carter."

Z flashes an impishly innocent smile. "Truth."

"The cops have his name," I add. "If I go missing, they'll know where to look," I assure my brother.

Teller and Z both choke on their laughter.

My brother isn't amused. His brows draw down in a scowl. "That's not funny."

"She'll be safe at our clubhouse," Teller says. "Chuck's supposed to be transferred to Empire County Jail, but you can come too if you're worried about him."

"He doesn't give a shit about me," Carter says.

"You don't want to stay here," I warn him. "The kitchen's still a mess."

"I'll go stay with Bianca." He gives me a hug. "Call me later."

After he leaves, Z chuckles and glances at Teller. "Now I understand why you like him so much."

"Thanks for not shooting him," I mumble.

Z seems offended. "He's just worried about his sister. Although I hope he has some skills to back up that mouth. Not everyone he runs into is gonna be as understanding."

I shake my head. "Not so much."

Teller lifts his chin. "Good call not mentioning the cameras."

"It would've traumatized him to find out you…" I say, nodding at Z "…watched him sleep all night long."

Z laughs. "I wasn't watching twenty-four-seven like a fuckin' creeper."

"There's more to it than what you told the cops, isn't there?" Teller asks. "Now that it's just the three of us, what did you leave out?"

My gaze darts between Teller and Z. "Personal, family things."

Thankfully, Z takes that as a cue to leave. "I'm heading to the clubhouse. I'll let Rock know what happened. Tell the guys you'll be up later so we can sit down at the table."

I don't like the sound of that at all. *Sit down at the table* is obviously biker code for *discuss how to kill Merlin*. I hold my tongue until Z leaves.

"Talk to me, Charlotte," Marcel says, running his hand over my hair. "I'm so sorry I wasn't here."

"Don't, Marcel. It's not your fault."

"Yes, it is. Carter's right." He flicks his gaze across the room. "I almost fuckin' lost it when I saw the cops in front of your building." He holds me against him, and I soak up his comforting warmth for a few minutes before pulling away.

Where to begin?

"He was pissed that I told you about what happened. Told me you wouldn't want me because of it."

"Fucking asshole." He stares down at me. "You know that's not true."

I acknowledge that with a nod. "I pushed him. Hard. About the truth of that night. He had to know who it was or have some clue, but it only made him angrier." Bits and pieces of what Chuck said click into place and my stomach lurches.

"What's wrong?"

"Nothing." Composing myself, I begin again. "He said I was pathetic for still thinking about it and I said *that's* why I told you, so you'd understand why I didn't respect him or have any loyalty to him when it came time to choose."

"Sunshine," he croaks, holding me tighter.

"He lost it. I thought he was going to hurt me again. You know the rest."

Violence shimmers in his eyes. And I know exactly what it means.

Someone touched me. Hurt his woman. Marcel's planning my uncle's death as we sit here.

Gently, I touch his arm, pulling him out of his trance. "Marcel, don't. Please don't do anything. I'm okay."

He meets my eyes and gently rubs his thumb over my bruised cheek.

"In no way is this okay. He hit you. Hurt you."

"Well, I did stab him. So, I think we're even."

He doesn't crack a smile. "Honestly, his club will probably punish him before I even get the chance."

"What? No. Whisper wouldn't—"

"Something like this brings too much unwanted attention. Makes him seem unstable. They might view him as a liability."

My uncle's words come back to me.

"You don't want to keep trying to unravel this."

I hope there's time to pull the truth from my uncle before his club has him murdered.

Teller

WHEN WE ARRIVE at the clubhouse, everyone's clearly heard about Charlotte's attack. Hope and Trinity meet us in the living room.

"Rock's waiting for you," Hope says. She leans in closer and in a lower voice adds, "I'll take her back to our house and keep an eye on her while you're at the table."

My throat tightens, and Hope wraps her arms around me for a quick hug.

"Teller! Let's go!" Z barks from inside the war room.

I give Charlotte one last kiss before Hope and Trinity lead her out of the clubhouse.

Z smirks when I step in the room. "Waitin' on you, brother. Bricks, Dex, and Birch are down at CB. I'll fill them in later."

"One of you better fill me in now," Rock growls.

I recount the story and when I get to the part about Charlotte plunging a knife in Merlin, Wrath lets out a low whistle.

"Go, Charlotte," Murphy mutters.

"This was all over what happened to her seven years ago? Why is it suddenly an issue for him?" Rock asks.

"Carter suggested it was grief from his mom's death, but I don't know."

Rock taps the table in front of him. "What do you want to do?"

"He hurt my girl." My fists tighten. "I want to fucking rip him apart."

"Wolf Knights will get to him first," Wrath says. "No way Whisper's gonna let that slide. They're probably at the table voting in a new president right now."

I turn to Rock. "If he makes it out alive, I want a piece of him."

"Done." Rock glances around the table. "Anything else?"

Z raises his hand. "I think we should all take a second and acknowledge the fact that Charlotte barely blinked when she found out we'd set up cameras in her apartment."

Rock snorts and then laughs. "Poor girl." He turns to me. "You explain it to her?"

"Yeah. She was pissed, but she understood. It also probably kept her from spending the night in jail."

Z shakes his head and laughs. "Girl's brave. Merlin knocked her around pretty good and she still had enough spunk to give me lip about the cameras."

"She did? When?"

"When you were talking to your cop buddy."

"He's not my buddy," I grumble.

"I didn't take what she said as disrespect," Z clarifies, glancing around the table. "She's opinionated and has a backbone. But she's also smart. She definitely understood the why of it."

"Good," Rock says.

Z shrugs and continues. "She wanted to know how hard we were on Trinity and Hope."

Wrath leans forward at the mention of his wife's name. "What about it?"

"Ease up. She was asking what else she could do to prove herself to us."

If it's possible, I love Charlotte even more. For her understanding of my world and her acceptance.

"You trust her?" Rock asks Z.

"I do, yeah."

"Glad to hear it," I say. "Because she's staying here with me for a few days."

Rock nods. "Good. Safest place for her right now." He glances at Wrath. "Reach out to Whisper and ask for a sit-down. We need to see where we stand with them before this goes any further."

"Yeah, okay."

On my way out, Wrath stops me. "I'm glad she's okay. Never expected something like this from Merlin."

"Me either."

Charlotte's swaying on her feet when I pick her up from Rock's house. Outside, she blinks at me and I rub her cheek with the back of my hand. "Hungry?"

"Hope fed me." She yawns. "I'm exhausted."

We don't say much as I lead her back to the clubhouse and up to my room. It's still daylight out, but I take her into the bathroom and strip her down. Try to keep myself calm when I find multiple bruises and marks on her body that her clothes kept hidden.

"How'd this happen," I ask, gently tracing the deep purple mark running from her hip to the top of her ass.

She turns and glances down. "Jesus, no wonder my whole back hurts." I stand and grab a bottle of Advil out of the cabinet, shaking a few tablets into her hand and giving her a glass of water.

When she's finished, I ask again. "How'd it happen?"

"He shoved me into the counter." Her bottom lip trembles. "I was trapped between him and the counter. I thought...I thought..." She drops her head, hair falling around her face. "I don't know. I was terrified. That's why I stabbed him."

Taking care to keep her injured hand dry, I lead her into the shower and clean her up.

"Is it okay that I'm here?" she asks.

"What kind of question is that?"

She shakes her head.

"This is where you're supposed to be. Right here with me. You're safe here."

Finally, she meets my eyes. "I know."

Like a zombie, she follows me out of the shower, lets me dry her off and slip one of my T-shirts over her head.

"You look good in that."

The corners of her mouth turn up just a bit.

"Bedtime. You can barely keep your eyes open."

Under the covers, she can't get comfortable. I pull her into my arms and eventually, she settles down.

"I'm so sorry, Charlotte." It's easier to say this in the dark. "Your brother was right. I should've protected you better. I saw how pissed Merlin was the other day. Claiming you only made him angrier—"

"Caveman," she teases.

"Stop. I'm serious."

She presses her hand against my chest and lifts her head. Her eyes glitter in the darkness. "No, *I'm* serious. I understand you better than you think, Marcel. You want to take this and twist it so that it's somehow your fault. And I'm not going to let you do that. The only one responsible for today is my uncle."

I hesitate, and she keeps going.

"Don't fight me on this, Marcel. I argue for a living. You're just going to lose."

How can I not laugh?

"I love you so much. I can't stand anything happening to you, Charlotte." My voice lowers even more. "I felt fucking helpless today and didn't like it."

"I know you're not used to it, but sometimes things happen we can't control."

"It's how we react to them that matters."

She laughs softly and lays her head against my chest. "Exactly. See, now you're learning."

"I want you to get your concealed weapon permit. I know a guy who can push yours through quickly."

She lifts her head. "What makes you think I don't have one already?"

"Do you?"

"Yes. I even have a fancy little revolver."

"Well, aren't you full of surprises?"

"It wouldn't *be* a surprise." She inches up and brushes a kiss over my jaw, down to my neck. "If you weren't so fascinated with my vibrator, you would've found the little gun safe in my bottom drawer."

I growl and gently roll us, pushing her back flat to the mattress. "Is that right?"

She loops her arms around my neck. "Yup."

"I'll have to investigate better next time." I turn my head, taking in the space I've called home for years. "Or have you move in with me."

"Here?"

"Why not?"

"I don't know. Would your brothers really approve? Especially after today?"

I roll to the side, but keep my arm around her waist. "Today's not your fault either."

"It's still going to drag your club into something with the Wolf Knights."

"No one's going to blame you for that."

She yawns, and I kiss her forehead. "Get some rest. We'll talk more about it in the morning."

A few minutes later she stretches out on her stomach. I run my hand over her hair and down her back until her soft snores tell me she's out.

I lay there, one arm resting on my chest, the other behind my head and stare at the ceiling, thinking of everything that happened and everything that's coming.

Sleep evades me and eventually, I give up. Charlotte's sound asleep and safe here.

The clubhouse is dark and mostly quiet as I pad down the stairs. Light spills out from under the war room door.

Looks like I'm not the only one up.

At this hour, it used to be Rock we'd find in the war room. Since he's in his own house now, it's probably Z.

There's also a light next door in the office, but that doesn't register for me right away. I open the war room door, expecting Z to be at the table.

Instead, I get an eyeful.

I recognize Hope first. Or rather her long hair cascading down her bare back as Rock strips off her sweatshirt. She's sitting on the table facing him and they're obviously about five seconds from fucking. He leans over her, pushing her down against the table, then catches sight of me.

One hard *get the fuck out* stare is all I need to snap me out of my shock.

I jump back and quietly shut the door.

"What're you doing up, bro?"

"Shit!"

Z's standing by the office, corners of his mouth turned up in a smirk.

"Nothing much. Just been traumatized," I whisper loudly, as I stride over to him.

He waves his hand, inviting me to follow him inside. "Rock came over earlier to talk. Hope followed a little later. They're going through some stuff. Thought I should leave them alone."

"Next time hang a sock on the door or something to warn the rest of us."

"Aw, nothing you haven't seen before, little brother."

"That's different." I shake my head. "I'll never look at our table the same."

"Christ. On the table? Figured they'd do it on his throne, or one of the couches—"

I cut him off. "Can we *not*."

Z chuckles. "What's got you up?"

"Take your pick."

"Rough fuckin' day." He drops into his chair and one of the dogs pops out from under the desk and sets his head on Z's leg. "Wrath set that meeting up with Whisper."

"When?"

"Tomorrow."

"I want to be there."

"You think that's a good idea?"

"Come on, Z. Give me some credit."

He sits, stroking his hand over Zipper's head for a few seconds. "Seems unimportant now, but I looked into those transcripts."

"And?"

"It fit her story."

I grunt in response. Never expected different.

"I've been thinking about who they might have been in business with six or seven years ago."

I raise an eyebrow, surprised Z's still interested.

"You think it's possible he set her up?" he asks. "Some way to get in with another club?"

"After today, anything's possible with that asshole."

He nods and works his jaw from side to side as if he's contemplating whether he should say what's on his mind. I brace myself. Z's not one to second-guess giving his opinion.

"Is it possible *he* did it?"

"Fuck. Not gonna lie, it's crossed my mind." I run my hand over the back of my neck, considering how much to share. "At the hospital, she was told there was more than one."

Z sits back and sighs. "Jesus. Any man who thinks that's okay to do to a woman deserves a bullet to the head." He points at the door with an imaginary gun and pulls the trigger. "One bullet."

I stretch my legs out in front of me, getting comfortable in Rock's office chair. "Now I understand why she didn't believe me when I told her we didn't tolerate that stuff here."

"Please. Clubhouse or college campus. Seems like that shit goes on *every*where lately. Some days I think *we're* the only ones who actually have a moral compass." He snorts. "Which is really fucked up."

"Agreed." I put my hand down at my side, snapping my fingers. Ziggy lifts his head and trots over to have his ears scratched.

"I'm patching Charlotte."

Z glances up. "She'll make a good ol' lady."

I take that to mean Z will vote yes. "Thanks."

"Give it a little time, though," he cautions.

"Because of this?"

"Because of everything." He pins me with a more serious stare. "Let her interact with the girls more."

"Oh, man," I groan, understanding what he's saying. "*Trinity* even said she's over it."

"I've known Trin a long time." Z's mouth quirks. "You know how it is. Talk shit about me, I'll let it go. Talk shit about my friend, I won't be as quick to forgive."

I snort at the truth of his sentiment. And I'd be pissed, except I know that down the road, he'll defend Charlotte the same way. Hell, he already announced in front of everyone that he trusted Charlotte.

After what Charlotte went through today, his suggestion might seem cruel, but no one gets voted into this club out of pity. Not even the old ladies. That's not how things work in our world.

Every person *earns* their place in the Lost Kings MC.

CHAPTER SIXTEEN

Charlotte

THE NEXT MORNING, I feel like someone worked me over with a baseball bat.

Groaning, I stretch and roll over, bumping into Marcel. "You're here."

"Where else would I be, Sunshine?"

"I woke up last night, and you were gone." I hesitate for a second, hating that I sound so needy. "Was everything okay?"

Marcel pulls me into his arms, and I take refuge against his warm, bare skin. "I couldn't sleep, so I went downstairs. I didn't want to wake you up."

"Oh."

Marcel must sense my unease or doubt. He brushes the hair off my forehead. "Look at me. I went downstairs and talked to Z. That's it."

I don't want him to think I don't trust him. Not after everything he's done for me. "I trust you. Yesterday was so—"

"Your uncle put a lot in your head. I get it." He throws the covers back and taps my leg. "Come on. You must be hungry. Let's get you fed."

"Ugh, if anything, I feel sick."

"Even more reason to get up and face the day."

"You're mean."

Marcel ignores my reluctance, and thirty minutes later I find myself downstairs about to sit down and have breakfast with Z, and two other brothers whose names I don't remember.

"How are you feeling today, sweetheart?" Z asks.

"Like a truck full of baseball bats ran me over," I answer as Marcel pushes in my chair.

Z seems to read the uncertainty in my expression correctly. "Charlotte, I don't know if you met him before, but this is Dex," he says, tipping his head toward the bigger guy sitting next to him. "And that's Ravage."

Both of them give me a nod and tell me they're sorry about what happened. No one even pretends that they don't know about my uncle's attack. It's oddly refreshing.

As we're finishing breakfast, Hope and Trinity join us.

After we go through the whole *how are you this morning* ritual, Hope asks, "Do you know when you can go back to your apartment?"

To my surprise, Marcel has an answer. "Liam is supposed to call me when her place has been cleared."

Trinity reaches over and squeezes my hand. "Let me know when, and I'll come over and help you."

"Thank you."

Teller

AFTER BREAKFAST, I meet Rock, Wrath, and Murphy in the living room.

"How's your girl?" Wrath asks.

Surprised that's his first question, I answer with a clipped, "Fine."

"You good?" Rock asks. His way of asking if I'll behave when we meet with Whisper.

"Won't say a word, Prez. Promise."

Z and the girls find us outside.

"You ridin'?" Z asks.

"Yup."

"All right, brother." Z holds out his fists for a bump.

"When did that happen?" Wrath asks.

"Murphy and I went out yesterday." My gaze moves to Charlotte. "Before everything…"

"Got it." Wrath holds out his hand and as I slap it, he pulls me in for a hug and smacks me on the back a few times.

Charlotte watches the whole scene with wide eyes and a hint of a smile.

"You taking this rat bike to our meet?" Z bitches. "Makes us all look bad."

Murphy and Rock share a look, but neither of them tell Z to shut up, so I guess that's up to me. "Fuck off."

Everyone—including Z—gets a laugh out of that.

Heidi meets us in the garage with Alexa and I hold my arms out for her. "Morning, baby."

She squeals and makes her usual morning happy noises along with clapping her hands. She's even happy to have Charlotte hold her for a minute.

"Are you sure you don't mind, Hope?" Heidi asks.

Hope waves off my sister's concern. "I'm meeting Mara for lunch, and she's bringing her daughter. Cora *loves* Alexa. They always have fun together."

"Thank you. I always worry she doesn't have any other kids to be around."

"I have an easy way to fix that," Z says. "I see three fertile couples right in front of me."

"Shut the fuck up," Wrath snarls, while everyone else laughs.

Murphy opens his mouth "I'm—"

"If you say you're working on it I'll kill you," I say, cutting him off.

Heidi rolls her eyes and turns to Hope. The two of them move away to talk without us bothering them.

Charlotte settles her hand on my shoulder. "You know eventually they're probably going to have more kids, right?"

"Not you too. What did I say about conspiring with him?" I point at Murphy who's shaking with laughter.

"I didn't even tell her to say that," he says.

The rest of my brothers can't hide their laughter either.

Z must deem me "healed" or some shit because he gives me even more grief when we get to my bike. "Look at that thing. Where the hell is Charlotte supposed to sit?"

Well that certainly quiets everyone down.

Charlotte glances at the single seat. "I'm fine."

"I've had it since I was a prospect," I explain to her. "It's seen better days. The other one, The one I crashed was newer and a lot nicer, I—"

She stops me with a hand on my arm. "You don't have to explain yourself." She leans into me and bumps me with her shoulder. "When you're ready, I'll go shopping with you and let you know what I like."

I wrap my arms around her waist and pull her close, sliding my hands down to cup her ass. "Is that right?"

"Well, my ass won't fit on one of those tiny pillion seats."

Leaning down, I brush my lips against her ear. "What did I tell you about trash-talking my girlfriend's ass?"

Her eyes glitter with mischief. "I don't remember. I guess I need another lesson."

I groan and close my eyes. This isn't the time for the painful erection only Charlotte can cause me.

She kisses my cheek. "Your brothers are waiting for you."

"You're evil."

No denials, only wicked laughter from my girl.

"Let's go!" Z shouts. Rock, Wrath, and Murphy are all busy saying goodbye to their women. "For fuck's sake, we're gonna be gone for two hours max. Not two months. Jesus."

We ride in our regular formation to a park that borders Empire and Slater counties.

Neutral ground.

Whisper's waiting for us with Hudson and Keeper.

"Rock," Whisper greets. The rest of us get a nod.

Instead of, Sergeant-at-Arms, Whisper's patch now reads President.

Whisper gets right to the point. "Appreciate you giving us time to sort this out."

"Our clubs have a long history of working together, Whisper," Rock reminds him.

He acknowledges that with a nod. "Merlin's been distracted." He slides his gaze my way. "It's been interfering in a few areas."

"Seems he's been a little too interested in our business lately. Both club and personal," Rock says.

"Merlin wanted in on Ironworks," Keeper explains.

"That why he's been bringing South of Satan MC into our territory?" Rock asks, staring Whisper right in the eyes.

Keeper shifts and looks away.

Whisper dips his head but doesn't acknowledge their interference in our business.

"That's a relationship Merlin was pursuing on his own," Hudson says, earning a stern look from Keeper.

"Where we at, Whisper?" Wrath asks.

"Voted this morning. We don't want any action in Ironworks. We got our own ventures we're committed to. But Merlin got us into some things and I need him to get us out," Whisper explains.

Rock glances at me and I let Whisper know what it's going to cost him. "That's fine. I need some answers from Merlin about a couple things, though. That gonna be a problem?" I ask.

"He's staying in lock-up for the time-being," Whisper says. "But when I can, I'll make him available to you."

"Is that acceptable?" Rock asks me, and I nod my agreement.

Whisper pulls an envelope out of his cut and hands it to me. "I think this is yours."

I recognize it as the money I gave Merlin to pay off Charlotte's loan and take it. "Thank you."

"We done here?" Rock asks.

I lean in and lower my voice. "I'd like to have a word with Whisper."

Rock nods, giving me the okay to speak to the Wolf Knights' President.

"He's got a few questions," Rock says.

Whisper jerks his head toward some picnic benches and we walk away from our brothers.

"You got something on your mind, Teller?"

"What other clubs were you doing business with six or seven years ago?"

Whisper stops, turning to stare at me. I shouldn't be asking about their club's business.

"What's this about?"

"What clubs would have been invited to one of your Christmas parties back then?"

He narrows his eyes at my persistence. "You need to give me some context, Teller."

"A party Charlotte attended."

His brow wrinkles and he takes a step back. "Someone hurt her? In our clubhouse?"

I nod once.

"Shit, Teller. I don't know. I'm always down in Florida that time of year."

Another dead end. "I figured you didn't know."

"Wait a minute." Whisper narrows his eyes. "You saying Merlin knew she got hurt? And never handled it?"

"That's what I'm saying."

He kicks the toe of his boot into the dirt a few times. "Fuck. I'll see if I can ask some of the other boys and find out."

"Thank you."

He holds out his hand and I shake it.

I guess Merlin lives to see another day.

CHAPTER SEVENTEEN
Teller

"YOU GOT A few minutes?" Rock asks after Whisper and his crew leave.

"Sure. What's up?"

"Need to talk to you for a bit. In private."

Well, that doesn't sound ominous or anything.

"Follow me back to the house." He nods at Murphy. "You too."

It's not unusual for Rock to ask us to stop by his old house. Bricks and his family rent the place now, but Rock kept his custom bike shop there. He and Bricks work out of the garage.

I haven't been there in a while now.

For the briefest second I wonder if I'm in trouble.

Murphy and I follow Rock. As much as I love this old bike, and have all sorts of warm, fuzzy, sentimental memories attached to it, the suspension is non-existent and I feel every bit of Empire's poorly maintained roads. Something I don't think I gave much thought to before my accident.

The gate at Rock's house is open and we ride into the driveway, stopping outside the garage.

Rock meets me at my bike.

"How's it feel?" A hint of amusement twitches at the corner of his mouth.

"Honestly, a little rough."

"We should probably find you something else."

Murphy claps a hand over my shoulder. "Nah, that piece of shit is older than he is. He loves that thing. He doesn't want to upgrade."

These two are definitely up to something.

Rock strides over to the garage and lifts the door. "That's too bad." He gestures toward the HD Low Rider S in the middle of the garage. "Had a weekend rider bring this in after some cager tapped the rear. Guy decided riding was too scary after that. I bought it off him, thinking I'd find a home for it."

Murphy moves around the machine, running his hand over the two-up gray leather seat with blue stitching and glances up. His raised eyebrow and subtle smirk communicate that I'm being set up.

"Am *I* the home for it?" I take a few steps closer, taking in more and more details. It's gorgeous and my fingers are already itching to wrap around the specially upgraded grips.

Rock shrugs, completely casual. As if this isn't a huge gift.

I'm stunned stupid.

"You like it?" Rock asks.

Like it?

Still too stunned to speak, I bob my head up and down a few times.

"I love it." Jesus, now isn't the time for my throat to tighten up and my words to get lodged in my throat. "Thank you for thinking of me."

He slaps my shoulder and pulls me into his side. "Always thinking of you, knucklehead."

Now that my brain's starting to function again, I narrow my eyes and take in more details. All the custom modifications that just happen to be so perfectly tailored to my tastes.

"Someone traded this in?" I ask.

Rock senses the suspicion in my tone and smirks. "Yeah."

"And it just happened to be club colors and have all the mods and upgrades I'd pick out for myself?"

He gestures to Murphy and shrugs. "Murphy and I might have made a few adjustments."

"Rock, this must've cost a lot. Let me—"

He stops me with a hard stare. "Are you rejecting a gift from your president?"

"No, but it's too much."

He shakes his head. "It can never make up for…everything, but it's my way to say I'm glad you're riding again."

Way too many emotions bubble up inside me to respond. I turn to Murphy instead. "How long you been helping him with this, you sneaky ginger?"

He just laughs.

"Actually, we can't take all the credit. The whole club helped."

Yeah, since no one asked me to withdraw any funds, I know the guys paid for this out of their own pockets. Or more likely Rock paid for it out of *his* own pocket and is giving the club credit so it doesn't seem like a big deal.

"You can leave the XR here. I'll have someone trailer it up to the property for you." Rock says.

I cock my head. "You sure you're not going to junk it on me?"

"Didn't even cross my mind," he says with a smirk. "All kidding aside, I'll take care of it."

"Are you going to show it to Charlotte?" Murphy asks.

I'll admit, after the shock wore off, sharing this with Charlotte was the first thing that came to mind. But the thought of having her on the back—having *anyone* I care about sitting there again—still leaves me uncertain.

"I don't know if I'm ready for that yet. Baby steps, Prez."

He pulls me in for another hug and slaps me on the back a few times. "Go ahead. Give it a try."

Eager to get my hands on it, I flip the switch and start it up. "Sounds great."

I straddle it and mess around with the gauges, get comfortable with the seat and foot pegs. "You coming, Prez?"

"You two go ahead, I have a few things to take care of here. Tell everyone else to be ready to sit down at the table when I get there."

Murphy starts his bike. "Ready?" he shouts over the combined noise of our engines.

I am.

This ride's a completely different experience. Much smoother. Just as loud, but a more deliberate rumble.

On the way back to the clubhouse, I notice a "for sale" sign at the end of a long driveway. Instinct has me signal to Murphy that I'm turning in and he follows.

He pulls alongside me. "What the fuck?"

I get his concern. Showing up unannounced in someone's driveway in rural New York, is a good way to get an ass full of buckshot.

Still, we keep going.

Ahead, a large farmhouse comes into view. White with green trim. A three-car garage to the right. A smaller house and another outbuilding farther back.

No cars in the driveway. No one on the porch with a shotgun.

We shut our bikes down. "What're we doing here?" Murphy asks.

"I wanted to see what's down here. This place is close to our property. Never really noticed it before."

"Some yuppies from the city probably own it."

I point to the front door. "Looks like it's in foreclosure."

"Then they probably stripped the place bare before they got kicked out."

We walk around the house, checking out the garage and other buildings.

"What's on your mind?" Murphy asks.

"Just curious. I want to look it up on an aerial map. See if it butts up against our property line."

He shrugs.

"Let's go back and look it up."

THE RIDE BACK to the clubhouse did a lot to clear my head. Because we stopped off to look at the house, Rock makes it to the clubhouse before us. We back our bikes into line and Rock meets us.

"Where'd you two go?"

"Took the long way home," I answer before Murphy spills. For some reason, I want to keep my interest in the house to myself.

Charlotte's still out with Heidi. Sparky and Stash are waiting upstairs, and we all file into the war room to sit down and discuss what we learned this morning.

Rock silences everyone by rapping his knuckles against the wood table. "All right, had our talk with Whisper. He's been voted in as president. Merlin has had his officer patches stripped, but they haven't kicked him out of the club yet."

"That's fucking bullshit!" Dex explodes.

"Simmer down," Rock says. "Not our call to make."

"They gonna let Teller have a piece of him?" Ravage asks.

"When the time's right."

Wrath sits forward so he can see everybody. "Whisper claims Merlin pulled the club into some deals that not everyone was on board with. He says they need him to get out of those deals." Wrath turns to me. "What did you guys talk about?"

My gaze slides to Rock before answering. "I asked him to try to get some information for me. I gave him an idea of what happened. He was pretty upset. I don't think he knew. He was going to look into it." My hands tighten into fists in front of me. "I'll fuckin' beat it out of Merlin if I have to. Charlotte needs to know the truth. And that fucker's hiding something."

"I wouldn't let her go talk to him alone."

"Wasn't planning to." By the look on Wrath's face, it's obvious Charlotte's safety isn't his only concern. "She won't try to finish the job if I explain that his club needs him breathing for the time being. Obviously, you know we can trust her."

"No, I don't," Wrath says. He gestures to everyone at the table. "None of us have spent a lot of time around her."

"Whose fault is that?" I shoot back.

Next to me Z places his hand on my arm. "Easy, bro."

"Hear me out," Wrath says. "We're taking a run down to Sway's next weekend. Bring her along."

Rock snorts. "We gotta stop using Tawny as some sort of old lady approval system."

"It will give her a chance to interact with the girls. And around another chapter." Wrath says, ignoring Rock's comment.

I hate like hell admitting in front of all my brothers that I'm not ready to have someone on the back of my bike yet. Instead, I nod. "She doesn't have a patch yet."

"I'll get her a T-shirt," Z promises.

Sparky raises his hand practically wiggling out his chair. "Boss! Boss, I want to go too."

All heads turn in Sparky's direction. "And leave your plants?" Wrath asks, and for once I don't think he's just being a cocky asshole.

"Stash can handle it for a couple days."

"You bringing anyone special, Sparky?" Z asks.

"No. I haven't been there in a while. Last time he was here, Sway said he wanted to set up a small grow opp for personal use. Figure I'll go down and help him with that.

"Sounds good," Rock says. He turns his gaze to Murphy. "You coming?"

We already know the answer, but it's nice of Rock to ask. "I was just there. I'm good, Prez."

Rock nods. "You and Heidi can hold down the fort."

CHAPTER EIGHTEEN

Teller

AFTER CHURCH, I grab Murphy before he runs off to find my sister. "You got a minute?"

"Yeah, what's up?"

Too many brothers are still in the clubhouse. I jerk my head toward the stairs. Murphy follows me up to my room.

He doesn't crack any of the usual jokes. Instead, he seems concerned. "What's wrong?"

Before answering I run my hands through my hair a couple times. "I'm not comfortable yet having Charlotte on the back of my bike," I say in a rush. Feeling like a fucking pussy here. Murphy nods in understanding and keeps the jokes to himself.

"Why don't we go for a short ride tonight when the girls get back?" he suggests.

"Yeah, I'd like that."

"That accident wasn't your fault, bro. No one's running you off the road while I'm around. I always got your back," Murphy says.

"I know you do."

"Charlotte even like to ride?"

"Shit, I think so. Guess we'll find out."

The door to Murphy's room slams shut. As Heidi and Charlotte's voices filter through, Murphy squirms. "Damn, these walls are thin," he mutters, staring at the floor.

"No fucking shit, asshole."

He sniggers and glances at the door. "Do you want to go for that ride now that the girls are home?"

It's almost as if he's worried I'll back out or something.

"Yeah, I'd rather go while it's still daylight."

Charlotte's standing outside my door about to knock when we open it. She takes a step back her lips curling into a smile. "There's a joke in here somewhere," she says. "And here I thought I'd have to worry about finding bunnies in your room, not Murphy."

Murphy gives my shoulder a have-fun-with-that pat. "Where're my girls at?" he asks.

Charlotte nods toward his room. "Alexa's still out with Hope. Heidi's in your room changing. She spilled milkshake all down the front of her shirt."

A growl erupts from Murphy and he leaves without saying anything else.

"Get in here." I pull her inside and press her up against the back of my door. Fitting my hands over her hips, I stare into her eyes. "You want to explain that bunny comment?"

Her lashes flutter and she looks away. "I was just kidding."

"Don't kid about stuff like that."

She loops her arms around my neck. "Sorry."

"Did you miss me?"

She nods vigorously. "Am I allowed to ask how the meeting with Whisper went?"

Having her pinned up against the door like this has my mind on things other than the Wolf Knights. "There isn't much to tell, honestly. They voted Merlin out as president. Whisper is in." That's something Charlotte can easily find out on her own, so I don't consider it club business I need to hold onto. "Your uncle is alive and well for the time being."

"That's good, I guess."

I raise an eyebrow. "After what he did? Really?"

"I'm not saying I want to have him over for Thanksgiving. But I still need to get some information from him." She looks away and softly adds, "He's unfortunately my last connection to my parents. To my dad." She shakes her head. "Fuck. I see this all the time with my clients. Some of my most abused children remain the most loyal to their parents. I never understand it. And here I am the same way."

I slide my hands over her shoulders and squeeze. "You have a good heart. And I love that about you."

She meets my eyes. "Thank you." After a deep breath, she prompts me to finish telling her about the meeting.

"I gave Whisper the gist of what happened to you," I say carefully, waiting to see what her reaction will be.

Her cheeks turn pink and she tugs on her bottom lip with her teeth. "And?"

"I got the impression he didn't know. He wasn't happy about it that's for sure. He promised to see what he can find out."

"Thank you."

Next-door, there's a thud followed by a rattling noise and then a steady thumping. "Godfuckingdammit! Seriously?" I shout, picking up a sneaker and hurling it against the wall.

Charlotte bursts out laughing. "Aw, it's sweet that they can't keep their hands off each other."

Groaning, I take her hand. "It is *not* sweet. It's fucking disturbing." I give her a gentle tug. "Come on. I want to show you something outside. I can't listen to this shit."

"Oh, I figured you'd want to rattle your own headboard." She barely gets the words out before they're swallowed up with her giggles.

I yank her closer. "After listening to that, I couldn't get it up if I tried."

More laughter. "Oh, I bet you could." She glances at the wall and wrinkles her nose. "Maybe not. Let's go."

More unholy noises burst out of their room once we're in the hall-way. "Jesus. Fuck," I grumble, hurrying down the stairs.

Outside, I walk her to the neat row of bikes parked along the fence and stop in front of the one I still can't believe is mine. "What do you think?"

"You bought this today?"

"Rock gave it to me." I shove my hands in my pockets and lift my shoulders. "It's like a 'glad you're riding again' present."

"That's some present." She studies it closer, walking around to the opposite side. "I like the paint. He must've put a lot of work into it. The blacked-out forks, brushed chrome. A lot of upgrades. The shotgun exhaust is nice." She leans down and runs her hand over the straight pipes. "High enough not to scrape every time you make a right-hand turn."

"And here I wasn't sure if you even liked to ride."

She wraps her arms around me, sticking her hands in my back pock-ets and tips her head back. "Is that your way of saying you want me on the back of your bike?"

"No, this is." I lean down and brush my lips over hers.

She pulls me closer. "I'd be honored," she whispers. "Whenever you're ready."

"Wanted to go this afternoon." I jerk my head toward the clubhouse. "Those two fuck monkeys were supposed to come with us."

"I heard that!" Heidi yells.

Charlotte and I turn to find Murphy and my sister coming toward us.

"You want me to tell you what *I* heard, little sister?" I shout back and laugh as Heidi's face turns red and she smacks Murphy.

"What did I tell you about that?" I say, punching his arm when he's within range. "I'm right next door for fuck's sake."

Murphy barely hides his satisfied grin. "I don't know what you're talking about."

"Fucker."

"Are we going for a ride?" Heidi asks, ignoring our whole exchange.

"I think that's the plan," Charlotte answers. She flicks her fingers at me. "Whenever they stop comparing the sizes of their cavemen clubs."

"Eww," Heidi groans.

"He's definitely the bigger caveman," I grumble. "But that's about it."

Heidi gags. "Make it stop, Charlotte."

"So, we doing this or not?" Murphy asks.

"We're going today?" Heidi's gaze slides to Charlotte. "You too?"

I glance at Charlotte to make sure she's still on board.

"Hell yes. I can't wait," she answers with more enthusiasm than I expected.

Heidi's bottom lip trembles and her eyes shine. "That's good." She throws herself at me and gives me a tight hug. After a few seconds, she lifts her head, resting her chin on my chest. "So you like the bike?"

"You knew about it?"

"Of course I did."

"Yes, it's perfect."

Heidi and Murphy end up running to Rock and Hope's for some gear. I take Charlotte inside the clubhouse.

"We don't have to do this right now if you don't want to," I tell Charlotte.

"I'm ready when you are."

I brush the back of my hand over her cheek, blood boiling at the marks Merlin left on my girl. "Do you trust me?"

"More than anyone, Marcel."

"Let's do it."

Opening the front closet, I search through extra jackets and other crap we store in here along with the club's massive gun safe. I pull out a leather jacket and hand it to Charlotte. "This should fit you." Her mouth twists as if she's doubtful.

"It's a little snug."

"You look hot as fuck. Here. Put these on too." I hand her a pair of leather gloves. "Shit, you need a helmet." Why didn't I plan this better, instead of doing everything half-assed?

The corners of her mouth twitch.

"Why are you laughing at me?"

"You'll see."

"I'm serious, you can't ride without it."

She rolls her eyes as if I'm being ridiculous. "Come on."

She takes my hand and leads me outside. Heidi and Murphy are back, waiting for us. Murphy's mouth twists, a little too smug for my taste. He hands Charlotte a helmet and she takes it. Not surprised at all.

By the looks of it, it's brand-new. On closer inspection, it matches the faded blue paint of my bike. Except the helmet is sparkly where my bike has a matte finish.

"Did you? What, how, do you know about this?"

Charlotte slips the helmet on and tightens the strap under her chin as if she's done this many times before. "Murphy asked me to meet him at the shop on Central Avenue a couple weeks ago to pick this out."

"A couple weeks ago?" I stare at Murphy with my jaw hanging open for a few seconds. "You didn't know if I'd ever be able to ride a couple weeks ago."

"You were always going to ride again," he answers. "It was just a question of *when*."

Shaking my head, I slip on my own helmet. "More conspiring between you two," I joke to hide the emotion welling up in my throat.

"Stop running your mouth. Let's go," Murphy says.

Even though it's new, the second I straddle the bike, it feels like home. Even better when Charlotte climbs on behind me.

She sits too far back, and I grip her legs sliding her closer, so her thighs cradle my hips. Having her wrapped around me, her body so warm against mine, sends my senses into overdrive and the ride hasn't even begun.

Charlotte

THE LOUD RUMBLE of pipes around me vibrates through my body. I wrap my arms around Marcel tighter, pressing my cheek against his soft leather jacket, inhaling his familiar scent.

"Park and back?" Murphy shouts.

Marcel gives him a thumbs-up.

Heidi reaches over and taps my bicep with her fist. I glance over and she mouths "thank you" to me.

We start down the driveway slow. It's a bumpy ride over the dirt, gravel, and uneven ground. It's really more rolling than riding. He slows at the gate. "You still okay back there?"

"Yes! Let's ride," I shout.

The roads out here aren't wide enough for the guys to ride side-by-side. Murphy takes up a position behind us. My hair blows all around my face under my helmet. I haven't been on the back of a bike since I was a teenager.

We pick up speed and I tighten my arms around him. I close my eyes, enjoying this feeling. Knowing that with him is exactly where I'm meant to be.

CHAPTER NINETEEN

Teller

W ITH THE VIBRATION of the new bike beneath me and my girl tight against my back, I'm harder than fucking steel when we reach the park. Instead of the overlook, I pull into the gazebo area where Wrath and Trinity held their wedding. It's not so I can reminisce. There are a lot of private trails through the woods and a small building with a public restroom.

"Why'd you stop here?" Murphy asks.

Heidi already ran over to the gazebo when I stopped, but I captured Charlotte's hand to keep her next to me.

"What? The view here is just as nice and there're fewer people."

His gaze strays to Heidi who's waving us to come join her.

"Give us a second," I say, tugging Charlotte toward the woods. "I need her to help me with something."

This section of the park is empty today, which is fortunate. I pull Charlotte into the men's room with me, locking the door behind us.

"What are you doing?" Her laughter echoes in the small space. "Do you need me to hold it for you?"

"I'm fucking you." I spin her around to face the sink and mirror and she braces herself against the cool, white porcelain.

"Murphy and your *sister* are right outside."

"I know," I say, unbuttoning her jeans and yanking them to her knees. "That's why I'm fucking you in here instead of bending you over my bike in the parking lot, which was my first choice."

I keep one hand on her hip while freeing myself.

Her laughter turns to a sigh as I drag my cock through her wetness. I lean in and kiss her neck. "Did the ride excite you?"

"Yes," she whispers, pushing her hot little ass into me and spreading her legs wider.

"Good, because I don't think I can be gentle."

She huffs out an annoyed breath and lifts her head staring at me in the mirror. "Stop talking and start fucking."

That's all the incentive I need to slam into her. My arm bands around her waist lifting her. She clings to the edge of the sink, holding herself steady for every quick thrust.

I slip my hand down to rub her clit determined to satisfy her before we leave this room.

"Fuck, just like that," she begs. "Right there."

"Shh, people outside."

She makes this grunting-growly noise that's sexy as fuck. "Harder."

"Fucking love the way you take my cock, Sunshine."

"Love the way you give it. Now fuck me harder."

I bury my face against her, scraping my teeth against her shoulder enough to make her shiver.

When I look up and meet her eyes in the mirror again, they're wild and desperate. I slide one hand up to her neck, and she tilts her head back, giving herself to me. Watching her reflection closely, I gently squeeze until her eyes roll back and her pussy tightens around me.

When she opens her eyes again, I kiss her cheek. "Was that good, Sunshine? You came so hard for me."

"Yes," she mumbles, still dazed.

I grip her hips with both hands. "Now it's my turn."

"Yes, yes, yes." And a bunch of other frantic sounds come out of her mouth.

My balls tighten, and streaks of white-hot pleasure shoot down my spine. I bury myself inside her, coming so hard my legs shake with the effort of holding us up.

We're both breathing hard and take a few seconds to slow our racing hearts. When I think I can function, I reach for some paper towels to clean her up.

She wiggles away from me. "Ouch, those are rougher than the fucking you just gave me."

I close my eyes and press my forehead against her back, trying not to laugh any louder.

"I don't know how I'm going to face your sister and Murphy now," she says, pulling up her pants.

"Serves them right." I clean myself up in the sink. "Was I too rough on you?"

"No." She leans in, placing her hand on my cheek. "You're always perfect for me."

"Good."

We kiss and I groan into her mouth. "Careful or I'm taking your pants off again and this time you won't get them back."

There's banging on the door. Charlotte's eyes widen and her hand flies up over her mouth.

Moving her behind me, I open the door. But it's just Murphy wearing an exasperated expression. Charlotte slides her hand into mine but stays behind me.

"Seriously, bro? Your sister's traumatized now. I hope you're happy."

With my free hand, I pat his cheek.

"I don't know what you're talking about."

WHEN WE RETURN to the clubhouse a couple hours later, Trinity calls us into the dining room. The whole club's waiting for us. Whoops and shouts erupt from everyone.

Shaking my head, I move through the crowd, accepting hugs and handshakes from my brothers until I reach Trinity.

"Was this your doing?"

"I had some help."

"You're embarrassing the shit out of me, so I hope you at least made a cake."

She laughs. "It's in the kitchen."

"I'll help you out, Trinity," Charlotte says, pulling her hand from my grasp.

First, we have dinner. The guys set up one of the long dining room tables, instead of the round ones we usually use so we can all eat together. There're plenty of questions about the new bike and the first ride.

Charlotte elbows me in the ribs, so I leave out the part about the bathroom sex at the park.

After dinner, Trinity and Swan bring out the cake. They even stuck a candle in the middle of it. "It's not my birthday," I protest.

"Sure it is," Rock says.

Shaking my head, I nudge Charlotte to help me blow out the candle, then turn and catch her lips for a quick kiss.

Her cheeks turn red when everyone heckles us.

I'm distracted by an incoming text.

"Everything okay?" Charlotte asks, peering over my shoulder.

I show her the text. "Your apartment's been cleared."

"I can imagine the mess they probably left it in."

"I have a photo shoot in the morning, but Heidi and I can stop by and help you afterward," Trinity offers.

Heidi nods. "That'll be fun. I'll finally get to see your apartment."

"Don't get too excited, your brother keeps saying it's a shithole."

Across the table, Z snorts.

Heidi leans back and reaches behind Charlotte to poke my arm. "You're so rude."

Alexa squeals and Heidi stops hassling me to pull her daughter out of her highchair, settling her in her lap.

"Your man tell you about the vacation he's taking you on yet?" Wrath asks with a wide smirk. He knows damn well I haven't had a chance to bring it up with Charlotte.

"Vacation?" Confusion strains her voice, and she turns to me with a raised eyebrow.

"We're running to our downstate charter next weekend and I want you to go."

"Oh." Her gaze pings across the table, studying Wrath for a moment before answering. "Sure. Who else is going?"

"Most of us."

"Not me!" Ravage calls down to us. "Someone needs to stay and guard the homestead."

"Guard the pussy is more like it," Z grumbles loud enough for everyone to hear.

"It's a difficult job, but someone has to do it," Rav shoots back.

Trinity covers her mouth and cough-laughs. "You're going to *love* Tawny."

"They run things a little different than we do up here," Hope adds. "But it will be a good time."

"Way to sell it, First Lady," Murphy jokes.

Charlotte turns to Heidi. "Are you guys coming too?"

"We were just there not that long ago. And I'm not comfortable bringing Alexa down there."

"I'll be here to guard the fort and keep Ravage in line," Murphy says.

Later that night in the room when we're alone, Charlotte asks, "This is a test, right? Can your old lady behave in front of another club?"

She says it with a smile, but I sense the unease under her words. "I'll be there. Hope and Trinity will be there too. You'll be fine."

"I'll make you proud."

My chest tightens. "I'm already proud you're my girl. Now I just want to show you off."

CHAPTER TWENTY

Charlotte

To my surprise, Trinity and Heidi show up early the next day to help me clean up my apartment.

"Hey, I didn't expect you for a couple hours," I say, inviting them inside.

"My model canceled at the last minute," Trinity fumes.

"You're the photographer? I assumed you were the model."

Trinity chuckles as she hands me a box of industrial-strength Hefty bags. "That's sweet Charlotte," she says as if she thinks I'm just trying to be a kiss-ass.

"I carry the equipment and help her set up the shoots," Heidi explains.

I vaguely remember her explaining this before and feel silly for not paying better attention.

The two of them check out my apartment, which feels weird. "Oh, I love that bed," Heidi says, peeking into my bedroom. "Murphy told me to start thinking about the furniture I want for the house, so now I'm noticing everything."

Trinity shakes her head. "I see lots of trips to furniture stores in Murphy's future."

"Uh, your brother bought it. You can ask him where he found it."

Heidi blinks. "I so did *not* need to know that."

I shrug. "Don't snoop then."

Trinity ends up herding us into the kitchen and handing out the cleaning assignments, which is kind of funny since it's my apartment. She has me scrubbing down the kitchen floor when I ask, "On a scale of one to ten, how worried should I be about this trip downstate?"

She stops and taps her finger against her chin, pretending to think about the answer. "An eleven?"

"She's not that bad," Heidi calls out from the living room.

In a lower voice Trinity explains, "She's known Heidi since she was a kid, so she likes to mother her. She's always had a soft spot for Teller. You're new to the club, so I'm sure she'll like you just fine."

I suddenly realize what Trinity's really saying. If Tawny's a more typical biker's old lady, and Trinity used to be a club girl, well, I don't need to ask more questions. "I'll make sure to stick with you and Hope."

She winks at me. "We'll keep you safe from Tawny's talons."

Heidi wanders into the kitchen, glancing down at her phone.

"Hope's at her office," Heidi says. "She said she'll swing by if we need any supplies."

"Tell her we're all set." Trinity chuckles. "Hope's not so much with the manual labor," she says with affection, not judgment.

"Rock's okay with his old lady not doing menial work around the clubhouse?"

Trinity raises an eyebrow. Opening my big mouth and inserting my foot around Trinity seems to be a common theme for me.

"You should probably spend more time with them," Heidi says. "They're totally relationship goals."

"She's very much his Queen," Trinity adds in case I don't get Heidi's Instagram-speak. "He doesn't want her waiting on anyone but him and even then, I think he prefers taking care of her."

"That's, uh, unusual for bikers, no?"

"Bossy, dominant, alpha men? Not really." Trinity shrugs. "Even if it is, our club's unique in a lot of ways."

"That's what I keep hearing."

"Now, Wyatt and I have a different relationship. I enjoy catering to him." She shakes her head and laughs. "*And* I don't want him messing around in my kitchen."

"He seems to appreciate it though," I say because if even Wrath makes me want to pee my pants every time he turns his scary eyes my way, I can't help but admire the affectionate and respectful way he treats his wife.

"He does," Trinity agrees.

I glance at Heidi who shrugs. "Murphy probably cooks more than I do. But I used to love helping out at the clubhouse as much as possible just so they'd let me hang out there."

I bump her with my shoulder. "Are you sure it wasn't to be near Murphy?"

I was teasing, but Heidi hesitates. "Yes and no. I just liked being around family and the club has always been family to me."

"I guess what we're trying to tell you," Trinity says. "Is that everyone finds their own place in this club and helps out in whatever way they can. Hope's most important job is keeping our president happy, so no one cares that she's not the perfect hostess."

"She does a lot of other stuff," Heidi adds. It seems to bother her that we're discussing Hope at all, which wasn't my intention.

"I wasn't saying she doesn't, Heidi. Her role just seems different than what I grew up around."

"Honestly," Trinity says. "I don't think it would even occur to Hope to do some of that entertainment stuff that old ladies like Tawny do."

"Oh," Heidi says. "Yeah, you're probably right."

I snort out a laugh. "I'm pretty sure that's *all* my uncle thinks women are good for."

"Well, obviously that is the more prevalent attitude among bikers," Trinity says. "I'm not denying that. Our club is different."

"Teller cooking in my kitchen makes more sense now."

"Aw," Heidi sighs. "All my nagging finally paid off."

Trinity laughs and flicks her with a dish towel.

"Actually, he told me that was all your doing, Heidi." I relay the story about the two of them watching cooking shows together when she was little and she blushes.

"That's true. I forgot about that."

My front door opens, and the three of us turn to see who it is.

Trinity reaches for something under her pant leg. Christ, she's probably carrying at least one gun on her. "It's my brother," I explain before she shoots him.

"Hey, Carter!" I shout.

He walks toward us, then stops. Poor Carter. While he's known Mercy long enough to be comfortable joking around with her, overall he usually ends up tongue-tied around women.

I rush over to meet him. "Who's the porn star?" he asks loud enough that I'm sure Trinity heard him. Behind me, Heidi giggles, drawing Carter's attention to her. "And the model?"

"Stop right there," I grumble, placing my hand on his chest. "That's Teller's sister and Trinity is an old lady." Under my breath, I add, "Don't you dare embarrass me."

His cheeks turn bright red. "Too late."

Letting out a frustrated huff of air, I turn to introduce him. Trinity seems more amused and charmed by Carter than anything. And thank God for that, because the last thing I need is Wrath hunting down my brother.

After the official introductions, Carter holds up a bottle with some unidentified chemical in it. "I brought this, it's supposed to help remove the fingerprint dust."

"Oh, thank you," Trinity says, taking the bottle out of his hand to study it. "That's a bitch to clean."

Carter's wide, puppy dog eyes following Trinity around earn him another smack from me. "Knock it off. I'm serious. Her husband's the club's SAA."

"What'd I do?" he asks with complete innocence.

A few hours later when the place is spotless—probably cleaner than when I moved in—and there's no sign a man had been stabbed in my kitchen, Teller and Murphy show up.

"Hey, Carter," Teller says, holding out his hand.

My brother gives him a cool look but shakes his hand.

Heidi runs over and tackle-hugs her fiancé, which makes Teller groan.

Carter grins, picking up on the dynamics in play immediately. "How's that karma tasting, *King*?"

"Is Wyatt with you guys?" Trinity asks.

Please say no.

"No, but he wants you to call him," Murphy answers.

Trinity steps onto my back porch to call her man.

Murphy squeezes Heidi's side. "I got your unicorn decorations."

"He dragged me to three party warehouse stores, Heidi," Teller grumbles. "You realize Alexa isn't gonna know the difference between a unicorn and a horse right?"

"Yes, she will," Heidi says.

Carter busts up laughing. "Oh, man. The scary bikers shopping for glittery unicorn party hats. That's priceless."

Murphy scowls, and I smack the back of Carter's head. "Knock it off."

I turn in time to see the *told you so* face Teller shoots at Murphy.

"We're having a big party for my daughter's birthday in a couple weeks. You should come, Carter," Heidi says, ignoring Murphy who glances down at her as if she's lost her mind.

"Uh, sure," Carter says. "Thank you, Heidi. Sounds like fun."

"Hey," Trinity calls out. "Wyatt needs me to come pick him up. I'm going to head out." She glances at Heidi and smiles. "I assume you'll be riding with Murphy."

"Does he need help?" Murphy asks.

"No, I have his truck." She turns and gives me a big hug.

"Thank you so much, Trinity. I never would've gotten this done without your help."

"No problem." She squeezes Carter's shoulder which leaves him tongue-tied. "Nice to meet you, Carter."

"Make sure he calls if he needs something," Teller says as Trinity reaches for the door.

"I will. Promise. Later."

"Shoot, I wanted to at least buy her dinner," I mumble after she whirls out the door.

"You can buy *me* dinner," Carter suggests.

"You didn't do anything," I tease.

"Murphy's buying dinner," Teller announces. "He owes me for the seventeen Party Warehouse trips."

"Two. Two stores. Stop exaggerating." Murphy's mouth curls into a wicked smirk. "How're you gonna get Charlotte to make babies with you if you can't go shopping for kid stuff without running your mouth?"

Heidi and I burst out laughing while my brother groans. "I don't need that visual."

"Don't you want a niece or nephew to spoil?" Heidi asks.

I'm not sure it's something Carter's ever considered. To end the awkward silence, I grab my purse. "I'm buying, but only if there's no more baby-making talk."

"That's all it is, Charlotte," Heidi says. "Talk. They really just like baby-making *practice*."

Now Teller's the one groaning. "For the love of fuck."

Heidi giggles and grabs Murphy's hand, dragging him out the door.

Carter stops me with a hand on my arm. "I'm gonna go...you don't want me tagging along."

"Sure we do," Teller says, inserting himself between us. "Murphy told me about this mural he wants designed for Alexa's bedroom and I told him you'd give it a go."

"You what?" Carter asks.

Teller ignores the question. "Fair warning, it probably involves a unicorn, a crown, and a four-leaf clover."

"Well, now I'm intrigued," Carter says, marching out the door.

Teller winks and slips his arm around my shoulders. "Thank you," I say, reaching up to kiss his cheek.

"You can thank me later with some *baby-making* practice."

CHAPTER TWENTY-ONE

Charlotte

FRIDAY EVENING, MARCEL arrives at my apartment a few minutes after me. I can't lie, I've been freaked out about this trip all week. But I packed my backpack last night, and I'm ready for a weekend away with him.

"Where is everyone?" I ask, locking up my apartment behind me. Not that I expected the whole club to rumble down Lark Street, although it would be impressive.

"Waiting for us near exit twenty-three."

"Everyone's held up because of me? I'm sorry."

He picks up one of my braids and flicks the end over my cheek. "It's not a problem. We all ride together."

I slip my backpack over my shoulders and hop on the bike behind him, clinging to his body.

We ride out of downtown Empire and meet up with everyone at a gas station next to the Thruway entrance.

"You good?" Marcel shouts.

"Yup!"

He circles the parking lot and pulls up behind Z. When there's a break in traffic, Rock signals everyone to move and we roll out.

It's a cool summer night, but I'm still sweaty when we arrive at the downstate club two hours later. My ass is numb and my legs don't seem to want to move for a minute. "You all right, Sunshine?"

"My butt fell asleep."

"I'll help you wake it up."

Chuckling, I use his shoulders to balance myself while I climb down.

He takes my helmet and sets it on the bike. "I'm all sweaty and gross. I'm going to make a terrible impression," I grumble, undoing my braids and finger-combing my hair.

He snorts. "You're surrounded by bikers."

Hope hurries over and wraps her arm around my shoulders. "Ready?"

"As I'll ever be."

I take Marcel's hand and I'll admit, the confident way he swaggers across the parking lot is a huge turn-on.

We receive a respectful greeting from two prospects at the front door before entering the downstate clubhouse.

Now *this* clubhouse atmosphere is more familiar to me. Naked girls laid out on the bar top, the sweet stench of pot in the air, and a lot of drunk bikers. Sparky pushes past us, diving into a group of brothers gathered around a huge skull-shaped, glass water bong.

"Why doesn't that surprise me?" I mutter. Teller squeezes my hand, the only warning I receive before Tawny arrives.

Yes, the woman in the skin-tight leopard print pants and six-inch heels can only be the president's old lady.

Hope takes over and introduces us.

Tawny reminds me of my mother in the early days. Or who my mother could have been if my father hadn't died, leaving her broken and unable to cope. In other words, she's a tall, stacked, helmet-haired bitch on wheels. Although the patch on the front of her "property of" vest says Queen B. I assume the B stands for *bitch*. And I don't think my assumption would offend her one bit.

"Go on boys," she says, waving the guys off with a regal flick of her wrist. "Sway's waiting for you in the chapel. Let me catch up with the girls."

Teller raises an eyebrow, and I give him a brief nod. I can do this.

Once our men leave, she holds out her arms and gives me a welcoming hug. "Aren't you pretty?" She turns, her gaze landing on Teller across the room. "Seems like you've managed to turn his frown upside down." Her lips twist in a teasing way.

"How was your ride?" she asks Hope.

"Not bad. Thanks for having us again so soon," Hope says in a perfectly gracious manner. She's basically the opposite of Tawny and yet they seem to get along.

Trinity remains quiet during this exchange. Tawny finally seems to acknowledge her with a quick hello. Hope, who very obviously doesn't like anyone showing a hint of disrespect to Trinity links her arm through hers. "I'm dying for a drink, do you mind if we go raid your kitchen?" Hope asks. She doesn't really wait for an answer. Tawny stops me from following them by wrapping her arm around mine and turning us to face the room. "You stay here so I can get to know you better."

Oh goodie!

TAWNY ZEROED IN on Charlotte the second we arrived, which I kind of expected.

Wrath chuckles as he watches the two of them. "I *almost* feel bad."

"Don't lie."

He laughs harder, not offended at all.

Sway pulls us into the chapel. "Thanks for coming down. Smoke's been a mess since he got out of the hospital. I was hoping a big party with a couple chapters would lift his spirits."

Sway doesn't know us all that well, or maybe he does but just doesn't care. From what I've seen, since Rock settled down with Hope, he's *over* his partying days. Same for Wrath, so I'm not sure how the two of them are going to cheer up anyone.

Not to mention, word that's spread through the club—because yes, bikers gossip as much as any group of women—is that Smoke laid down his bike because he was drunk.

Having seen a lot of carnage in the early days of the club, Rock's always had strict rules about drinking and riding. It only made sense, so no one in our club's ever fucked up on that one. If one of us pulled what Smoke did, we'd be on the receiving end of an ass-kicking, and possibly a temporary patch-stripping, not a party thrown in our honor.

"Yeah, no problem. Where is he?" Rock asks.

Sway cocks his head, a filthy smile in place. "With a couple girls. Shoulda left your ol' ladies at home."

"We're good," Rock says.

"Oh, Christ." Sway turns to me. "This new girl of yours got your dick in a cage too?"

"Nah," I answer with a big grin. "Couldn't find one big enough."

SWAY SENDS US back to the rest of the party. Charlotte's red hair catches my attention, and I lift my chin. She waves and blows me a kiss.

This is different. I've never brought a girl who was one-hundred-percent *mine* with me on one of these trips. Besides loving the way it felt to have her at my back the whole way here, knowing who I'm going to bed with leaves me free to concentrate on the conversation around me.

I lose sight of Charlotte in the crowd, but I'm reasonably sure she's safe with Tawny, Hope, Trinity, and my brothers looking out for her. Rock bumps my arm. Leaning over he says, "She's fine."

"Do I look that worried?"

"Worried? No."

Before he has a chance to expand that thought, Sway joins us. "You free next month to escort Stella around?"

Because he's standing so close, I both hear and feel the irritated groan emanating from my president. Somehow I manage to keep a straight face.

"Z's on board," Rock answers. "I don't think it'll be hard to find a couple other brothers to help out."

Escort the hot porn star while she picks up random dudes to fuck in her hotel room as part of her "film project?" No, I don't think Rock will have trouble filling that job at all.

Sway's normally sleazy-jovial mask slips and he adopts a more serious expression. "I'd really feel better if I have the president watching her. I got a lot of money tied up in this project and I know you'll make sure she's safe."

Rock's expression turns to stone. "None of my guys are sloppy. If you're that worried, why aren't you going 'on tour' with her?"

Sway's eyes stray to somewhere behind us—Tawny if I had to guess. "Not *everyone* gave the green light for this project and it's caused some friction, so I need to be here."

Holy shit. Is Sway admitting his ol' lady gave him some sort of ultimatum? I'm not sure why she'd choose now to put her foot down. The whole organization knows they've fucked around on each other for years. It's not a well-kept secret.

Rock seems to have drawn the same conclusion. "Tawny got your nuts in a cage now?" he taunts—not a level Rock would normally stoop to, but Sway's earned it over the years.

"Steel vise is more like it," Sway admits.

I choke and sputter, trying not to laugh.

"Listen," Rock says, finally taking mercy on Sway's situation. "Z and Dex run Crystal Ball tight. They're not gonna let anyone mess with your girl."

Sway flicks his gaze across the room. "You'd trust them to watch Hope?"

Jesus Christ, is Sway in love with his little porn star?

"Without a doubt," Rock says.

"You'd trust Wrath more."

Oh, hell. We *all* know this isn't a job Wrath wants to be signed up for. Rock snorts. "Yeah, I trust Wrath to look out for my wife. I wouldn't trust him with Crystal Ball. He's got no patience to sort out glitter thong thefts among the girls."

"Fair enough," Sway says. "Thanks for this. I'll make sure you're compensated." He flashes a dirty grin. "Stella will too. If you ask her nicely, she'll even do it off-camera."

Gross.

Sway takes off, leaving Rock and I shaking our heads. "Someone needs to cut off his Viagra prescription," Rock mutters.

"Someone needs to cut off *something* of his."

Rock's mouth curls into a smirk and he gives my shoulder a push. "Surprised Tawny hasn't by now."

We're interrupted from mocking our brother's love life by a brother from our charter in Virginia.

"T-Bone," Rock says, shaking his hand. "How you been? You can't drive the extra two hours to come visit us?"

"Fuck that. Too fucking cold."

"It's summer," I say.

"Your crew was supposed to come to us." T-Bone pulls Rock aside and as I lose track of their conversation, a soft hand grazes my arm. Thinking it's Charlotte, I turn with a smile.

And find Serena.

Shit.

"Sorry," she says, glancing away. "I didn't mean to bother you. I just wanted to say hello."

"No problem," I answer. Is it too much to ask for her to hook up with T-Bone so she leaves me alone?

No such luck. Rock and T-Bone move their conversation to the bar so I guess I can't count on them to distract Serena.

"So, you're riding again?" she asks.

"Yup. First run since the accident." I shift, uncomfortable with where our conversation might lead. While I've never fucked her—at least I don't think I have—she and Murphy were pretty tight for a while after Heidi got married. And I just know she's dying to ask—

"Did Murphy come with you?"

There it is.

"No, he's home." Fuck, I have no way of knowing what Murphy's said to her. But I want her to understand my best friend is *forever* off-limits. "You know he's with my sister now, right?"

"Oh." Her eyes widen as she digests the news. "Heidi, right. I remember her. I'm sorry. I didn't know."

Before she can ask her next question—which I'm pretty sure will involve an offer to warm *my* bed tonight—Charlotte slides her arm around my waist, tucking herself into my side.

"Hi, Serena? Right?"

I tip my head in Charlotte's direction. "Serena, this is my girl, Charlotte."

To be fair, Charlotte isn't catty. She holds out her hand and after a second Serena takes it. I'm probably an asshole, but I really like how it feels having Charlotte assert herself this way. The sweet but confident expression on her face clearly says "he's taken" and it gives me an unusual jolt of satisfaction.

"Nice to meet you, Charlotte." Serena lets out a bit of nervous laughter. "I guess it's not a good time to ask if I can come hang out upstate?"

I lean over and kiss Charlotte's cheek. "I'll be at the bar."

Charlotte

AFTER TELLER LEAVES, Serena flicks her gaze around the room. I guess I don't blame her for being nervous. I practically ran over here and peed on Marcel's leg to mark him as my territory.

"How did you know who I was?" she asks with an almost hopeful eyebrow raised.

"Tawny."

"Let me guess. She told you to come over and get your man before I blew him."

Now I'm the one with the nervous laughter. Yes, Tawny ended up being the kind of ol' lady I expected. "Sort of."

"That's exactly why I was thinking about moving back upstate." She flashes a quick smile. "Hope's always been nice to me. And I guess word has spread through some of the LOKI chapters, that upstate has the nicest president's old lady."

Something about that strikes me as both sweet and sad. "Hope's good to everybody from what I've seen." I hurry to add, "But I'm pretty sure she'll kill anyone eyeing her man."

Serena laughs. "Probably. Can't blame her." She hesitates, then tilts her head. "Teller said his sister and Murphy are together?"

At once it clicks who this chick is, Murphy's sort-of ex. That's a relief. When I first saw her talking to Teller, I assumed she was a bunny he used to shack up with when he visited this clubhouse.

"They're engaged, yes." I'm not sure how much I should say, but surely that's common knowledge.

"Wow. Never thought. Wow." Her gaze strays across the room to Teller. "He probably forced that, huh?" Another nervous giggle rolls out of her.

"Uh, not really. I don't think Murphy was going to let anything stand in his way."

Her pretty smile falters and I have a small twinge of regret for my words. But I also feel protective of Heidi and don't like this stranger making assumptions about their relationship.

Before the conversation turns any more awkward, a rough looking, dark-haired Lost King walks up, grabbing Serena around her tiny waist. "Where've you been, sweetheart?" he asks, slurring each word.

Serena's mouth turns down. Maybe he's not her favorite of the Lost Kings, I don't know.

"Hi, Shadow," she says. "Have you met Teller's old lady Charlotte?"

Busy licking Serena's neck, he barely throws me a greeting. Serena wiggles her fingers at me as he drags her way. "I'll catch you later, Charlotte."

I'm not alone for long. An older Lost King swaggers over, but before he opens his mouth, Teller's at my side. "She's with me."

"No disrespect, was just coming to say hello. How you been, T?"

My gaze and mind wander while they talk, leaving me in the perfect position to notice the biker at the door pulling out a gun.

Teller

"MARCEL!" I CAN'T miss the anxiety in Charlotte's voice.

Before I determine what caused it, a blast silences everyone in the room. "Get behind me," I say to Charlotte. She doesn't argue or hesitate. In seconds, her soft warm body molds to my back.

At the front door, an older brother who I recognize waves a pistol around. My only concerns at the moment are keeping Charlotte safe and locating my president.

I don't have to say anything to her. She follows my lead and slowly backs up toward the bar with me. I slip into a spot next to Rock, leaving Charlotte protected between my body and the thick wooden bar.

"Jesus Christ," Sway says. "It's Smoke. Told you he hasn't been right since the accident."

"He need to blow off steam or is he an actual threat?" Rock asks. I don't see any sign of Wrath or Hope and Trinity, so I assume they're safe somewhere else in the clubhouse. Rock hasn't lost his shit, so he must be certain Hope's okay.

I drew my pistol at the first shot and have it at my side, pointed at the floor, waiting to see how Rock wants to handle this. We may be standing in Sway's clubhouse, but I'll still take my directions from *my* president.

Z quietly slips in the front door while Smoke's busy ranting a bunch of nonsense. While's Smoke's distracted, Z wraps one thick arm around the old guy's neck, keeping him in a chokehold until two of Sway's crew disarm the wild biker.

"Take him downstairs!" Sway shouts.

Sway slaps my arm. "Always something exciting down here, right? I need to take care of this, you two hang out."

"Show's over, people. Party on!" Sway shouts as he moves through the room.

Rock meets my stare. "You all right?"

"I'm fine." Reaching behind me, I pull Charlotte forward.

"Well, that was exciting," she says.

"Wrath has the girls in one of our rooms," Rock explains. "I need to go find them."

"Yeah, go ahead." I nod at Charlotte. "I think we're done for the night."

While she put on a brave face for Rock, Charlotte's trembling body says she's not okay. "Let's go to our room, Sunshine."

"Boy, Trinity wasn't kidding about your club being unique," she mumbles.

"Sorry about that," Tawny says, joining us.

Inwardly I groan. I'm ready for this night to be over and not in the mood to force polite conversation with the Queen B of our downstate charter. She rakes her nails through my hair, which is creepy as fuck with Charlotte holding my hand and Tawny old enough to be my mother.

Instead of being annoyed by the older woman's fake-as-fuck display of affection, Charlotte looks like she's trying not to laugh.

"It's certainly lively down here," she says to Tawny.

"We do our best." She finally stops touching me, but she opens her mouth which is almost worse. "You've grown into such a handsome young man, Teller."

For the love of fuck. Why?

"I've known him since he was a teenager," Tawny says to Charlotte.

"I'm sure he was a handful." Charlotte nods.

"Well," Tawny taps her finger over my lips and I barely fight the urge to shake her off. "This mouth of his almost got him in trouble more times than I can count."

"Oh, it still does on occasion," Charlotte says.

I narrow my eyes and raise an eyebrow at her.

Tawny laughs and pats my shoulder. "I like her," she whispers in my ear. As if she thinks I'd been waiting for her approval.

"Me too."

Satisfied that she's done her ol' lady duties, Tawny saunters into the rest of the crowd. When I glance down at Charlotte, she's shaking.

With laughter. Not fear.

"Are you *laughing* at me?" I ask in a low voice.

"A little." Her gaze strays to Tawny. "She's so *predatory*."

That's a good word to describe Tawny.

"Did you two ever...?" her voice trails off without finishing the question, but I don't need her to complete the thought. Let alone say it out loud.

"Fuck no." Internally, I shudder at the idea. Slipping my arm around her shoulders, I steer her toward the hallway. "I think that's enough fun for the night."

CHAPTER TWENTY-TWO

Charlotte

"COME ON! WE'RE going to be late," I yell to Carter.

I haven't spent a whole lot of time at my apartment in the few weeks since we returned from our trip downstate. But I wanted to make sure Carter came with me today, so I spent the night here.

"Are you sure you want me at this party?" he asks for the millionth time. "I feel weird."

"It's a family party. They invited non-MC people too."

"Well, I didn't receive an invitation."

"Carter, I stood right there and heard Heidi personally invite you. Next excuse?"

"She was just being polite. I've never even met her kid."

"Well, today you'll be able to finally meet her," I say with exaggerated patience. I feel like we've been having this conversation all morning long.

Oh, wait, we have.

Since Chuck's attack, Carter's been down on MCs in general and my boyfriend in particular. He doesn't seem to care that the attack was about my uncle and not about the Lost Kings.

He blames Marcel.

Giving Carter a complete picture means I'll have to disclose what happened to me too, and Marcel knows how much I don't want to burden my brother with that, so he hasn't bothered to correct him. Honestly, I don't think it would help at this point.

"You're sure you want me there?"

"Yes! Oh my God, stop dragging your feet. We're going to be late."

When I emerge from my bedroom, he's waiting by the front door with a big box covered in white paper with rainbow unicorns scattered all over it, topped off with a big pink bow.

"What's that?"

"It's a birthday party. Aren't we supposed to bring presents?"

"Well, yes. But I already bought something from both of us."

"And I'm bringing this from *me*."

"What is it?"

"It's this unicorn. She plays different songs and melodies. I don't know. It lights up and does some other stuff." He shrugs. "Teller said his sister's into cognitive development toys and this is supposed to be good for that."

I'm not sure what to say. Instead of responding in some meaningful way, I stand there with my mouth open.

"What's with the face?" He opens the door. "Come on, now you're the one making us late."

Even though I plan to stay over, we take my car. It makes sense. Carter's been using it more than I have lately.

A prospect lets us in the front gate after I wave to him.

Carter whistles as we climb the driveway. "Well, I feel better now. I think you're pretty safe out here."

"Have you been worried about me?"

"Yes, I worry about you, Charlotte."

I reach over and pat his leg. "I worry about you too."

Teller meets us in the driveway and points out where we should park. He opens my door and pulls me into a hug. "Hey, Sunshine. Missed you."

"Missed you too."

"Jesus. You saw each other yesterday," Carter grumbles.

"What's up, Carter? I see you're full of cheer this afternoon."

Carter flashes a fake smile and pulls the present he brought out of the back seat.

Teller raises an eyebrow. "I thought you—"

"That's from Carter."

"This is quite a place, Teller. Seems too classy for a bunch of bikers."

"We like it out here."

Teller introduces Carter around. Thankfully my brother seems too uncomfortable to say anything too obnoxious.

"HAPPY BIRTHDAY TO you." The club, the whole club, and everyone else in attendance, finishes belting out the last verse of Happy Birthday to baby Alexa.

Marcel leans in to help her blow out her birthday candles, and I slip my phone out to capture a picture. This is a side of him few people probably know, and I'm happy Carter's here to witness it. Maybe it will put his mind at ease.

Once the candle's out, Alexa promptly plants her face in the cake.

Trinity has her professional camera out to capture every bit of pink frosting that gets in Alexa's hair.

"Oh my God. Look at you." Heidi giggles as she attempts to clean her daughter's face. "Did that taste good?"

Alexa chortles and plunges her little fists into the cake next.

Trinity leans over and whispers in my ear. "Good thing I made two cakes. The other one's tucked away in the kitchen."

"Thank God, I've been drooling over it since we got here."

Marcel's absolutely enamored with his niece. Every time I see them together, thoughts I never, ever expected I'd have, start running through my head.

Murphy cuts the side of the cake that escaped Alexa's grabby hands and Hope passes it out. While Marcel's busy feeding Alexa cake, Murphy comes over and gives me a one-armed hug. "Can you check on Heidi? She went inside."

"Sure. Is everything okay?"

Although he nods, he seems unsure, so I leave to check on her.

I find Heidi in the kitchen standing at the sink with the water running. After a few seconds, I realize the water masks the sounds of her crying. "Heidi, what's wrong?"

"Oh!" She leans over the sink and splashes water on her face before facing me. "Nothing."

I take measured steps and gently touch her shoulder. "The party's lovely. Alexa seems so happy. What's wrong?"

"Who am I talking to? Charlotte my friend? Or Charlotte my brother's girlfriend?"

"Whoever you need."

She takes a deep breath. "It's nothing. I just feel bad Axel's not here for Alexa, you know? Even if we weren't together...I don't know...I'm not...Murphy's so good to her. To me. I can't help feeling bad, though."

Her admission stuns me a little. I'm used to seeing the worst sides of broken families. Women who *wish* their exes were dead. Men who'd rather spend their day with the new girlfriend than at a one-year-old's birthday party.

Even though she won't turn twenty for a few more weeks, she has more depth and compassion than so many people I've encountered in my life.

I choose my words carefully. "That's understandable. That's what makes you a good mom, Heidi."

"Yeah, but it makes me a shitty fiancée."

Remembering the concerned way Murphy asked me to check on Heidi, I say, "I think Murphy understands."

She hiccups. "He does. We talked about it this morning. That's why I don't want him to know it was still bothering me. I was fine until she blew out her candle." Her mouth pulls into a half-smirk. "Or rather, my brother blew out the candle and she face-planted in the cake."

"Trinity got a great photo of that."

Heidi chuckles. "I saw."

"Have you tried reaching out to Axel's parents?"

"God, no."

"Maybe it will help you feel better if Alexa connects with Axel's family."

She shakes her head. "They've never wanted anything to do with her."

"Well, maybe now that some time has gone by…"

"I don't think I can stand—"

"To have them reject you?"

She snorts and waves her hand in the air. "Please. I've been rejected my whole life, Charlotte. I couldn't care less if they like *me*, but I won't have my daughter treated like she's not good enough for them. Absolutely not."

The little girl in me whose mother never showed up for a single parent-conference night, school play, or graduation weeps with her. The attorney who's seen a lot of parents lacking the strength to stand up for their children, cheers for her.

"Well, she's one lucky little girl. She has an entire club full of overprotective men happily attending a unicorn-themed birthday party."

That finally puts a smile on her face. "We're so lucky. I love our family."

The door that leads into the dining room swings open, halting our talk. "Everything all right?" Hope calls out.

Heidi sniffs once then forces a bright smile. "I'm okay, Aunt Hope."

Now it makes sense why Heidi's so tight with Hope and practically worships her.

"Oh, Heidi." Hope sweeps her up in a hug and flashes a quick smile. "Teller's looking for you," she says to me.

"I'll find him in a minute."

Heidi snorts and turns sideways, still keeping her arms around Hope. "That's right. Make my brother wait for it."

"Well…"

"Actually," Heidi says, her lips curving into a wicked grin. "I wouldn't mind a niece or nephew. Then Murphy can stop worrying about Alexa not having any siblings."

"Oh my God." I burst out laughing. "Yeah, we're *definitely* not there yet." I sneak a sideways glance at Hope. "Besides, I think it's the duty of the First Lady to start making some baby Lost Kings."

Hope snort-giggles but surprisingly doesn't disagree.

Instead, she pulls me into her other side, hugging me tightly, making me feel like I finally have a place.

With this family.

Teller

"NO GOOD CAN come from that, bro," Murphy says, backing away from the kitchen door. He shakes his head, but there's a grin forming at the corners of his mouth.

I step up and take a peek at whatever it is he thinks is so funny.

"Fuck me," I mutter.

Hope has one arm wrapped around Heidi and one around Charlotte. The three of them look like they're plotting world domination.

Murphy jerks his thumb over his shoulder. "Your brother-in-law-to-be is out there unchaperoned."

"He'll be okay."

"How have you not kicked his ass yet?"

I lift one shoulder. "The same way I stop myself from kicking *your* ass every day, I guess."

"Har, har."

"What are you two creeps doing?" Wrath's big voice echoes through the room.

"Shh." Murphy tilts his head toward the door.

Wrath, using one massive arm to brush Murphy out of his way, takes a look and comes away laughing. "You two are fucked for sure."

Murphy glances in the window again and loses the smile. "Heidi had a rough morning. I'm glad she's talking to Hope."

"About what?" I ask.

Murphy shrugs off my question. Whether it's because he doesn't want to talk about it in front of Wrath or it's his way of reminding me to butt out, I'm not sure. Either way, I leave it alone. If they want me to know, one of them will tell me.

"At least the only advice Hope gives my wife is what kind of sexwear to buy for me," Wrath says.

"What?"

"Gross." Murphy shakes his head. "I don't want to hear *Hope* and *sexwear* in the same sentence ever again. I'm already subjected to enough living with them."

Wrath laughs so hard there's no way the girls can't hear us out here.

"What are you three knuckleheads doing?" Z calls out, striding into the dining room carrying Alexa in his arms. He lifts his chin at Murphy. "Where's your woman? Our little princess here, has frosting in her ears, up her nose, in her hair, and hell knows where else."

Murphy snorts and holds out his hands. "Give her to me."

"Aw, such a modern dad," Z snarks.

Murphy flips him a discrete middle finger behind Alexa's back, then nods at the door. "Guess I'm going in."

After he's gone, Wrath claps me on the back. "You gonna rescue your girl?"

"From Hope?" No fucking way. The two of them have been spending more and more time together since our trip downstate, which was exactly what I'd hoped for. I want Hope on Charlotte's side, especially now.

"You want her teaching your girl the art of withholding sex?"

Z lets out a sharp bark of laughter. "I don't think Hope's familiar with that one."

Wrath's eyes widen and he lets out a dramatic gasp. "Are you calling our First Lady *slutty*?"

"No, I'm calling her dick-whipped."

I place a hand on my stomach. "I'm going to throw up."

Z pats my head, similar to how he pets the dogs. "Sorry, little brother." He turns to Wrath. "He still hasn't recovered from catching Mom and Dad doing it on the war room table."

"Oh, for fuck's sake," Wrath says. "They have their own damn house."

"Why are you all in here?" Rock says as he pushes through the dining room doors and throws his hands in the air. "The party's outside."

"These two were spying on the girls," Z explains.

"I wasn't," Wrath says. "Teller and his ginger wonder twin were."

Rock heaves out a deep breath, searching for patience to deal with us, I'm sure.

"Tell me, Prez," Wrath says, stroking his hand over his beard. "Did you and your ol' lady desecrate our war room table?"

"Asshole," I hiss at him.

Rock's mouth twists into a smirk and he gives us a casual shrug. "Man's gotta do what a man's gotta do."

Wrath leaves to find Trinity and Z leaves to take the dogs for a run.

"How you doing?" Rock asks.

"Good." I stop and take a breath. "I want to patch Charlotte and ask for the officers' votes."

"All right. Today?"

"Yes."

Together, we push into the kitchen and find Murphy and Heidi fussing over a pissed-off Alexa who's getting bathed in the sink.

"Blake, can you grab me a towel?" Heidi asks.

Murphy holds a towel open while Heidi hands Alexa to him. He wraps her up tight, and she stops wailing. Leaning over, he gives Heidi a quick kiss and they share a few words.

Rock walks up behind Hope and wraps his arms around her middle while she continues her conversation with Charlotte.

I join them and slip an arm around Charlotte. "Where've you been?" she teases.

"We're gonna sit down for church in a few," Rock says.

"You want me to round everyone up, Prez?" Murphy asks.

"No. You're busy with our birthday girl." He nods at me. "Bring everyone in."

"You got it."

Murphy lifts his chin at me, grateful I think, to have a few extra minutes with his family.

I take Charlotte outside. Before we return to the party, I stop and back her against the side of the clubhouse.

"Kiss me."

She wraps her arms around my neck, rises up on her toes, and presses her lips to mine.

I pull back, staring down at her face. "Do you want kids?"

Her big blue eyes widen in surprise. "Eventually, yes."

"You ever think about *us* having kids?"

A bright smile lights up her face. "Only every time I see you with Alexa."

"Yeah?"

She nods and pulls me down for another kiss.

"What made you ask that today?" she murmurs against my lips.

"Realized I've never really asked."

"And what if I said no?"

She's teasing me, so I pin her to the wall and grind my hips into her. "I would've convinced you."

Her soft laughter warms me all over, confirming my decision to patch her. Hopefully it won't be hard to convince my brothers.

CHAPTER TWENTY-THREE

Teller

CHURCH IS QUICK. Rock passes out assignments to everyone for the week. I pass around some cash. Wrath updates us on the rebuild of the gym.

Rock dismisses the general members but asks the officers to stay. Murphy gives me a smile and a nod, knowing what I'm about to do.

"I want to give Charlotte my property patch."

"Are you asking for our votes as well?" Rock asks.

"Yes."

Rock's the first one to say yes. Then he moves to Z.

"Yes." He pats my shoulder. "She cured this moody prick. She's a loyal girl."

Murphy's a 'yes' as well.

All of us turn to Wrath. He doesn't ask questions or dick around, which is a bad sign.

"No."

He might as well have taken one of his giant fists and hammered it into my gut.

"What the fuck?" I shout.

Unmoved by my outburst, he holds up his hand. "I'm not saying no forever. Just right now, I think it's too soon. We should see how things shake out with her uncle first."

"Motherfucker," I grumble even though I'm not really surprised. "You know she and Trinity patched things up, right?"

He rolls his eyes as if I'm dense. "That has nothing to do with it."

"Like fuck it doesn't."

"All right. Simmer down," Rock says. "You still want to give her your patch?"

I glare at Wrath. "No. I'm not making her feel like she's *less than* since she won't have the officers' patches like the other girls do."

Wrath shrugs. "Give it to her. If she gets pissed, it's a sign she's not cut out for this. If she understands, maybe she is."

"Fuck you."

He leans over the table. "I've been humoring you since I know why you're pissed, but watch yourself, little brother."

"Knock it off." Rock swings his right arm out, pushing Wrath back in his chair.

I take a few deep breaths and compose myself. "I have another announcement."

Rock raises an eyebrow and waits for me to continue.

"I'm moving out of the clubhouse."

Everyone just stares at me for a few seconds.

Except for Murphy, who slowly nods, not at all surprised.

"Where are you going?" Z asks.

"Bought a house right down the road. The property actually borders ours."

"The old farmhouse that's been up for sale for over a year?" Wrath asks. "That place?"

"Yup. People who owned it blew all their cash restoring it, couldn't pay the mortgage, and lost it. There's still some work that needs to be done, but it's solid. I'm showing it to Charlotte today."

"She doesn't know about it?" Z asks.

"No. It was a surprise." I glare across the table at Wrath again. "I *was* going to give her the patch when I showed her the house."

Wrath rarely, if ever, shows remorse and his expression remains blank.

Z's already in planning mode. "We can break an access trail between the two properties, that'll be cool. So you'll have a back way in."

"Not a bad idea," Rock says. He gives me a nod. "Congratulations."

STILL PISSED ABOUT the vote, but excited to show Charlotte the house, I leave the table.

Hope, Trinity, Heidi, and Charlotte are in the living room playing with Alexa. I tug my girl up off the couch. "Did your brother head home already?"

"A little while ago."

"Come take a ride with me, Sunshine."

The girls hoot and make obnoxious catcalls at us. "Perverts," Charlotte calls out as I lead her outside. "What's the hurry?"

"No hurry. Just want you to myself."

I hand over her helmet and straddle my bike. Carefully, she gets on behind me, snuggling up close. She doesn't ask where we're going, just holds on tight.

When I turn down the unfamiliar driveway ten minutes later, her body shifts and I feel her turning her head, checking out the surroundings.

"Where are we?" she asks after dismounting. Her eyes are wide with curiosity. A bemused smile plays over her lips.

"You'll see."

I take her hand and lead her up the steps. She watches as I take out a key and open the front door.

It's not furnished yet, but the place is beautiful. Dark, gleaming hardwood floors. Large windows with plenty of light.

I follow as she moves through the living room and up the stairs, checking out each bedroom. "This was two bedrooms, but they converted it to one master suite."

It's the one room with any furniture.

"Hmm." She runs her hand over the gray comforter on the bed. "This looks familiar."

She checks out the master bathroom, which is one room that still needs to be finished. "We can do whatever you want in here. There's plenty of room."

So far, she hasn't said a word and a sense of dread begins to form.

We end up downstairs in the kitchen, where I lift her up to sit on the counter. "Move in with me."

Her hands frame my face and she brushes her lips against mine. "We're pretty much already living together."

"Let's move into our own place."

A bit of nervous laughter flows out of her. "What did you do?"

"Let's make *this* our place."

"Is it yours?"

"It's ours."

She blinks and throws her arms around me. "Oh my God! You bought us a house? Thank you. This place is amazing."

"You like it?"

"I love it! I didn't want to get too excited since I didn't know why you were showing it to me."

"Sorry about that. I wanted it to be a surprise."

She pulls me down for another kiss. "I'm surprised."

"There's something I have to tell you, though."

"Oh, no. It's not haunted, is it?"

I drop my head and chuckle. "No."

"Is there a family of cannibals living in the basement?"

I laugh even harder. "You and Trinity need to stop watching so many horror movies together."

"Is it clowns?" she asks in a fake-serious voice. "Are there killer clowns in the attic?" She stops goofing around, but her smile remains. "Heidi said she thought you were asking the guys to vote me in today."

Goddamn it, Heidi.

"She knows better than to talk about club stuff."

Charlotte's smile falters.

"I did ask," I say gently. "The verdict was not yet."

"Oh." She blinks a few times. "But not a solid no, right?"

"Right."

She presses her palms against my face again. "I understand. Chuck's still in jail. Your club's relationship with the Wolf Knights is still questionable until that gets sorted." She narrows her eyes. "I hope you didn't give your brothers a hard time."

This woman's perfect for me in every single way. "Shit, I love you." I lift her off the counter, and she wraps her legs around me. "I can still give you my patch. It just won't have the officer patches on the side."

"Nope." She shakes her head and hugs me tighter. "I want it all, Marcel and I'll wait for it."

Charlotte

MARCEL STARES INTO my eyes with nothing but love. "I *do* want to give you everything."

"Is that why you're moving away from the clubhouse?"

"No, I already had this place," he explains, but a small part of me wonders if deep down he knew it would take a while before all his brothers accepted me completely.

Overwhelmed with love for this man who has risked an awful lot to be with me, I wrap my arms around his neck.

"Thank you."

"You're not upset?"

I pull back, so we're eye-level. "Hell, no. How could I be upset? Are you *sure* you want to be away from the club?"

He sets me back on the counter and tucks my hair behind my ear. My eyes close and I lean into his touch. "I want to be where you are."

"But you won't be near your sister and Alexa."

"We're only ten or fifteen minutes from the clubhouse. Easy enough for Heidi to drop Alexa off when she needs me to watch her. Close enough for me to be up there when the club needs me."

"What did Heidi say? Was she upset?"

"I haven't told her yet."

My eyebrow quirks up. "Really?"

"I wanted to show it to you first. Murphy probably guessed because he was with me when I found the place, but this is about you and me. No one else."

I hug him tight, inhaling the scent of the man I love so much. "I love you, Marcel."

He kisses my forehead. "Come on, I want to show you the rest of it."

I slide down off the counter and stroll to the side door that seems to lead to the yard. Beyond that, there are a few smaller buildings. "What are the other buildings?"

Marcel comes up behind me, wrapping me up in his arms, and pulling me against his chest. "That," he says, pointing to the one that from here looks like a miniature of this house. "Was the caretaker's cottage. It was converted into a workshop downstairs and an apartment upstairs."

"Neat. What are you planning to do with it?"

"Thought we'd offer it to Carter. He can use the workshop as an art studio or something and live upstairs. Or just stay there when he visits."

Unsure I'm hearing him correctly, I turn and stare at him.

"You bought a place." Each word comes out slow and full of awe. "For us. That has a place. For my brother?"

Doubt creeps into his expression. "Well, yeah. When I saw it, I knew it'd be a great setup for our situation."

"Our situation?"

"Well, he can't stay under our roof. Not with us being all *depraved* and stuff."

Wowwowow.

I practically jump on him. "You're the sweetest. I can't even. Thank you."

He truly seems perplexed by my reaction. How can I even explain it?

Uncle Chuck kicked Carter out of his house and my boyfriend, no, my *old man*, is offering this amazing, beautiful, wonderful home as if it's the most normal thing in the world. Because to Marcel, it's the right thing to do.

That's his moral code. To take care of and provide for his loved ones.

"I know how important he is to you, Sunshine. He's family."

"You're my family now too."

He gives me a half-smile. "Yes, I am."

CHAPTER TWENTY-FOUR

Charlotte

WE SPEND MORE time exploring the house and property. After Alexa's birthday party, a regular club party had been planned and we're supposed to be there.

Marcel's almost hesitant, as if he's worried I won't want to visit the clubhouse again after the guys didn't vote me in.

"We have to go up. They're expecting you."

He still doesn't say anything.

"I'm fine, Marcel. I'm not even supposed to know about it, right?" I remind him.

"True."

"It doesn't change how I feel about you or the club."

Besides, I can take a good guess at who cast the *no* vote.

When we arrive, Marcel stops to talk to Murphy, and I search for Wrath. I find him in a corner of the living room, back to the wall, arms crossed over his chest, surveying the party with the terrifying intensity that has to be partially responsible for his road name.

Deep breath.

I walk over and stare up at him for a few seconds before he acknowledges my presence with a raised eyebrow.

"Can we talk?"

Pretty damn ballsy of me, right?

But I went over this in my head a few times on the ride up here. There are two things I figure Wrath respects above everything else. Brutal honesty and bravery.

To confirm my suspicions, there's a twitch at the corner of his mouth. I can't tell if he's trying not to laugh or wants to tell me to fuck off. He jerks his head toward the front door and I follow him outside.

"What's on your mind, Charlotte?" he asks in his deep, rumbling voice.

Since I'm pretty sure a long speech will piss him off, I dive right in.

"I'm guessing you didn't vote for me."

His expression doesn't change. "You mad about that darlin'?" he asks with an edge of sarcasm.

"No. I get it. I wouldn't think you were so good at your job if you let me in right away."

He snorts. "That so?"

"Yup." I lean in closer and drop my voice so he has to bend down to hear me. "You should know, though, I love Teller and I'm not going anywhere."

I think the big, scary enforcer for the Lost Kings MC is speechless so I continue. "I'll prove to you that the club can trust me and I understand it will take time to earn that trust."

After a few seconds, I'm on the receiving end of a genuine smile from Wrath. My very first. "You're fearless, I'll give you that."

"I *am* concerned he's moving away from the clubhouse, though. I don't want him to resent me later because of it."

Wrath seems surprised. "He didn't *have* to move."

"I don't want it to interfere with his relationship with the club, with his brothers."

"No one questions his dedication or loyalty to the club, Charlotte." He flicks his gaze to somewhere over my shoulder, then back to my face. "I'll be honest with you, he's been taking care of everyone else his whole life. He deserves to have something just for himself and a good woman he can trust."

"You can trust me."

He raises one blond eyebrow.

"I know how to keep my mouth shut."

"Lawyer-client confidence." He rolls his eyes. "Yeah, I've heard."

I snort because I guess Hope has laid some groundwork for me here. "I understand why you're hesitant. And, honestly, you're right. I have no idea what's going to happen when my uncle gets out of jail."

He crosses his arms over his chest and if I didn't know better, I might think he's mad on my behalf.

"I understand the importance of the club in your lives. It's clear that you're more than a club. You're a family. I respect that."

He doesn't respond or move, so I continue. "It's different from the club I grew up around. So much different. I already love Teller and I'm halfway in love with the club."

"You realize those patches are more symbolic than anything, right?" he asks.

"Not having them means if we're somewhere and I fuck up, Teller's the only one responsible for me, right?"

"Charlotte, I can tell you right now, no matter where we are or what you're wearing, not one brother in this club is gonna let anyone lay a finger on you."

"Even you?"

"Even me. As long as you treat my brother well, we'll always have your back."

My eyes well up a little and I sniffle. "Thank you." I hold my arms out. "Can I hug you? Truce?"

His expression darkens. "I'm not a hugger."

"You let Hope hug you."

"I don't *let* Hope do anything, she just does it," he grumbles, sliding his gaze toward the clubhouse. Probably to make sure Rock's not around to catch him saying anything negative about his wife.

Finally, he relents and gives me a quick squeeze that knocks the breath out of me. "Trinity must be sturdier than she looks," I mutter.

"What was that?"

"Nothing."

Before we go back inside to the party, he says, "I think you're good for him, Charlotte. Whether you're good for the club, I'm not sure yet."

"Fair enough."

Again, he seems shocked.

Score one for me!

"You seen Rock?" I ask Z.

"War room."

"Oh, Christ, is Hope in there too?"

He shakes with laughter and nods at the bar where Hope's talking to Swan.

"Thank fuck."

The party's too loud to bother knocking, so I just open the door.

Wrath and Rock are sitting at the table sharing a bottle of scotch.

"She's got big brass ones." Wrath laughs. "Came and told me she wants to earn the club's trust." He shakes his head. "And that I'd be shitty at my job if I just accepted her right away," he finishes, laughing even harder.

Rock nods and glances up. "Hey, Teller."

"Hey."

Wrath turns and grins when he sees me. "Pull up a chair. We were just talking about you."

"That's what I'm afraid of."

I take Z's chair and Rock passes me a glass. Wrath leans over and pours.

"I was just telling Rock, maybe after you've settled into your new place, you should ask for another vote."

CHAPTER TWENTY-FIVE

Charlotte

ARCEL AND I leave the clubhouse late and decide to spend the night in our new house.

Our new house.

I still can't believe it.

It's not ideal. Although he made sure we had a bed—*of course he did*—the only finished bathroom is downstairs. I almost break my neck in the middle of the night trying to find it.

"Maybe tomorrow we sleep downstairs," I say when Marcel wakes up.

He runs the back of his hand over my cheek. "You should've woken me up."

"To take me to the bathroom? Let's save something for our old age."

He closes his eyes and shakes with laughter. I flick his side with my fingers. "Stop laughing at me."

He's warm and pulls me closer as I run my hand down his body. "Ooo, are you naked under there?" I ask, peeking under the sheet.

He growls and rolls over on top of me. "Fuck, yeah I am."

He takes his time, kissing and licking my neck, slowly sliding down my body.

"Oh, God," I gasp when he parts my legs and runs his tongue over me. My hands grab his hair and he groans. "I want to wake up with your face in my pussy every day."

"Done," he mumbles, licking and sucking harder. "Come all over my face, Sunshine. Then I'm going to fuck you."

Whatever witty comeback I had dies as he latches onto my clit. "Fuck. Don't stop."

His phone buzzes on the nightstand next to me. "Ignore it," he murmurs. "I'm not done."

I stretch, arching my back to give him better access and he slides two fingers inside me, rubbing the exact spot that makes my toes curl.

"Marcel, I'm so close." My breath comes out in harsh little panting noises. "Please make me come."

His phone goes off again.

I scream in frustration and punch the mattress. "Just answer it."

"What?" he answers his phone, kneeling up to give me a fantastic view of his glorious morning wood.

I reach out and wrap my hand around his cock, slowly stroking.

His expression morphs from annoyed to furious. "What? When. Where is he now?"

Alarmed by his tone, I sit up and try to listen in.

"All right. Thanks for letting me know, man. Appreciate it."

"What?" I ask as soon as he hangs up.

He's stopped from answering by his phone going off again. "Fuck me," he grumbles. "Yeah?"

He flashes a tight smile while he listens. "Where are you taking him? Okay. Thanks."

This time he shuts the phone off and sets it on my nightstand.

"What's going on?"

"Nothing," he says, lowering his body over mine. "It can wait. I need to finish what we started."

I stop him with a hand against his chest. "I don't think I could come if you put a gun to my head now."

"Let's not get that extreme. Give me a minute to work my magic."

I don't even crack a smile. "You don't need to make some phone calls?"

"No," he answers, drawing out the word. "At the moment, I want to finish fucking you."

His morning-rough voice is sexy as hell, but I can't help laughing.

He dips down and nuzzles my neck. "I can't love you up right if you're laughing at me," he murmurs against my ear.

"Aw, you wanna love me up?" I tease, inching my body down the bed.

"Where do you think you're going?" he asks, as he lands on the mattress next to me.

Without words, I tease and lick my way down his chest, trace his abs with my tongue. "God, I could bounce quarters off you."

"I want something bouncing on me and it's not quarters."

"In a minute."

He raises an eyebrow, and I feel even bolder. He presses his elbows into the mattress and lifts himself up, all the muscles I just spent time admiring flex and tighten, reminding me of how powerful he is.

I reach down and wrap my hand around him. "Let's get you nice and hard again."

"You calling me soft, Sunshine?" He lies back and tucks his hands behind his head, watching me with an amused smile playing over his lips.

My lips move in closer, lightly grazing the tip.

"My girl wants to get her mouth on my cock bad, huh?"

My girl.

Wow. I used to hate anyone calling me *girl*. But in this moment, warmth spreads through me.

In my hand, he's hard and hot. I grip him tighter and wrap my lips around the head of his cock.

"Aw fuck," he moans, letting his head fall back. His eyes close and he gives himself over to me as I suck and lick. He shifts his hips, allowing me to take him deeper. He rests his hand on the back of my head.

"Your mouth is fucking heaven." His fingers twist in my hair. "But I want your pussy."

Shaking with desire, I pull back. He holds out his hands. "Come on. Show me how much of my dick you can take."

"Fuck," I moan as I slide down. "All of it. I want all of it."

When he's buried inside me, he grips my hips and rocks me back and forth. "Good girl. Love being deep inside of you."

I lean back and sigh as his hand tightens around my neck.

"Keep riding me. Don't stop."

His hand squeezes tighter, matching the need rising inside me. He keeps speaking soft, dirty words of encouragement but I'm lost, gasping with pleasure and grinding against him.

My orgasm exhausts me and I'm ready to collapse.

"No, no, dirty girl. My turn."

I nod frantically, always wanting him to find as much pleasure as I do.

He bucks me off easily, and I land on my hands and knees.

"That's right," he murmurs. "Ass up." He squeezes one cheek and grabs my hips, sinking inside me.

"Oh, fuck," I mumble against the blankets.

"What's that, Sunshine? You gonna come for me again?"

"I don't think I can."

"A few minutes ago you didn't think you were going to come at all. So, let's see what we can do."

"You're relentless."

He laughs and slides his hand between my legs, rubbing my clit until I'm climbing that peak again.

This time, he follows me, groaning in pleasure as his orgasm hits.

"That's better," he mumbles as he falls down next to me. "Now I'm ready to start the day."

I chuckle and snuggle up against him. We lay there in a naked heap, catching our breath together.

"Now will you tell me what those calls were about?"

He sighs and turns to face me. "Merlin made bail this morning."

"Shit. Really?"

"The first call was from my buddy, Liam. The second was from your boyfriend, Hudson."

"He's *not* my boyfriend."

"Who's your boyfriend?" he teases.

"I don't *have* a boyfriend. I have an old man," I say, climbing over him.

He cups my cheek with one hand. "Yeah, you do, Sunshine."

"So, I guess I better get ready for my chat with Chuck," I say as I sit up.

I don't even make it to the edge of the bed before Marcel pulls me back down.

"No."

"I'm not asking your permission." I stroke my fingers over his cheek. "I would like your help though."

"I'm not leaving you alone with him."

"Good." I press a soft kiss against his lips. "I don't think I could do it without you."

Teller

WE GET DRESSED and I take Charlotte up to the clubhouse. While we were busy and my phone was off, Whisper apparently called Rock to set something up.

"Where the fuck you been?" Z says as soon as he sees us. "I've been calling you for half an hour and it keeps going to voicemail."

"Oops."

"Christ, you spend one night in your new house and you're slacking off."

"If it helps, he was in the middle of some very important business at the time," Charlotte says with a straight face.

"Unless you're gonna give me details, I don't want to hear it," Z grumbles. "Get your ass in the war room, Teller."

I nudge Charlotte toward the couch. "Hang out here. This won't take long."

Rock, Wrath, and Murphy are waiting at the table when Z and I enter.

"At least we know he was serious about helping us out," Wrath says.

"A biker's word is all he's got sometimes." Rock taps his knuckles against the table. "That's why I can't believe this shit. Ulfric was always decent." He glances at Wrath. "We go way back with their club."

"I remember." Wrath shrugs. "Whisper definitely worked my last nerve from time to time—"

Z butts in. "Who doesn't work your last nerve?"

"You're working it right now, asshole." Wrath faces Rock again, dismissing Z. "Overall, Whisper's usually honest."

"So how'd they miss that Merlin was such an asshole?" I grumble because I'm not in the mood to listen to anything resembling praise for the Wolf Knights right now.

"What are you going to do?" Murphy asks.

"Beat the truth out of him," I answer. Dead serious too.

No one laughs or disagrees with me.

"You bringing Charlotte?" Murphy asks.

I run my hands over my hair and down the back of my neck a few times, considering all the ways this can go wrong. "Fuck, I don't want to. But she knows what questions to ask better than I do."

Rock slaps the table. "Let's do it."

"Now?" I ask.

"Whisper's waiting for us," Wrath explains.

Charlotte's waiting in the living room and doesn't question where we're going.

Rock, Wrath, Z, and Murphy all ride to the Wolf Knights' clubhouse with us. Charlotte feels so good at my back, I want to continue down the highway. Keep on riding and take her far away from any more pain.

Because I know whatever we learn from Merlin today will hurt.

When we arrive at the clubhouse, Whisper's waiting outside. He shakes all our hands before settling his gaze on Charlotte.

"I'm so sorry, sweetheart. I never knew." He seems genuine in his concern. Charlotte straightens up and nods in response.

"Did he give you anything?" I ask.

Whisper doesn't hesitate to answer. Even though my president's standing right behind me, this is my show today. "Not yet. Said he won't discuss it with anyone except her."

"She's not going in alone." I crack my knuckles. "You okay with what's about to happen?"

"We owe you a debt." That's a *yes* as far as I'm concerned. He glances at Charlotte again. "You too. Cash and blood. That's how we pay our debts."

"Amen to that," I grumble.

Charlotte remains silent and I'd give anything to hear her thoughts.

We follow Whisper inside and he leads us downstairs, someplace I've never been in their clubhouse. The way Charlotte shivers and holds onto my hand, I don't think she's been here either.

Whisper opens a dark wood door with a small window at the top.

Merlin's inside, sitting behind a metal table. On closer inspection, I notice he's actually handcuffed to the table.

"You son of a bitch, Whisper. We've been brothers for decades and you're handing me over to this fucker?"

"I ain't handing you over to anyone, but you owe this girl some answers."

"That's it?"

Whisper strokes a hand over his beard. "Well, if he roughs you up a little, you kind of have it coming, no?"

It seems Whisper might've had a few beating-the-shit-out-of-Merlin fantasies of his own lately.

"Fuck you," Merlin spits.

Whisper backs out of the room, pulling me along. "Give me your word he'll still be breathing when you're done."

"I want some answers from him. That's all," Charlotte says.

But Whisper wasn't asking her, he was looking at me. He raises an eyebrow, waiting for my answer.

"As long as he doesn't try to hurt her again, you have my word."

I don't think Whisper expected anything other than a 'yes' from me, but he can't argue either.

After he leaves, I turn to my brothers, lifting my chin, silently asking them to wait here in the hallway.

"We're right here, Teller. Go on," Rock answers.

Settling my hand at the small of her back, I guide Charlotte into the room ahead of me.

Merlin finally seems to notice that she's here. "Come to stab me again?" He laughs. "Never saw that coming." He holds his fingers an inch apart. "Doctors said you came this close to killing me."

"You make one move toward her and *I'll* fucking kill you," I warn him. "Don't give a fuck what arrangement our clubs have made."

Merlin dips his chin, acknowledging my threat. I pull out the chair across from him and Charlotte takes it. I'll move to the back of the room in a minute to give them the illusion of privacy, even though the room's so small, I'll be able to hear every word between them.

I have a feeling Charlotte's going to need me. And I intend to stay right here with her.

CHAPTER TWENTY-SIX

Charlotte

TELLER LEANS IN and kisses my cheek. "You've got this, Sunshine," he whispers against my ear. "I'll be right here."

My uncle locks eyes with Teller. Cold electricity crackles between them. On the outside, Teller appears calm and doesn't flinch.

"I know you think it's insignificant," I say, drawing Chuck's attention away from Teller, "but I need you to tell me the truth about the night I was raped." Saying the words out loud gives me a sense of power over the situation. Something I desperately need to carry me through this meeting.

Teller steps back, giving me space. He's right, I can handle this. His presence surrounds me like a warm blanket of safety.

Uncle Chuck drops his head, staring at his hand that's bound to the table. "Char, I know I'm a bastard. I've given you a lot of reasons to hate me and don't deserve your trust. But please, for your sake, let this go. You have a good life. Forget about that night."

It's the most sincere, honest statement that's come out of Chuck's mouth in years. Maybe I should heed the warning, but I can't. Not after everything that's happened. "You're right. My life was perfectly fine without you and your club in it. *You're* the one who brought all of this up again. If you stayed out of our relationship none of this would've happened. You could've kept your awful secrets."

He picks up his head and glares at Teller. "Known you since you were a little girl, Char. Lawyer or not. You're too fucking honest. I knew if you two got close, you'd end up confiding the whole story to him. And I *knew* that motherfucker wouldn't let something like that go."

"Fucking A," Teller grumbles behind me.

Chuck scowls even harder at Teller. "Christ, you've always been a self-righteous prick. Just like your prez."

Teller sneers. "Thank you."

"Leave Teller out of it. He's a decent guy. I understand that's confusing for you."

Chuck snorts. "Bikers can't afford to let women make them soft."

"Stop fucking around and tell her what she needs to know," Teller snaps. "Before I beat it out of you."

"Jesus Christ, he reminds me a lot of Dean," Chuck mumbles, shaking his head.

My jaw drops. "What are you talking about? You told me he was nothing like Dad."

Chuck glares at Teller. "I don't suppose you'll wait outside, so I can have this conversation with my niece in private."

No. No. No.

"*One*," Tellers says. "If you're not talking—*two*—by the time I get to five—I'm going to—*three*—break—every finger in your—"

"All right. Jesus. Fuck." Chuck drops his gaze again. "Did you know I met your mother first?"

Now that we wore him down and it seems like he's finally ready to tell me the truth, ice settles in my stomach. Maybe he was right, and this is a truth I should leave buried. "No," I finally answer.

He takes a deep breath and sits back, staring straight ahead, but I don't think he's looking at Teller. It's more like he's trying to capture a glimpse into the past.

"She was a grade below me in high school. Dean was a year behind her."

"I knew they met in high school."

"I saw her first." He meets my eyes and a hint of a smile curves his lips. "She was beautiful. You really do look so much like her when she was younger."

Instead of glowing from the compliment, icy fear shoots through my veins.

"Anyway, we dated through my senior year."

Holy shit. That's news to me. I always assumed whatever their strange relationship was, it started *after* my father died.

"After graduation, I start hanging around here more. I don't have to tell you what goes on in the club. Or out on the road." He smirks at Teller. "What happens on the road stays on the road, right, son?"

"Maybe for you," Teller fires back.

"So, you cheated on Mom?" I ask.

"Even when she was a teenager, she had a vicious little temper. She got even with me in the most perverse way."

Trying not to seem too hopeful, I ask, "Did she cut off your balls?"

One corner of his mouth twists up. "That might've hurt less."

What he's hinting at becomes clear. "She hooked up with Dad? To get even with you for cheating on her? Is that what you're saying?"

"She didn't know a single one of those girls." He presses his free hand against his chest. Not in a dramatic way. An unconscious gesture as he searches for the right words. "But she knew how close Dean and I were."

"So you're saying their whole marriage was based on getting even with you. Christ, your ego has no bounds."

He snorts out a laugh. "I wish it was that simple. But no, she loved him. And he was crazy about her. I loved both of them and wanted them to be happy, so I stayed out of their way."

"Well, aren't you a martyr."

"Not really. I brought him into the club. Figured he'd fuck up the same way I did and teach her a lesson."

"So much for staying out of their way," I mumble.

"It didn't work. They had you. Went on about their happy life. He never strayed once that I know of."

After that he's quiet and something awful occurs to me. "Did you kill him? To get her back?"

"What kind of question is that?" I think I actually hurt his feelings, if he has any. "No, Charlotte. I should've died in that accident. It should've been me. I didn't have a wife and kids depending on me. No one would've given a shit if I'd been the one to slam into that semi."

"Mom would've cared. Dad would've cared."

"After Dean died, she lost it. I did all I could do to keep her out of trouble. She was constantly running up debts with dealers and fucking around with shady characters."

I want to scream when he stops talking to take in a deep breath.

"I tried reasoning with her. I tried being with her." He glances down. "But she hated me for being alive when he was dead and she never let me forget it."

Tears burn my eyes. I remember a lot of their back and forth. The times Chuck tried to stay at our house and inject some normalcy into our daily lives. Not that he was perfect. Or could ever replace my dad. But as much as I hate him, I have to admit I remember times when he *tried*.

"Go on."

"That last time I was inside, was the worst. She was a mess when I got out."

"I remember."

"I was really proud of you when you went to college. And when you said you wanted to go to law school. Your dad would've loved that. I wasn't lying that day." He pauses to glare at Teller. "He didn't want this life for you."

A lot of little things Mom said to me when I graduated from college come back. Things I probably pushed to the edges of my memory. "Mom wasn't happy about it though, was she?"

"No," he admits. "She wasn't. She got pregnant with you and had to drop out of college."

She never let me forget it either.

"Christmas was the worst time for her," he continues. "I think Dean's death always hit her hardest during the holidays. That particular year, she was into her dealer for a lot of money. No matter how hard I tried to keep these fuckers away from her, she always found a way. I beat and ran off more dealers, other clubs, gangs, you name it. When that woman wanted something, she was relentless."

"I'm sure having a woman in your life who you couldn't control, made club life awkward for you." He doesn't so much as flinch at the venom in my voice.

"It wasn't easy keeping the two things separate when she'd drop my name as a way to get out of paying her debts. She did that more than once." He stops and stares at me. "I think that's enough."

"Don't you *dare* stop now. You haven't told me anything useful."

"I've said enough."

There's a scrape of the chair next to me being pulled over the concrete floor. Marcel sits and takes my hand. "Who are you protecting, Merlin? Charlotte or her mother?" he asks quietly. No hint of anger or judgment in his tone.

Chuck meets my eyes. "Both."

"What are you saying?" I ask.

Chuck blows out a long breath. "Your mother was into some gangbanger for a lot of money. Without warning me, she invited him to come to the party with the promise he'd get paid."

A memory fuzzes at the edge of my brain. The parking lot behind the clubhouse. A bedroom. A black T-shirt. The harder I try to focus on it, the fuzzier it becomes, and then it's gone.

"Charlotte?" Teller squeezes my hand. "Are you all right?"

"I'm fine." I meet Chuck's curious eyes. "Go on."

"At this point, Cindy had been bleeding me dry for months. I didn't have enough on me to cover the whole amount." He takes a long deep breath, letting it out maddeningly slow. "When I left to get the cash, she worked out a different deal."

"What?"

Marcel squeezes my hand tighter. "He's right. That's enough, Sunshine."

I seem to be the only one missing a giant piece of the puzzle.

A puzzle that's right in front of me.

Or my mind just can't bend around the dark truth.

"I don't understand. What different deal?"

Chuck can't meet my eyes. "When I returned to the clubhouse, he was gone—or so your mother said. Made up some bullshit story about how he decided to wait for the money. She claimed you'd gotten into an argument with her and went back to your apartment."

"I don't remember fighting with her that night."

He hesitates, and I almost scream in frustration.

"She asked me to take her home." He drops his head and in a lower voice adds, "Then she asked me to stay."

"So you were busy *reconciling* with her mom, while Charlotte was getting raped?" Teller spits out.

Chuck doesn't respond to the accusation. "I didn't know what she'd done."

"Wait." Shards of awareness slice into me. "*Mom* set me up? My own mother? To pay off a drug debt?"

I shoot out of my chair so fast it tips over, clattering to the floor. The agony of betrayal burns through my veins. Blinding pain steals my vision and breath. Blood roars through my ears, drowning out everything else.

My mother?

Marcel's at my side, wrapping his arms around me, pulling me against his warm solid body. My fingers curl into his shirt as my tears soak the fabric. He continues stroking my back.

"It's okay, Sunshine. It's okay." He holds me, whispering soothing words in my ear, rocking us from side to side until I can breathe again.

I sniffle and wipe the dampness from my cheeks.

Marcel hugs my face with his hands, staring into my eyes. "You don't have to keep doing this."

"Yes, I do."

When I face my uncle again, he's watching us with an unreadable expression.

Marcel picks up my chair and guides me into it. I take a breath, composing myself before addressing Chuck. "Finish. Please."

He sighs, his gaze darting around the tiny room as if he's trying to search for the right words. "When you came to me days later, I put it together right away." His eyes find mine and he reaches across the table with his free hand and grasps my fingers. "It fuckin' gutted me that she was capable of something so malicious. Of hurting her own daughter."

"Way to rewrite history, Uncle Chuck. You remember what you said to me? Do you remember blaming *me* for being raped?"

He flinches and averts his gaze. "I handled it badly."

Chuck admitting he made a mistake. That's new.

His helpless blue eyes meet mine again. "I didn't know what to do. I put your story together with your mother's, but I couldn't tell you my suspicion. I wanted to be wrong." He shakes his head and stares down at the table. "After you left, I had it out with Cindy. First, she claimed she didn't remember. Then she cried and said she was high and didn't know what she was doing."

"Bullshit," I snort.

"She begged me not to tell you. I promised to keep her secret in exchange for something else."

"What?" I can't keep the exasperation out of my voice. "Please don't tell me you blackmailed her for sex."

I'm tired. So tired of trying to pull this information out of him. Sick from learning how disturbed my mother truly was. Embarrassed Marcel's sitting here listening to the twisted tale of my family tree. Humiliated to have the man I love discover what kind of evil runs through my blood.

To his credit, Chuck doesn't try to defend himself. "I made her call the guy to the house. Then forced her into rehab."

I snort. "Well, that didn't work."

This conversation seems to have aged him twenty years. He lets out a heavy sigh. "It did for a while. It got her off the hard drugs at least. After that, she only drank to forget."

"Don't you dare try to make me feel sorry for her."

"Who was the guy?" Teller asks.

"Some mid-level dealer, who ran with the 18th Street Boyz back then," Chuck answers. "I made him suffer, Char. I promise you. But I couldn't tell you the truth."

"Why?"

He tilts his head, dropping the tough-biker mask he usually wears. Probably the saddest expression I've ever seen settles over his face.

Marcel squeezes my hand under the table. "He still loved her," he says in a low voice.

"I did." Chuck dips his chin. "But I never looked at her the same after that and she knew it."

In light of his story, all the anger and dysfunction in their relationship makes more sense.

"I thought I found the best solution, Char. Even though it drove you farther away. I figured that was for the best. That it would keep you from getting hurt again."

"Did anyone else in the club know?" Teller asks.

"No one until you told Whisper." He faces me. "I wouldn't expose you. I made sure no one else knew."

I snort. "Don't act like you were protecting my honor. You just didn't want your bros finding out that you lost control of a situation."

He doesn't bother with a denial.

"Who was the other guy?" Teller asks.

Chuck's forehead wrinkles. "What other guy?"

"Chuck, at the hospital," I whisper. Red-hot shame washes over me as I explain it to him. "They ran tests. When the report came back. More than one person…" I'm so mortified, I can't finish.

He slams his fist into the table and tries to stand, but his cuffed hand holds him in place. "What the fuck are you talking about?"

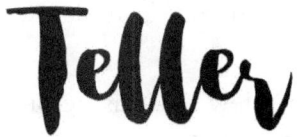

JESUS CHRIST, THIS is so much worse than I ever anticipated.

Merlin looks like he's been sucker-punched in the gut, but I refuse to feel sorry for him. I don't give two fucks that the reason he lied to Charlotte was out of some twisted love for her mother. The result's the same. Charlotte's innocent in all of this, yet she's the one who got hurt back then and the one who's hurting now.

My love for my own mother died when I realized she wasn't capable of returning affection and didn't care about my sister's safety. Protecting *Heidi* became the most important thing to me. Not my mother. Some things are unforgiveable in my book. Always have been.

So, no, I'm not in the mood to empathize with Merlin today.

Maybe Charlotte can't process everything or maybe she senses our time here is limited and has other questions she needs answers to before Whisper kicks us out. She ignores Merlin's outburst and sits forward. Her calm, professional mask slides into place. "Why'd you take my money then?"

He shrugs. "You were adamant. So angry. I didn't know what else to do. I was dealing with your mother at the time too. Trying to keep her straight. I put it away for you. Figured I'd give it to you eventually. Or just leave it to you when I die."

It's a shit answer, considering how much Charlotte's been struggling these last few years. It also makes me love her even more for being so determined and resilient.

"Why are you so awful to my brother?" she asks in a small voice.

Merlin's jaw tightens and he glances away.

My body twitches, anticipating his answer.

"He's your *half*-brother." The words fire out of his mouth like bullets, ricocheting around the room.

"What?!" Charlotte explodes. "You claimed they were so happy together."

He works his jaw for a few seconds before turning his cold eyes my way. "You know as well as I do how sometimes our women end up victims of our club disputes."

Considering I helped Rock take out the Viper who planned to hurt Hope a few years ago, as well as murdered the man responsible for Mariella's death, I'd say I know a little about it.

"Yes."

He nods. "That's one thing neither of our clubs ever engaged in. Only the lowest harm innocents."

"Agreed."

"But you also know not everyone in our world sees it that way. You remember what happened to Ulfric's sister-in-law?"

"Not really."

He lifts his chin at the door. "Rock probably knows then."

"Stick to Charlotte's mother." I don't know how much more of this Charlotte can take. We can't afford for him to veer off-topic now.

"Right. That wasn't the first time the Vipers went after one of our women. That's one of the reasons our clubs always worked together."

"Yeah, by the time I started hanging around the club, Wolf Knights were considered friends of the club."

Merlin snorts. "Shit, you were a scrawny piss-ant back then."

Charlotte's head swivels between us as if it just occurred to her that Merlin and I have moved in the same circles for years.

"We kept most of our affairs to ourselves." He gives me a pointed look. "No matter how tight two clubs are, they're never gonna share everything. But we always knew we could count on Kings to back us up."

"Same."

"Even if we don't trust each other one-hundred percent."

"Kings first."

"Right.

"Um, can you guys wax on about the joys of brotherhood some other time, please?" Charlotte says. "We were discussing my mother."

Merlin huffs out a laugh. "God help you, Teller."

Charlotte growls in frustration, and Merlin turns serious again. I get the feeling it's a painful story he's worked hard to forget. Unfortunately, my sympathy for Merlin is in short supply.

"Cindy got caught in the middle." Merlin's non-explanation doesn't satisfy Charlotte.

"How?" The word slides out of her mouth as an impatient growl and I squeeze her hand to keep her from lunging across the table.

Chuck glares at her in a way I don't care for. "She didn't know her damn place."

"Thanks for clearing that up," she mutters.

"She didn't listen when her man told her to stay out of Viper territory," Merlin says with a dose of bitterness.

"Did Dad know?"

"Of course Dean knew. They'd been trying for years to have another kid. Your father didn't care she was carrying some rapist, bastard's baby."

Charlotte gasps and falls back against her chair. "Jesus Christ. Did he...did he make her...?"

"She didn't realize it until it was too late. Dean didn't care. He wanted a son and he made damn sure no one ever knew the truth."

Charlotte nods. "He never treated Carter differently. But Mom—"

"He was a constant, painful reminder to Cindy."

"That's not his fault," Charlotte whispers.

Merlin shrugs as if he couldn't care less.

Asshole.

"Does Carter know?" I ask.

"No. Dean made me promise." He looks away. "I wouldn't have disrespected Cindy like that anyway."

"But you treated him like shit instead? Good job, Uncle Chuck."

He spreads his free arm wide. "What do you want from me, Charlotte?"

Cheeks pink with anger, she leans over the table, a little too close to Merlin for my taste, and lowers her voice to a seething whisper. "You claim you loved my mother so much. Whatever the circumstances, he's her son and you've been awful to him his whole life."

All he does is nod as if he agrees with every word. "Told you, it should've been me who died on that highway, not your dad."

Tears fill her eyes, but she doesn't respond. Merlin sits back, watching her come apart with shining eyes of his own.

"We're not finished," I inform him.

His startled gaze swings my way. "What else is there?"

I lean forward, slapping my hands on the table. "Who else was here that night?"

"No one." He glances at Charlotte and shakes his head. "Your mother told you that story about a visiting club later, so you'd forget about her dealer. She was ashamed of what she'd done and paranoid you'd figure it out." He shakes his head. "She didn't need to worry about it, though. Your mind was all fucked up from whatever the fuck she gave you."

"I swear to fuck, Merlin, if you're lying—"

He cuts me off, any regret he'd just displayed vanishing. "You think

I'm going to give up her mom after I protected her secret all these years, but hide someone else? Fuck you."

"Yeah, if you were trying to strike a deal with another club behind your president's back. You know, like what you've been doing with South of Satan MC."

"Sit down and shut up, boy. You don't know fucking shit about anything."

"I know you promised to patch over South of Satan to try to push us out of Ironworks. Maybe you were working with them back then too?"

He snorts and then laughs. "Nothing got by Ulfric back then. The deal I was working on *now* is none of your fucking business." He waves his hand at the door. "Besides, I'm pretty sure, thanks to your crew, Whisper has killed that arrangement."

"You'd protect one of your brothers over me," Charlotte whispers. "It's always been club first, family last for you."

"I deserve that." He slides his gaze back to Charlotte and his hard expression fades. "Are you sure there was someone else?"

She shakes her head. This whole thing has completely unraveled her. "Yes, but I threw all the paperwork from the hospital away years ago."

I lean in closer. "Who was part of the club back then?"

"How do you expect me to give up a brother?"

"You owe her. That's how."

He sits back and shakes his head. "Ulfric was away. Whisper was away. Hudson was a member of another charter back then."

"What about Tiki? Keeper? Dolph?" I'm dangerously close to an ass-kicking if Whisper overhears me accusing his brothers and don't even care. "Come on, think."

Merlin shakes his head. "These are men I've shared a patch with for years, Teller. I can't fathom one of them disrespecting me that way."

"It's not about *you*," Charlotte snaps.

"I honestly don't know."

I hate that I actually believe him. He seems as distressed as I am.

Probably because he's doing the math and realizing, whether he likes it or not, the other person *had* to be one of his brothers.

Christ, I'm torn between beating the shit out of him for hurting Charlotte, for lying to her all these years, for everything. And if we were alone right now, my fists would be flying. But after everything she's had to take in today, I can't stand the thought of more violence invading her mind. And I can't send her outside. Not even when I know my brothers will look after her while I deliver the punches Merlin has coming.

I just can't leave her side.

Besides, somewhere in this clubhouse, there's a Wolf Knight who knows the truth.

Now to figure out which one.

CHAPTER TWENTY-SEVEN

Charlotte

I'M NUMB AND broken as we leave my uncle's cell.

Teller leans in and whispers something in Merlin's ear, then walks us into the hallway.

Rock places his hand on my shoulder. "You okay, sweetheart?"

"I don't know," I mumble.

"Let's get her home, then we'll regroup," Wrath says to Teller. He raises an eyebrow and tilts his head toward the room, asking Teller some unspoken question I can't decipher.

Teller shakes his head and squeezes me tighter.

"I got you, bro" Wrath says in a low voice, stepping away.

Rock and Z follow us up the stairs into the common area where we meet with Whisper.

"He still alive?" Whisper asks.

"Unfortunately," Teller grumbles.

Whisper glances down at me. "Get your answers?"

"Maybe a few too many." Another damn tear rolls down my cheek and I swipe it away with an angry flick of my wrist.

Keeper strolls into the room and stops when he sees us. "What's going on?" he asks.

"Nothing," Whisper answers without turning around. "Not your concern."

Teller narrows his eyes, watching Keeper closely.

Wrath joins us and pulls Whisper aside. Rock and Z walk out ahead of us and we follow.

As we pass Keeper, his dark eyes drill into me while his mouth tightens into a creepy smile. A shiver of fear skitters down my back.

Keeper throws out one hand, stopping Teller. "Merlin's out now. Better watch your back."

Teller's eyes narrow. "How's that, Keeper?"

"Well, her last thug boyfriend disappeared. Guessing she never mentioned it."

"Fuck you, Keeper. You fucking asshole," I shout. I haven't forgotten the way he pushed to have my uncle bug my phone or the nasty things he said about me.

Teller unwraps his arm from my shoulders and presses both hands to Keeper's chest, shoving him into the wall. "Don't talk to her or even look at her again, or you're dead. We clear?"

"Hey! What's going on?" Whisper shouts, storming over to us.

"Your VP needs to learn some fucking respect," Teller growls, still pressing Keeper to the wall.

"Easy, brother," Wrath says in a low voice. Even though he seems to be trying to diffuse the situation, his fighting stance suggests he's ready to attack if anyone lays a finger on us.

Keeper finally holds up his hands. "No disrespect intended."

"Go on," Whisper says to us. "I got him."

Teller gives Keeper one last shove before taking my hand and storming out.

AT HIS BIKE, I stop, tugging on his hand. "Take me home. Please."

He hesitates, glancing at Rock and Z. "I need to go back to the clubhouse."

To discuss all the dirty details he learned about me, I'm sure.

I can't be around the guys for that. I won't be able to look at any of them in the eye ever again.

"Drop me off at the house then."

His fingers brush my chin, tipping my head back. "I don't want you alone right now."

"I can't see anyone. Especially if. If..." I can't even complete my thought.

"Hey," he leans in closer, brushing his lips against my ear, "everything we learned from Merlin today stays between the three of us. That's what I told him before we left."

"Really?"

"Yes." His gaze darts around the parking lot. "Except that I want to figure out which Wolf Knight hurt you. Everything else stays buried."

"Carter?"

"We'll talk about it more later, but honestly, I don't see what good comes from telling him. It's only going to hurt him and bring up questions he'll never be able to get answers for."

"Thank you," I whisper.

He hugs me to his chest and I soak in his warmth for the few brief seconds before he lets go.

"All set?" Wrath's big voice startles us apart. He settles one hand on Teller's shoulder and my gaze falls on his scraped knuckles.

"Let's go."

STILL WORRIED ABOUT Charlotte, I watch her trudge up the stairs at the clubhouse. I should go with her, but I'm too eager to sit down at the table and figure out my next move.

At least I know she's safe here.

"How'd it go?" Rock says as I close the war room door behind me.

"Awful. Merlin's an asshole, but at least he's not as twisted as I feared," I answer, glancing at Z.

"Are we done with this?" Rock asks, sounding as confused as I feel.

I think about how to say it without revealing too much, but fucking hell, do I finally want some justice for Charlotte.

"What I didn't say before was that…more than one person hurt her that night. Merlin found out about one back then. Turns out he *did* handle it."

Wrath scowls. "He did? Why the fuck didn't he just say so?"

"It's…complicated."

Rock throws a hard look at Wrath before addressing me. "That's not important. Continue."

"He didn't seem to know about the other person."

"How's that possible?" Z asks.

"I don't know. But I'm pretty sure it was another Wolf Knight. And after he thought about it, Merlin seemed to agree. He just didn't know who."

"Ulfric and Whisper are out," Z says, jumping straight in.

"Tiny died a couple years ago, but that fucker was so old he could barely move, let alone get it up," Wrath says.

Murphy sits up. "Tiki likes younger women."

"So do you," Z jokes.

"Stay on track," Rock warns.

"What did Keeper say to you tonight?" Wrath asks.

"Nothing useful." I actually think about the words Keeper used. "He implied Merlin has gotten rid of Charlotte's boyfriends before and to watch my back."

"What a tool."

Charlotte's never told me much about any of her boyfriends, something I probably wouldn't have wanted to hear anyway, but the fact that Keeper described one as a thug, gives me pause.

"I need to think on it and talk to Charlotte some more."

"All right." Rock holds up a hand indicating I should stay for a second. "If you come up with anything or Charlotte thinks of anything, call me."

"Thanks, Prez."

Charlotte

AFTER TELLER ENTERS the war room, I can't shake off the ugliness swirling and pulsing in my head. Finally learning what really happened should've set all the demons chewing at my insides free. So, why does uncovering the truth hurt so much worse than living with the lies all these years?

A need to run and be alone consumes me, but since I came here with Marcel, I'm trapped.

"Hey, Charlotte," Heidi calls out. "Everything okay?" She's leaving her room and when I meet her eyes her smile falters.

"Hi. Are you busy right now?" I ask.

She frowns. "No, not really. Hope's watching Alexa while she naps. I just ran over here to—"

"Do you think you can run me home? The guys are at the table and I need to do a few things."

"Uh, sure. I guess."

The whole way downstairs, she chatters about Alexa, school, and her job. I nod and try to follow along, but the need to get home overwhelms all my other senses.

"Are you sure you don't want to wait for my brother? They probably won't take that long," Heidi says when we arrive at her car. She glances back at the clubhouse and worries her bottom lip with her teeth.

"Nah," I say, trying to inject some casualness into my voice. "Who knows how long they'll be there."

After Heidi drops me off, the first thing, hell the only thing I can think about, is taking a shower. Hot enough to scrub the filth of the afternoon off.

Under the steady beat of water, shame makes its long, overdue appearance and I slump against the wall.

Marcel heard *all* of it. If I'd had any idea the full story would be that awful, I would have begged him to stay outside.

My mother.

I can't.

How is he ever going to forget everything he learned? Or want to have children with someone who comes with so much toxic baggage? What I learned today stung like being violated all over again.

Actually, it's worse, because it's not a stranger who betrayed me. It was my own blood. The person who should've protected me instead offered me up to the wolves.

With no clear plan in mind, I shut off the water, dry myself, and head upstairs to pack.

My mind's spinning so fast, I can barely breathe as I pull out a small suitcase and a backpack. A bitter smile forces my mouth up. A few days ago, I unpacked these same bags thinking I was starting a future in a new home with the man I love.

Now? Any future I thought I could have is stained with the painful truths we learned this afternoon. The little blond mini-Marcels I'd allow myself to picture having one day? *Gone.* Our sweet little girl I secretly dreamed about dressing in "daddy's girl" onesies? *Nope.* My hand absently settles over my stomach. How could he ever trust me with his children after what we learned today?

I pause in the middle of tossing a shirt in my suitcase. It's actually Marcel's and I stop to inhale his scent.

Should I stay and try to explain it to him?

No. He may have looked at me with nothing but love after we left my uncle. But eventually the details will sink in and I can't be there when that love is replaced by disgust.

I'm not sure where I'm going, but I can't stay here.

CHAPTER TWENTY-EIGHT

Teller

H EIDI'S CLOSING THE front door when we step out of the war room.
"Hey, beautiful, what're you up to?" Murphy asks, hurrying
over to her.

"Can't you keep your grimy paws off my sister for five seconds?" I
grumble.

Without turning around, Murphy throws up a middle finger and
continues molesting my sister. Eager to check on Charlotte, I leave them
and head upstairs.

"Hang on, Marcel," she says, pushing Murphy back. "I just dropped
Charlotte off at home, Marcel."

I pause mid-step. "You what? Why?"

"She said she had stuff to do and didn't want to wait for you." Her
gaze pings between Murphy and me. "Was that okay?"

"Yeah, it's fine," I say, reversing direction. "Thanks."

It's not fine at all. Dread settles over me. I shouldn't have left Charlotte alone after hearing all that garbage about her mother. Christ,
Charlotte's mother and my own could've been best friends. They sure
seem to have had the same set of twisted priorities.

"Hey," I say, pulling Heidi out of Murphy's grabby hands. I wrap
her up in a tight hug, wishing like hell I'd done more to protect her, but
thankful for the strong woman she's turned into. "Love you, kid."

"What's wrong, Marcel?" she asks.

"Nothing," I say, releasing her. "I'll catch you two later."

On the short ride to our house, I work out my thoughts on Keeper. Soon, I need to talk about it with Charlotte, but not tonight.

The house is quiet. She had to hear me ride up, but she's not downstairs. Maybe she was tired, drained from the day and decided to take a nap.

I take the stairs slowly, partially because my leg's bothering me today but also because if she's sleeping, I don't want to wake her up.

When I find her in the bedroom, she's not sleeping.

She's sitting on the edge of the bed staring at the floor.

A hot poker of pain hits me in the chest as my gaze lands on the suitcase and backpack at her feet.

She's *leaving me?*

"Charlotte? What're you doing?"

She whips her head around, surprise to find me in the doorway written all over her troubled face.

"What's going on?"

A soft sniffle reaches me and I can't stand another second of not holding her. I cross the room, avoiding the evidence of her intent to run and sit next to her on the edge of the bed.

"I'm sorry I took so long. It could've waited," I say, as I wrap one arm around her and tuck her against me. "Is that why you came home?"

"Marcel, I can't," she says, pushing me away and standing.

My heart hammers, but I keep my expression and voice calm. "Can't what? Talk about it? We don't have to tonight."

"No. I can't do *this.*"

Ice crackles through my veins. "Do what?"

"This. A relationship. Not after…Jesus, I wish you hadn't heard all of that."

"You're losing me, Sunshine." I reach for her hand and she steps back.

"Don't. I feel filthier than I did the day it happened."

"You didn't do anything wrong."

"No, but that same poison runs through me, Marcel. How could I ever…why would you ever?"

"What?"

"You don't want me to be the mother of your children. Knowing that's what I come from."

Utterly confused with her logic, I stand, running my hands through my hair. "Charlotte, you're one of the smartest women I've ever known, but that has to be the stupidest thing you've ever said."

"Don't call me stupid."

Her broken voice hurts so much as I struggle for the words to fix this. "Hey, I thought we cured that hearing problem of yours," I tease, reaching out to tickle my fingers over her earlobe. "Don't slide backward now."

The corner of her mouth twitches.

I move in closer, tucking a piece of hair behind her ear. "We're in this together, Charlotte. I'm not going anywhere."

She drops her gaze, shaking her head. "I'm not good for you."

"You're the best part of me."

She opens her mouth—probably for another denial—and I hold up my hand. "You're nothing like your mother. You're all sweetness and light and warmth."

"How could she do that?" she asks, sounding so lost and shattered.

What excuse can I invent that will ever make any of this hurt less? None. So, I go for honesty. "I don't know. I *do* know what a good person you are and how much I love you."

"Marcel, I love you too. So much." She rakes her nails over her arms and neck, leaving red streaks over her pale skin and I grab her hands to make her stop. "I hate that you heard all of that."

"It doesn't matter to me." I pause and take a deep breath, considering my next words. "Charlotte, do you know why my mother abandoned Heidi and me at my grandmother's?"

She tilts her head at the shift in conversation.

"Heidi said she ran off with a boyfriend or something."

"Probably. But that's not why she left us there."

"From what you've both said, it doesn't sound like she was a great mother before that."

"No, she wasn't. But it's my fault she left."

Some of her uncertainty disappears and her voice comes out stronger. "Marcel, all kids feel that way about a parent leaving."

"This time it's actually true." I run my fingers through my hair—at the rate I'm going, I'll be bald soon. "She used to have a lot of men in and out of our house. When Heidi was maybe five or six, one of them took an unusual interest her. I didn't like it one bit, but I was a kid. There wasn't much I could do other than tell her not to be alone with him and stay with her at night if he was at the house."

"Jesus, Marcel. How come she's never said anything?"

"Honestly, I'm not sure if she even remembers. You know I was already hanging around the club by then. I asked two of the older members to talk to the guy. I just wanted them to scare him away, so he'd stop coming around."

"And?"

"They talked to him. Talked to my mother too. She dumped us at my grandmother's not long after."

"That's not your fault," she argues in a fierce tone that sounds more like my Charlotte. "You were trying to protect your sister."

"Yeah, well, I didn't know it until recently, but my grandmother beat the hell out of Heidi for years after she kicked me out. So that's on me too."

She gasps and covers her mouth with her hand. "Goddammit. I *knew* things weren't right when I represented her, but Heidi never—"

"Because the old bitch filled her head with bullshit about how she'd get put into foster care if she said anything."

"That's ridiculous."

"She was a kid. She didn't know any better."

Charlotte seems so distressed, I almost feel bad for sharing this with her on top of everything else she's had to take in today.

"When I tell you that I've fucked up and failed—"

"That's not your fault, Marcel. Come on."

"It is, though. And I hate myself for it. Hate that for all those years she held it in and thought she couldn't tell me." My voice cracks and I stop. This isn't about me or my guilt. This is about Charlotte.

"But it's not your fault. You're so good to her. All she ever talked about was how much she loves you."

I close the distance between us and take her hands. "I'm sharing this with you because I want you to understand what kind of family *I* come from, Charlotte. People can say what they want about Heidi having Alexa so young, but she's a damn good mother. A hundred times better than our own mother ever was."

Her bottom lip trembles and she finally meets my eyes.

"From what your uncle said, it sounds like your mother was always a troubled, selfish bitch. That's probably *why* you ended up being the sweet, loving person you are. What's going through your head, Charlotte? You think you're going to magically turn into a monster one day?"

A faint smile ghosts over her lips. "You're trying to tell me I'm being ridiculous."

I throw my hands up in the air. "Finally! She gets it."

She doesn't laugh. Instead, she wraps her arms around my middle and rests her cheek against my chest, which is even better.

"Today sucked so bad," she murmurs.

"Yes, it did."

"Thank you."

"You never have to thank me."

One check of her face shows how much she's still hurting.

"What can I do to cheer you up, Sunshine?"

"I don't think anything can cheer me up right now," she says, shaking her head.

"No? How about if I do a strip tease for you?" I back away and slip off my cut, nice and slow, making a good show of it, add a few hip thrusts, and generally make a fool of myself. But it does the trick. She's laughing in no time.

"Oh my God. Make it stop."

"Stop? This isn't turning you on, babe?"

More giggles and she throws her hands over her mouth, but still can't contain her laughter.

"That's better." I stop gyrating around the room and point to her packed bags. "You want to explain this?"

"I panicked."

"No more panic. You don't have to hide any part of yourself from me." My smile fades and I look her in the eyes. "And don't you *dare* ever leave me like that."

"I'm sorry."

"You know I'd hunt you down, right?"

She huffs out a laugh. "And what? Drag me back by my hair?"

"No. Show you how much I love you until you believe it."

"I love you too."

"And *then* drag you back by your hair."

She rolls her eyes, but her smile remains. I hold out my hand and she curls her fingers around mine. "Come on, you haven't eaten all day."

"Ugh. I don't think I can keep anything down," she protests as she follows me downstairs.

"We'll see."

Turns out, my girl's starving. Together we cook a simple dinner of spaghetti and meatballs. It's not until we're almost finished that I bring up Keeper.

"What do you think that asshole meant by Merlin made your last thug boyfriend disappear?"

She sets her fork down and clasps her hands in front of her. "I have no idea."

That's what I was afraid of.

"You didn't date any gangsters in high school?" I say it in a teasing way, not wanting to risk upsetting her again.

"No. Never. My mother always hated the 'nerdy' guys I brought home." She narrows her eyes. "Why? What's on your mind?"

"I'm not sure yet."

CHAPTER TWENTY-NINE

Charlotte

A S MUCH AS possible, I try to put my uncle's revelations out of my head. Marcel helps by announcing he needs me to help him paint every room in the house.

First, we lure my brother over so we can show him the guest house.

To my surprise, Marcel's actually excited about showing it to Carter.

The house alarm lets out two short beeps, informing us someone's coming up the driveway. I glance at the monitor and relax when I recognize Carter's car.

"Why you so jumpy?" Marcel asks.

"I'm just excited to show him our place."

He kisses my cheek and we head outside to greet my brother.

Carter approaches us slowly. "Damn, this is some spread, Teller. I can't even be mad at you for taking my sister away."

"He didn't *take me away*. I'm probably closer to you now than when you were living at Mom's."

"Not the same."

He gives me a kiss on the cheek and hands me a bottle of wine. I raise an eyebrow and he shrugs. "I didn't know what else to bring and didn't want to show up with nothing."

"Thanks."

Marcel happily gives my brother the "guy" tour before bringing him into the kitchen for appetizers and drinks.

"How's my apartment?" I ask.

"Your landlord's such a dick. He stopped by and hassled me because I'm not on the lease. So, can you help me fix that?"

I tap my finger against my chin and pretend to consider it. "Well, I could, but I had something else in mind."

He narrows his eyes. "What?"

Marcel's grin seems to alarm my brother. "What are you two up to?"

"Come here, we want to show you something," I say, taking Carter's arm and leading him outside.

Marcel follows us and at the door to the guest house produces a key.

"Wow. This is cool." He moves through the space quickly, taking note of everything in his path. "So, I tell you two I'm on the verge of getting evicted and you're showing off all your fabulous space?"

"Actually," Marcel says, holding out a key. "This is yours if you want it."

Carter's eyes widen. "Mine?"

Marcel jerks his head toward the stairs. "Check out the upstairs."

He eyes us carefully before taking the steps one at a time.

"Oh, wow! It's an apartment." He's silent for a minute and then there's the sound of his feet racing above us. A few minutes later, he hops down the steps with an eager expression on his face. "Are you saying I can live up there?" he asks.

"Yup," Marcel says, handing over the keys.

"Wait," Carter says. "You two won't be doing any weird, naked, sex stuff in the yard, right?"

"We'll make sure you're out when we do our weird, naked, outdoor sex stuff," Marcel assures him.

"Gross," Carter mumbles. His eyes light up again. "Am I allowed to have girls over?"

"If you can find one who wants to come over, yeah."

Carter groans and meets my eyes. "I don't have to take that abuse from your old man, do I?"

"Afraid so, little brother."

His gaze sweeps the downstairs area. "What're you going to do with this space?"

"It's yours too," Marcel says. "Thought you could turn it into an art studio or something."

"Seriously?" He glances at everything again and his smile falters. "How much do you want for rent?"

"No rent," Marcel answers, beating me to it. Carter opens his mouth to protest, but gets cut off. "Just help me out around here and make sure your sister's safe whenever I'm away."

"You got it. Get me one of those big green tractors and I'll even mow the crap out of the yard," Carter says.

Marcel bursts out laughing and holds out his hand. "Deal."

CHAPTER THIRTY

Teller

CHARLOTTE'S BACK TO work. Taking time off after her uncle's attack left her with a lot of catching up to do. That's why I volunteer to help Carter clean out her apartment.

After I load the last box that's coming to our house into my truck, Carter takes off. "I'm stopping by Bianca's. She wanted to come over and see my new place." He hesitates. "If that's okay."

"It's your place."

"Thanks."

I wander inside the apartment to give it another look. Since her old bed couldn't take our furious fucking and left dents in her bedroom wall, I figure it's only fair I patch it up. I run over the materials waiting for me. Paint, tape, tarp, sheet, roller, pan, knife, and a few other odds and ends.

The knock at the door surprises me at first, but it's probably the landlord, so I open it, looking forward to scaring the piss out of him after the shitty way he's treated Carter.

It's Keeper.

He rears back when he sees me. "What're you doing here?"

"What are *you* doing here?"

He stuffs his hands in his pockets and pushes past me. I follow his gaze as he takes in the empty space. "Where's she going?"

"None of your business."

"She moving in with you?"

I cross my arms over my chest and don't bother with an answer.

"That ain't right. Her dad was a Wolf Knight, you know."

"Yeah, I'm aware."

I follow him into the kitchen. "This where she stabbed him?" He shakes his head and stares at the floor as if inspecting for blood drops.

"It's where he hit her first."

Keeper grunts and rocks back on his heels a few times before meeting my eyes. "Merlin's been asking a lot of questions since your visit."

Good. At least what little concern Merlin showed for his niece wasn't bullshit. "Anyone got answers for him?"

"He's asking about shit that happened years ago."

"You know something about it?"

"I know she brought some gangbanging lowlife to one of our parties one time."

Rage boils my blood and I take a step closer. "You want to say that again?"

"Never mind." He attempts to step around me, but I stop him with a hand to his chest.

"Finish your thought."

The hesitation he walked in here with disappears and he slaps my hand away. "Nothin' to finish."

In my pocket, my phone goes off and Keeper tries to shove past me. "Stay put."

I don't recognize the number, but that's not unusual, so I answer.

"Where you at, Teller?" Merlin shouts on the other end.

"At Charlotte's apartment. Your VP stopped by and we're having a chat."

He curses and there's a crash in the background. "You keep that piece of shit there. I'm on my way over now."

"You wanna tell me why?"

259

"Just fuckin' do it."

I'd laugh at the frustration in his voice if I wasn't so focused on keeping the man in front of me in place.

"We'll be here." My gaze searches the empty apartment for any potential weapons. We just cleaned my girl's apartment out, so it's bare.

"She's not there?"

"No. It's just me and Keeper right now."

"I'm on my way. Do *not* let him leave."

I hang up and shove the phone in my pocket. "Your prez is real eager to talk to you."

"He ain't my prez anymore, thanks to Charlotte."

"Yeah, it's all her fault he snapped and attacked her."

"I need to be someplace." He tries going around me again and I stop him.

"Where you off too in such a hurry? You obviously stopped by to talk to Charlotte about something, so speak."

"It's none of your business."

"That's where you're wrong. Everything about her is my business. And since you're never getting anywhere near her again, you might as well say what you gotta say to me."

Quick—but not quick enough—his fist comes flying at my face. I block it easily and use the momentum to turn him and wrench his arm behind his back.

"What's gotten into you, Keeper?" I snarl.

"You don't want to start this war, Teller."

"Oh, I think I do."

My gaze lands on a roll of duct tape on the counter. I can't exactly ask him to hold still so I can secure him. Instead, I hook my arm around his neck and use my other arm to tighten the hold, squeezing hard until he slumps to the floor. The fucker's so heavy, he almost takes me down with him. Once I'm sure he's out, I release him.

It takes a few seconds to bind his wrists behind his back with the tape and secure his ankles. When I'm finished, I drag him into the bedroom.

I spread out the tarp and roll him onto it.

A few minutes later he's still out cold when someone's banging on the front door.

I open it and find a steaming Merlin.

"Guess Whisper let you out of the basement," I say, opening the door wider.

He growls and shoves his way past me. "Where is that traitor?"

I shut the door. "He's in the bedroom."

Merlin's carrying a lumpy black backpack. I can only imagine the goodies inside.

My hand goes to the pistol in the holster at my side. A last resort, since the sound will draw too much attention. My other hand brushes against the hunting knife strapped to my opposite leg.

"This motherfucker still alive?" Merlin asks, toeing Keeper's leg with his boot.

"Where's the love for your bro, Merlin?"

He glares at me. "What do you think?"

"I'm guessing you asked him some questions and don't like the answers."

"Gee, you really are as smart as they say," he sneers. "He did it. Charlotte said there was a second guy. My money's on Keeper."

"Why?" Not that I disagree with Merlin's conclusion, but I'm interested in how he got there.

"He said something about 'don't I wish she was still dating thugs' instead of you."

"Yeah, he said something similar to us the other day."

"I asked him what he was talkin' about. Charlotte never brought any of her boyfriends around the MC. Always liked to pretend she wasn't related to us lowlife bikers."

"Can't imagine why."

Ignoring the dig, he continues. "His remark didn't sit right with me."

At our feet, Keeper groans.

He rolls and sits up, scooting in a circle until he's facing us. "What the fuck, brother? Untie me."

Merlin pulls his own hunting knife from a sheath at his side. "We need to talk first."

Keeper's eyes widen and his gaze darts between Merlin and me. "You're siding with him?"

"I'm siding with my niece. Explain what you meant before."

"What?" he asks, but by the fear in his eyes, he knows exactly what information Merlin's after.

"Charlotte never brought any boyfriends to our clubhouse. Why do you think she did?"

"I caught her fucking one of those punks from Eighteen's crew."

Blood roars through my ears.

"Caught how?" Merlin's low deadly voice should scare the piss out of Keeper, but he lifts his chin in defiance.

"You need me to draw you a picture?"

Tired of the bullshit, I lash out, kicking Keeper in the groin. He howls and falls back, rolling to his side.

Yeah, that's a dirty move I normally wouldn't pull, but it seems appropriate here.

Merlin nods at me in approval.

"What did you do, Keeper?" I ask.

To be fair, I let him have a few seconds to catch his breath.

"Nothing," he groans. "Nothing she didn't like."

My vision blurs red and hazy at the edges.

"You piece of shit," Merlin growls, kicking Keeper in the side.

Holding Merlin back with a hand on his arm, I tap Keeper with my boot. "Start from the beginning."

"Fuck," he groans, rolling over. "I found her in one of the back bedrooms gettin' railed. Recognized his tats. Figured she brought him to the party and snuck off with him. Always acted like she was better than us, but she'd do one of those guys?"

"And?" Merlin prompts.

"And what?"

"Don't fucking play games, Keeper. We're way past that now," I warn him.

Taking out my own knife, I squat down next to Keeper and show him the eight-inch steel blade. "Start talking or I'm gonna start cutting."

Keeper's pleading eyes lock on Merlin. "You're gonna let him slice me up right in front of you? We're fuckin' brothers."

"A true brother wouldn't touch my niece."

"Christ, she's a fucking piece of pussy, same as the rest of 'em. Needed to be taught a lesson for her disrespect. Bringing that trash into our clubhouse, then spreading her legs for him under our roof? That ain't right. Now you're letting her be his fuckin' whore and busting *my* balls?"

I grip his hair and tilt his head back, exposing his neck. "What did you do?"

"You gonna let me go if I tell you the truth?"

"Sure."

Keeper looks to Merlin for confirmation. "Yeah, brother. I'll make sure he lets you go."

"Fine. He finished and left her to go talk to Cindy and I took my turn."

Before I even realize what I'm doing, I drive the knife into his upper thigh and he screams.

"Shut him up," Merlin snaps.

Clamping my hand over his mouth, I push him flat on his back. "Was she even fuckin' conscious, Keeper?"

He shakes free of my hold. "She was moaning like a bitch in heat while I fucked every hole."

I can't listen to more. I've had similar conversations with rapist assholes before. The story's always the same. I love Charlotte too much to hear another word. Nothing he can tell me will change the past or the outcome.

Pulling his hair tighter, I run the blade over his neck, watching with grim satisfaction as blood pours from the line across his throat. Not deep enough to kill him—that's going to be too messy and I don't have the time I need for that sort of clean up.

His body jerks and he gags. He wrenches his shoulders, trying to get free.

I slip my arms under his and lock my hands behind his head, bending his neck forward until there's a snap and he stops moving. I'm breathing hard but don't let go until he's limp.

Merlin watches me with appreciation glowing in his ice-cold eyes.

"He done?"

"I think so."

"I wanted to fuckin' gut him."

"Yeah, well, her landlord's coming to inspect the place in about twelve hours, so I didn't think that'd be the best plan."

"My cage is parked in the alley."

"We can carry him through the backyard. It's so fuckin' overgrown, no one should see anything. Pull your truck right up to the back gate and put the tailgate down."

I unwrap the tape from Keeper's wrists and ankles, wadding it into a ball I'll take with me to throw away later. Merlin helps me roll Keeper up in the sheet and then in the tarp.

"Where you plannin' to dump him?" I ask.

"SOS has an abandoned hardware store across the border. Gonna dig a hole, throw him in, and light it up."

That'll certainly destroy any evidence.

"Let's go."

"You're comin' with me?" he asks, sounding genuinely surprised.

"You already did the dirty work. Least I can do is clean up."

"Yeah, I'll help you."

We may have just killed a man together, but it doesn't mean I trust Merlin not to fuck me over.

CHAPTER THIRTY-ONE

Teller

MERLIN AND I drive out to Vermont in his truck to dispose of Keeper.

It's a long drive. He's careful to stay under the speed limit and stop for every red light. Almost as if he's done this before.

I stare out the window.

"You move her up to the clubhouse?" he asks after we clear downtown Ironworks.

I turn and glare. Any information about Charlotte is off-limits to him as far as I'm concerned. "You can stop with the attempt to bond with me. This isn't exactly a family outing."

He laughs. "Isn't it?"

We're quiet for a few more miles. "You really despise me, don't you?"

"What do you think?"

"I came up in the club at a different time than you did, Teller."

"Don't use the *it was a different era* excuse. It's *never* been okay to hit a woman."

He nods as if he's glad he finally figured out what about him pisses me off so much.

"You hurt my girl," I continue. "Left *bruises* on her." I jerk my head toward the bed of the truck. "You're lucky you're not rolling around

266

with your bro back there."

Should I be shooting off my mouth and making threats when we're about to bury a body together in the middle of nowhere Vermont? Probably not.

"Everyone handles grief differently."

I want to growl out a *fuck you*, but what's the point?

"Wrath already shared his thoughts with me on hurting Charlotte. You want a crack at me too?"

He's not being a cocky asshole. I think he genuinely means it. Underneath that, I think he's considering the same thing I just did. Whether or not he's safe traipsing through the woods with me tonight. The idea that we're both wondering if one of us plans to kill the other is sort of amusing.

I stare at him for a long time before answering. "Charlotte seems to think stabbing you makes you two even."

His mouth quirks. "I said some real shitty stuff to her. Deserved the knife in the gut."

"Can't argue with that."

More silence stretches between us.

"Don't come near her again," I warn him. "You wanna see her, you go through me."

"Fair enough," he grinds out. I'm sure it's killing him to take orders from me. After a few minutes, he snorts. "My brother would've liked you." He glances over. "*I* don't like you, but he would've."

"Thanks."

"Where'd Carter end up?"

"Why do you care?"

"Maybe I thought about some of the things Charlotte said."

I seriously doubt that and I don't trust Merlin not to fuck with Carter. Maybe decide Carter should know the truth about his parentage just to be an asshole. "He's fine. I found him a place."

"Feel good to swoop in and play the hero?" He sneers. "Show me up?"

"I couldn't give a fuck less about that." How can I break it down in words he'll understand? "You may not have been able to look past…things, but he's a good kid. Loves his sister. Loved his mom too, even though it sounds like she didn't deserve it."

"You plannin' to bring him in as a prospect next?"

I snort and shake my head. "No. He's definitely not interested in that." Not to mention that, while Z and my brothers accept Carter in small doses, I don't think they'd tolerate him as a brother. I keep that to myself, though.

"How you plannin' to keep her safe?"

"I think you have a few stitches in your side that say she can keep herself safe."

He chuckles then turns serious. "This life is rough on women."

Is he for real? I turn so I can face him. "Her own blood served up the worst betrayal a woman can survive and you're worried about *my club*?"

"Fuck." He shakes his head. "I never wanted her to know what her mother did."

"Yeah, if I'd known that's where it was gonna lead, maybe I wouldn't have pushed so hard."

"I tried to warn you."

He's right and I have to live with that. Worse, Charlotte has to live with the truth. "I'll do everything I can to keep her safe and so will my brothers," I finally say.

"I believe you."

"I don't really give a fuck what you believe."

He sighs and flips on his turn signal. The road narrows and the tires kick up gravel. My hand strays to my pocket—just in case.

"I loved Cindy, but fuck did we bring out the worst in each other."

I keep my mouth shut, sensing he has more to say.

"Before you, I don't think Char ever woulda thought to fuckin' stab me." He laughs and shakes his head. "Maybe you bring out the best in each other."

A low, stone building comes into view and Merlin guides the truck around back.

"You're sure no one's here?" I ask, surveying the area.

"Shouldn't be."

"That's reassuring."

He puts it in park and jumps out. I slip my gloves back on before sliding out and meeting him at the back of the truck. He already has a shovel in one hand and a small LED lantern in the other. "Grab the other shovel and the gas can."

I nod. "Let's get this done."

CHAPTER THIRTY-TWO

Teller

I T'S LATE WHEN we finish erasing all traces of Keeper from this world. Merlin pulls up in front of Charlotte's building and we stare at each other for a few seconds.

"You plannin' to kiss me or kill me, Teller?"

"Neither."

"Figure, you're gonna run home and tell your prez, but I'd rather it not go much further than that."

Both of us have a lot to lose if *his* club finds out. Rock will understand my actions and I don't think I'll be punished for moving without taking it to my club first.

Merlin on the other hand—conspiring with me, someone from another club? Killing a brother? Without even attempting to discuss it at the table? Yeah, Merlin has a lot to lose.

"We're square. I got no reason to burn you, Merlin."

It's a poor choice of words, considering what we just finished doing, but he doesn't react.

"Where do you go now?" I ask.

He stares at the street ahead of us. "Maybe nomad for a while. Whisper will be a good president. He doesn't need me looking over his shoulder."

Before I step down, he holds out his hand and I shake it. He doesn't offer some lame "take care of my girl" banality. His brief chin lift says it all.

After he leaves, I clean up in Charlotte's bathroom, then roam through each room of the apartment carefully. Making sure there's no evidence of what took place tonight.

I glance at the wall in the bedroom. The landlord's gonna have to take it out of her deposit. I'll cover whatever it is.

Collecting the remaining stuff, I give the place one last inspection before locking up.

Outside, I run into her upstairs neighbors.

"Hey, Charlotte move out already?"

"Moved the last of her stuff out today."

"Sorry. We were camping all weekend or we would have helped," Brad—or Brian? I can never keep the two of them straight—says.

"No problem."

"Have her call us and we'll go out for drinks or something."

"Will do."

I shake hands with both of them before heading to my truck.

After tapping out a quick text to Charlotte to let her know everything's okay at her apartment, I head to the clubhouse.

Rock and Wrath are in their office when I arrive and I shut the door behind me.

"What's up?" Rock asks. His smile fades as he takes in my serious expression.

There's no need for a long, dramatic explanation. "Merlin and I took Keeper out."

Wrath sits back in his seat, speechless for once in his life.

"It was Keeper?" Rock asks. "You're sure?"

"He admitted it."

He stands and pulls me into a brotherly hug, patting me on the back. "You're sure you're covered?"

"I went with Merlin to take care of it. He was straight with me. He doesn't want anyone knowing either."

Rock nods, understanding the situation. "Anything else I should know?"

"What's left of him is on a piece of property owned by SOS."

Wrath smirks. "Nice touch."

"Charlotte know?" Rock asks.

"Not yet. Not sure she needs to." I think Rock realizes it's a matter of not wanting to bring up bad things for her, not a matter of not trusting her.

"What's next for Merlin?" Wrath asks.

"Says he's going on the road for a bit."

Wrath snorts. "Yeah, getting' stripped of his president's patch has to sting. Probably better for him not to be here buttin' heads with Whisper."

"He's gonna stay away from Charlotte?" Rock asks.

"We came to an understanding."

Wrath stands and gives me a quick hug. "Good job, little brother."

I head upstairs to shower and change. The clubhouse is quiet tonight, but I don't give it a lot of thought. All I'm worried about is getting home and holding my girl in my arms.

Charlotte

"ARE YOU SURE he was leaving right after you?" I ask again.

Carter squints as if he wants to tell me to fuck off, but can't quite bring himself to do it.

"He was staying behind to fix some of the damage in your apartment—which I'd rather not give a lot of thought to since they were dents in your *bedroom* wall—then he said he was coming straight home."

Marcel sent a text a while ago. He should've been here by now. I hate being the annoying girlfriend keeping track of her man's every move, but I'm worried. What if this stuff with my uncle's club isn't finished? Keeper's threat to Marcel the other day has bothered me ever since. What if my uncle decided he didn't care for Marcel's disrespect and decided to come after him?

The alarm chirps, letting me know someone's coming down the driveway.

"It's your man," Carter says, checking the monitor. "I assume you're either about to fuck or fight, so I'm leaving."

I roll my eyes and stick my tongue out, but don't bother explaining I'm not in the mood for sex or arguing.

Carter slips out the side door and a few minutes later Marcel parks in his usual spot. I meet him in the yard.

"Where have you been?" I call out, instantly cursing myself for my shrill tone.

"Get over here," he says, closing the short distance between us in seconds and wrapping me up in a ferocious hug. "Missed you." A shiver of fear works down my spine at the intensity of his raspy voice.

"Is everything okay?"

"Everything is fine," he murmurs against my hair.

My racing heart calms with his touch and I bury my nose in the crook of his neck, inhaling his clean scent.

His soapy, freshly-showered scent and damp hair.

"Where were you that you needed to take a shower before coming home?"

He sighs and pushes me back. "Let's go inside."

Far from satisfied with *that* answer, but unsure of what to do, I follow him into the house.

This feels like a conversation I should sit down for, so I pull out a chair at the kitchen table. "Marcel, you're freaking me out."

"I'm not trying to freak you out. I didn't want to discuss this at all tonight."

"Discuss what?"

He blows out a long breath and runs his hand over the back of his neck.

Ice swirls in my stomach. Maybe I don't want to hear whatever he has to tell me.

"Keeper showed up after Carter left."

"He did? Why?"

"Your uncle started asking questions and I guess it made him nervous."

The implications of what he's saying slam into me. "He had something to do with it?"

He swallows hard and then nods slowly. "Merlin was on to him. He called me and when I told him Keeper was at the apartment, he met us there."

"He did?"

"He wanted the truth too."

I absorb that for a second before prompting Marcel to continue.

"And, what did Keeper have to say?"

"He admitted what he did to you."

"Tell me."

"What?" I sense that he's dodging my question more than he needs clarification.

"What did he say exactly? What did he do? Tell me everything."

"Charlotte, please." He moves closer, taking the chair next to me. "You don't need this in your head."

For years, I've wondered what happened that night. If the horrifying flashbacks I'd occasionally have were real or products of my imagination. "I don't want to know, Marcel. But I *need* to know."

Beyond that need, I can't stand him holding a truth I don't have.

He sighs, slowly his hands slide over the table and cover mine. "It sounded like he thought the guy...your mom's dealer...was your boyfriend. That you brought him to the party and…snuck off with him. He found the two of you in one of the private rooms."

"And?"

"When the dealer left…Keeper went in—" his voice breaks and he shakes his head. "I didn't get any more details from him."

That means whatever Keeper said was probably disgusting. "He didn't realize I was unconscious?"

"I think he did, but he didn't care."

I squeeze my eyes shut tight. "Chuck heard this too?"

"Yes, but no one else ever will."

I gasp and sit back. "You…and Chuck?"

"Keeper won't be hurting anyone again, Charlotte. I promise."

"But…Chuck? A brother?" Surely he's joking. My uncle going against a member of his club? Over me?

"Maybe he felt guilty. Maybe it was his ego. Or maybe somewhere deep in his twisted soul he really loves you. I don't know. We did what needed to be done and I didn't ask what his reasons were."

Completely drained, I sit back and absorb what Marcel just shared.

"I'm not trying to tell you he's suddenly a good guy. And I still don't ever want you alone with him, Charlotte. But yes, he finally came through for you."

Heat creeps over my face and tears prick my eyes. Marcel didn't have to tell me any of this. He could've lied and said he did it all himself. Or tried to make himself look better. Or not told me at all, I suppose.

"Thank you."

He brushes his fingers against my cheek, prompting me to meet his eyes. "I love you more than anything in this world and I'll protect you until the day I die, Charlotte."

CHAPTER THIRTY-THREE

Teller

WE DON'T TALK about Keeper again.

After a few days, Charlotte seems much more like herself.

No, even better. Lighter and happier. It fills me with peace. Even if I'd gotten caught, it'd be worth it to know she finally has the truth and justice for what happened.

True to his word, Carter's been helping me with stuff around the house. In return, I've helped him out with a few things as well.

In my arms, Charlotte murmurs and her hair tickles my chest.

Several times throughout the night, I think she tried to extract herself from my embrace, but even in sleep, I held on tight.

My right arm's curled over her hip, resting on her stomach and my left arm's completely numb under her head.

Wiggling my fingers, I attempt to get some blood circulating through the limb when she stretches, arching her back, and yawning.

All hope of my arm waking up disappears as my blood rushes somewhere else.

"Marcel," she pats my hand resting over her stomach. "I need to turn over. Move," she mumbles.

I shift back a few inches and she twists around, tucking her face against my chest. I brush her hair from her face and run my finger over her soft cheek.

"Stop staring at me. It's creepy," she murmurs. Her hot breath against my skin makes the situation in my shorts even more critical.

"How do you know I'm staring at you?"

"I can tell."

"What if I want to do something else?"

She rolls to her back. "Do what you gotta do. I want more sleep."

Now she's just messing with me. "Careful, Sunshine," I tease, running my fingers under her shirt. "You give me an invitation like that, you know I'll take it."

She cracks open one eye. "You're horny this morning? Really?"

"Charlotte, if I'm breathing next to you, I'm horny. I only get to actually stick my dick in you about twenty-five percent of the times I *think* about fucking you."

"You're *so* romantic. I bet most guys average about two percent. You're lucky your girlfriend's so awesome," she says, rolling over and shoving her head under the pillows.

That's it.

Ripping the sheet off, I expose her plump little ass barely hidden by tiny hot pink lacy underwear.

Muffled laughter from under her pillows cranks me up even more. My hand lands on her left ass cheek and she yelps.

"Don't you dare," she warns a second before I lay a good smack on her right cheek.

She bursts out of her pillow cocoon and tackles me, pushing me flat against the bed. Her smaller hands pin my arms above my head—for now—and she stares down at me. "What did I tell you about waking me up on the weekends?"

My mouth quirks and I raise an eyebrow. "Do it with my dick in you?"

She glances down the length of our bodies. "And yet, here I am dickless." The last two words barely make it out of her mouth she's laughing so hard.

She trails one hand down my chest and pushes her way under my shorts, wrapping her fingers around my cock. "If you want the job done right, a woman's gotta do it herself."

I groan as she strokes her hand up and down my dick a few times and she hums with approval. "That's some impressive morning wood, Marcel."

"All yours." I close my eyes and let her have her way with me.

Her fingers tighten, squeezing hard. "Don't you fall back asleep on me."

"Couldn't if I wanted to." I slip my hands out of her hold and tug at her underwear. "Take these off."

"No."

I pull a little harder, but the material won't give. Opening my eyes, I pin her with a look. "What're they made of, indestructible fabric?"

She chuckles and spreads her legs, rubbing the soaked crotch of her panties over my eager cock.

Giving up on ripping them off, I slide the inch of fabric out of my way and run my fingers over her slickness. Her breathing hitches when I slip one finger inside her, then draw her wetness up to circle her clit. She scoots down, pressing herself against me.

"Oh, fuck. Stop teasing, Sunshine."

My hands grab her ass, holding her still and spreading her wider so I can thrust up inside.

Her nails rake down my chest and she throws her head back, moaning as she takes every inch.

She rolls her hips, trying to lift herself and I grip her tighter. "No. Stay there and take your punishment for being a bad girl."

"Me?" Her jaw drops with amused outrage. "You woke *me* up."

Releasing one hip, I fist my hand in her shirt and tug. "I want your tits. Take this off."

"What a caveman," she mutters. Slowly, she eases the shirt up and over her head. It lands on my face and while I'm distracted, she removes my other hand from her hip and rocks herself up and down faster.

"Fuck. I give up. Just don't stop riding me." I groan, closing my hands over her breasts and flicking my thumbs against her nipples.

Her head falls back and I press my thumb against her lips. "Suck." When my thumb's nice and wet I reach down and drag it over her clit, making her jump.

"Faster, Sunshine. Need you to come so bad."

"Uh, I, so close. Harder." She moans louder and I lightly pinch her clit, setting her off.

When her screams die down, I buck her off and sit up. I grip her legs behind her knees spreading her wide.

"Marcel, what—"

I cut her words off by shoving my face against her pussy, sucking and kissing in greedy mouthfuls.

"That's how you should've woken me up," she teases, running her hands through my hair.

"Tomorrow," I promise, sitting up and yanking her closer.

Sliding into her feels like absolute heaven. I fall down over her, kissing her cheek and she loops her arms around my neck. "I want to do this the rest of the day."

"Fuck?" she asks.

"Make you come."

Her laughter turns into moaning as I grind myself into her, hitting the spot that makes her eyes roll back. My hand closes around her neck and her lips part.

"Charlotte." I barely recognize the harsh rasp coming out of my mouth. Her eyes pop open, dreamy and unfocused. My fingers squeeze the sides of her neck then release. A faint smile curves her lips and that's when I lose it.

Pumping into her one last time, I pull out and cover her stomach in my cum. She's so out of it I don't think she notices right away. After a few seconds, she opens her eyes.

Her lips quirk. "Your aim is off. My tits are up here," she says, squeezing her breasts.

Out of breath, I fall down next to her laughing. "I'll keep that in mind next time."

She curls her fingers around mine and we lay side by side, staring at the ceiling while we catch our breath.

I roll over and kiss her cheek. "Stay there."

She waits while I run into the bathroom and grab a towel to clean her up with. "You're beautiful all naked and sticky."

"Get back in bed with me," she demands, tugging the towel out of my hands and tossing it toward the bathroom.

I'm about to crawl in next to her when my phone goes off.

"Noooo," she cries. "Don't answer it. You promised me a day in bed."

I glance at the phone and if it were anyone else but Murphy I'd probably ignore it. "It's Murphy, let me see what he needs."

"You're lucky I like that big ginger," she grumbles, rolling away from me.

"What's up, big ginger?" I answer.

"What?" he says.

"That's Charlotte's new name for you."

She slaps my leg and giggles.

"I'm afraid to ask," he says. "You're needed up here."

"Can't. I got a hot date all afternoon."

He blows out a frustrated breath. "It's not a request, man. Rock wants you up here *now*."

"You fuckin' serious?"

"Yeah, whatever you did just blew up, so get your ass here right now."

"Fine. I'm on my way."

"What's wrong?" Charlotte asks when I slam the phone down.

"I don't know. Rock wants me up there."

"Did you…Do they know?"

"Yeah. I had to tell Rock…in case something happens." I brush my hand over her cheek and down across her chest. "It's okay."

"I understand. He's not mad at you, is he?"

"No," I answer, even though after Murphy's ominous phone call, I'm not really sure.

CHAPTER THIRTY-FOUR

Charlotte

MARCEL RAN OUT so fast I can't help but worry. To keep myself occupied, I shower, dress, and run over to annoy my brother.

Although, as I open the downstairs door, it occurs to me maybe I should've called him first.

I walk in totally unprepared for the scene in front of me.

My brother's sitting on a stool with a sketchpad in his lap, drawing his friend, Bianca.

If Kate Winslet had been a goth girl, she'd look like Bianca. Her soft milky skin is set off by long, curly hair dyed jet black with streaks of cobalt blue and royal purple that falls to her waist.

Before today, I only knew about the piercings in her nose, lip, and eyebrow. Today, I notice silver rings glittering from a few other locations. Something I really didn't need to know.

She's been "friends" with my brother for years, but apparently their relationship has changed in the last few days. Currently, she's posing nude on a black velvet chaise lounge while my brother sketches every inch of her curvy body.

She waves when she sees me, but doesn't cover up or seem weirded out.

I must be turning into an old prude.

Carter turns around. Bright red lights up his skin from neck to forehead. At least someone besides me is embarrassed.

"A word, little brother," I say, jerking my thumb over my shoulder.

"Be right back, B."

She shrugs and picks up her cell phone, but still doesn't cover herself.

"What's up, sis?" he asks, leading me outside.

"I always knew I let you watch Titanic one too many times when you were a kid."

He blushes an even deeper red.

"So, I thought you two were *just friends*?"

"We are. I told her I needed to sketch some nudes and she offered to be my muse."

"Please tell me you're not using this as some weird way to get in your friend's pants?"

"Aren't you always hinting that we should get together?"

Yes, I have suggested that in the past, but Bianca's always kept my brother squarely in the friend zone and I can't stand the thought of him getting his heart broken.

"I don't want you to get hurt, that's all."

"I'm a big boy, Charlotte."

"You'll always be my little brother, though."

"It's not like I'm a virgin," he grumbles.

I slap my hands over my ears. "La, la, la, I did not hear that."

He rolls his eyes. "You're nuts. Can I get back to the hot, naked girl, I was sketching now?"

"Use a condom!" I shout over my shoulder as I run back into the house.

Teller

NOT ONE BROTHER lingers in the living room when I arrive at the clubhouse. The war room door is shut and I listen outside for a second before opening it.

Rock's at the head of the table—naturally. Wrath, Murphy, and Z are the only other brothers at the table.

"Where's everyone else?" I ask, rounding the table to take my seat.

Rock pins me with a hard stare. "This is officers only."

That doesn't reassure me.

Z stands and moves to the closet, but Rock snaps his fingers, drawing my attention to him. "We have some serious things to discuss."

"Okay." I glance around the table again. "I thought we were good last night? Do you need me to fill Z and Murphy in?"

"Nah, Rock told us while we were waiting for you."

"It didn't take me that long to get here, Prez, did it?" Christ, I sound like a whiny bitch, but I've been worried someone would complain I'm slacking now that I'm not living at the clubhouse.

Next to me, Murphy smothers a laugh, and oddly that relaxes me. If I were in trouble, he wouldn't be laughing.

"Christ, can't you keep a straight face for five minutes?" Wrath bitches at Murphy.

Now that he's been called out, Murphy really lets loose. "Did I take too long to get here, Prez?" he mimics in a high-pitched voice that sounds *nothing* like me.

Without turning my head, I punch his arm, which only makes him laugh harder.

"Jerk. What's going on?"

"How's Charlotte?" Rock asks.

"Fine. Why?"

"You talk to her?"

"I had to. I didn't give her details though."

"And?" Wrath asks.

"She was worried about me. And surprised Merlin finally did the right thing. Told her I still don't ever want her alone with him again."

"Good call," Rock mutters. He turns and jerks his head to Z who approaches me with a brown paper package.

"We got you something," Z says.

My heart thumps a little faster. I know that wrapper. Know what should be inside.

Z sets the package in front of me.

Patty's Patches is stamped in the top left corner. I run my fingers over it before looking up. First at Rock, then Wrath. "I didn't ask for another vote yet."

Wrath lifts his broad shoulders. "We took it for you."

Fuck me. We did the same thing for Murphy. But that was different. The two of them ending up together was inevitable and none of us could deny her commitment to the club or would ever vote her down.

Wrath already voted Charlotte down once before.

"You voted yes?" I ask him.

He nods. "I needed to know more about how committed she was."

"He just wanted you to move out of the clubhouse and get your own life," Z says, shaking his head.

Wrath snorts. "You give me too much credit. I'm not that deep."

I'm not so sure about that. If anyone's been telling me to get out of my sister's business and worry about taking care of myself, it's Wrath.

Too impatient to wait any longer, I open the package and check out the black leather vest.

Property of Teller
Lost Kings MC

The patch of each officer is sewn into the side while my dollar sign patch rests over the upper left side with "Sunshine" stitched underneath. I glance at Murphy who would've been the one to know to add that.

"Thanks," I say, nudging him with my elbow.

Meeting Rock's eyes, I lift an eyebrow. "You need me here?"

"No. Go give it to her." He stands, dismissing all of us.

I receive quick hugs from Z and Murphy. Rock pulls me in for a hug and slap on the back. "I like her. She's good for you."

"Thank you."

Wrath's a little rougher in his congratulatory hug. "I like her too. She's mouthy. Hope she gives you hell for years to come."

I huff out a laugh, because fuck, I hope so too. "Thanks."

I almost knock Heidi down on my way out of the war room. "What are you doing…" her voice trails off as she eyes the package in my hands. "No way! Really?"

"Don't you dare say anything. I want to surprise her."

Heidi runs her fingers over her lips. "Won't say a word." She reaches up and gives me a hug. "Love you."

"Love you too."

I race home, parking next to our house. I glance at Carter's place. He said his friend Bianca was coming over this weekend. Although I'd love to know if my suggestion to offer to sketch her nude worked, I'm way too eager to see my own girl.

Naked wearing my patch.

Charlotte

"GET NAKED. I have a present for you," Marcel calls out when he returns home.

Of course, I ignore the "get naked" part because it seems like he orders me to get naked in our new house fifteen times a day.

"Why aren't you naked?" he asks when he finds me in the kitchen.

My eye roll doesn't stop him this time. He stalks closer, setting something next to me on the counter.

"Your man wants you naked, you're supposed to be naked."

He's not fooling around. Sliding his hands under my shirt, he tugs it up and off.

"What are you doing? I'm cold."

"I'm gonna warm you up in a second."

I giggle as his rough hands brush my belly trying to unbutton my jeans. He finally gets them loose and tugs them down my legs, stopping to kiss my mound. "You can leave the pink lacy panties on. They're sexy as fuck."

"Gee, thanks."

I'm left standing in my bra and underwear in the middle of our kitchen, wondering if my old man has lost his damn mind, when he hands me a thick, black leather vest.

"Oh my God." I reach out with one shaky hand and unfold it.

Property of Teller.
Lost Kings MC.

The patch of each officer is sewn on the side. Even Wrath's.

"*This* is why they called you up to the clubhouse?" I ask, my voice shaking with emotion.

"Yup."

"You didn't ask for another vote?"

"Nope."

"You want me to have it?"

He cocks his head. "Are you or are you not standing half-naked in our kitchen right now?"

I turn it over and his dollar sign patch is sewn on the left, with "Sunshine" underneath.

"Was the dollar sign because you were treasurer?" I ask. "What if you want to run for another position one day?"

He laughs. "That's your question?"

"I realized I've never asked."

"The dollar sign is because I was a cocky little dick when I patched-in. I thought it was clever."

I hook my arm around his neck. "I love you. Cocky, clever dick and all."

"Good. My cocky, clever dick loves you too."

I snort and laugh, making him shake his head and snatch the vest out of my hands. "Turn around."

I turn and he helps me into the vest, then arranges the buckles at the side so it conforms to my shape. "Shit, that's hot," he mutters.

I'll admit it turns me on too and here I never, ever thought I'd be caught dead wearing something that declared I was "property of" anyone or anything.

Amazing how love has the power to change your perspective on almost everything. Before I would've felt degraded. Now, I feel cherished and protected.

Honored that he wants the world to know that not only do I belong to him, but that his brothers will protect me as well.

"I feel like I need heels to go with this," I tease.

"No. Bare feet is perfect."

"Oh, God. I can *not* be barefoot in our kitchen with a 'property of' patch. Absolutely not." I grin and duck out of his grasp, running into the living room where he easily catches me, tossing me onto the couch.

Touching his forehead to mine, he stares into my eyes and cups my cheek with his hand. "Sunshine, I'll take you barefoot and wearing my patch anywhere I can get you."

CHAPTER THIRTY-FIVE

Charlotte

MURPHY AND HEIDI were over earlier helping us paint the kitchen. Alexa kindly left us one of her tiny hand prints on the wall and we decided to leave it.

After they went home, Marcel and Carter went outside to work on a secret project.

I'm in the living room reading when my brother's car starts up and drives away.

Marcel sneaks up behind me, and kisses my cheek.

"Where's he going?" I ask.

"Out." He holds out his hand. "Come here, I want to show you something."

I set my book down. "Is it your dick? Because there are a few rooms in this house we haven't christened yet."

He bursts out laughing. "No. Get over here."

I take his hand and he leads me into the backyard. There's a grove of large trees. The woods thicken as the yard stretches up the mountain, but in this spot, it's flat and the trees provide a lot of shade.

The closer we get, I notice a hammock strung between two of the trees. A much bigger, nicer one than the one in my apartment.

Little white lights wrapped around the tree trunks sparkle, illuminating the area around the hammock.

"It's like a fairy wonderland." I glance at Marcel. "Is this what you two were working on?"

"Yes."

Marcel even has a small table set up next to the hammock. A thick black notebook rests on top.

"Remember when you told me you liked to sit in your hammock and picture your ideal life?"

"Yes." Heat creeps over my cheeks. We had our first fight that night too.

He points to the ground and grass under our feet. "Green grass." He points skyward. "Blue sky." He winks at me. "Well in the daytime."

"The night sky's even prettier," I whisper. My pulse races. "Marcel?"

He picks up the notebook and hands it to me. "Here's my ideal life."

I open to the first page.

Marry Me.

Not a question. A statement.

I fight the smile forming on my lips. "Are you trying to ask me something?"

He drops down on one knee and sighs. "I knew you'd be difficult."

He reaches into his pocket and pulls out a small box.

"Oh, shit," I gasp. "You're serious."

"Yeah, Sunshine. I'm serious."

He opens the box and pulls out a ring.

"Marry me, Charlotte."

"That's still not a question."

"No, it's not."

I give him my hand, and he slips the ring on my finger. I can't stand teasing him any longer and throw myself at him. Down we tumble to the wet grass, rolling over until I'm on top of him, staring into his eyes.

"Yes, I'll marry you." I lean down and press a kiss to his lips. As if I tripped a switch, his breath hitches and he cups the back of my head, holding me in place for deeper kisses. Underneath me, he hardens and I rub against his erection.

His hands move from my head to my pants. "Get these off." His hoarse voice leaves no room for discussion.

I wriggle out of them while he frees himself. Before he even has a chance to ask or order, I throw my leg over him. One of his hands grips my shoulder, applying light pressure, while he uses the other to guide me to his cock. We both groan as I take him all the way inside me.

He holds my hip, digging his fingers in, and I move it to my breast. His other hand rests on my shoulder, and I guide him to my neck. He strokes his thumb over my pulse. A light brush. "There."

I move faster and faster, my cries growing louder, but all I hear is the movement of our bodies and the blood rushing through my veins. Blinding pleasure gathers at my core, seizing me in place. I grind down harder, chasing the sensation for as long as I can. At the perfect moment, Marcel applies just the right pressure against my neck and I'm flying.

For a few seconds, there's nothing but the bliss of our bodies joined together. And our love binding our souls together.

He groans and arches up into me once, twice before stilling.

I blink down at him and smile.

After we catch our breath, we collect our clothes. He holds me in his arms and we tumble into the hammock, swinging side to side in silence.

"We should do this every night," I whisper.

A happy rumble rolls through his chest and his arms tighten around me. "Works for me."

"This is so beautiful. Can we leave the lights up?"

"Whatever you want, Sunshine." He glances down at me and strokes his hand over my cheek. "You light up my whole world, Charlotte. You're the something I was missing and didn't think I'd ever find. Anything that makes you happy, I want you to have."

Tears wet my lashes. Our lips meet. A soft brush of a kiss. "You make me happy Marcel," I whisper. "You helped me recover a piece of my soul I thought had been lost and damaged forever. I want to be your wife and your partner."

He wraps me up in an embrace, squeezing to the edge of breathlessness. "I'm all yours."

CHAPTER THIRTY-SIX

Teller

"MAKE SOME BABIES with me," I mumble against Charlotte's neck. While we planned to sleep outside under the stars, at a certain point we realized we were just getting chewed up by mosquitoes and ran into the house.

I flatten my palm against her belly, loving the way her body's curves fit my hands so well.

"What?" she murmurs.

"Let's make some babies."

"Marcel, if you want morning sex, just say so."

I run my hand up between her breasts, and turn her to face me. "No, I want to have a family with you."

I woke up with a clear vision of two kids playing on a swing set in our backyard. The vibrant image and feelings it brought on won't leave me.

"Well," she says, blinking and coming fully awake. "We need to *plan* for that. Like responsible adults, don't you think?"

"You've got my patch, my ring, we have our house. How much more planning you want to do?" I ask, kissing her neck. My teeth scrape her shoulder and she throws her head back, moaning softly.

"I need to go off the pill."

"Do it."

"It still takes a while."

"Good. We can practice a *lot*."

She laughs softly as I nudge her legs apart and settle on top of her. Her arms loop around my neck and she stares up at me while I tease my cock against her.

"I always wanted to be in a place where I could, you know take time off and be with my children until they go to school."

"So, do it." I reach under her, tilting her hips so I can slide into her. She clings to me tighter as I slowly thrust in and out. "Your man will support whatever you want to do."

I will *not* tell her how much I like that idea. Won't say how much the thought of her only job being the mother of our children for a little while appeals to me. Nope.

Instead, I brush my lips against hers.

I spend the rest of the morning alternating between pleasuring her and planning a future with the woman who took the shattered pieces of my soul and helped me meld them into something stronger than they'd been before.

THE LOST KINGS MC
AUTUMNJONESLAKE.COM

EPILOGUE #1

Charlotte

Somewhere down the road...

I CAN'T BELIEVE THIS.

My stomach heaves one last time, tossing up the last of my breakfast.

This is the third morning in a row.

Today is *not* the day for this.

In fifteen minutes, I'm arguing to a judge that one Blake O'Callaghan should be allowed to legally adopt his wife's daughter, Alexa Jade Ryan and change her name to Alexa Jade Ryan O'Callaghan.

It's a formality. The judge has had the petition for a while now. Still, I can't very well stand up and barf all over the table.

I take a few deep breaths.

"Charlotte, are you okay?" Heidi asks.

Of course she followed me in here.

"I'm fine."

When I emerge from the stall, she's standing against the sink with a huge grin stretched across her face.

"Get out of my way." I bump her with my hip and she giggles.

Running cold water over my wrists seems to help. I splash some on my face and then dry off with a stiff paper towel.

"Oh my God. Tell me I'm going to be an aunt!" She presses a hand against her own rather generous baby bump and sighs. "We can be birthing buddies."

"What the hell is that?"

"Oh, it will be so much fun not to do this alone again, Charlotte. And I can help you out too."

"Slow your roll, sister. It's just an upset stomach." I gesture to her belly. "Besides, you're way ahead of me."

"You're knocked up. I can tell. I know these things." She claps her hands and bounces up and down on her toes a little. "Oh my God, my brother must be so excited."

"I'm not sure about anything yet, so if you could *not* get his hopes up, that would be great."

"Okay, I promise not to say anything."

"Thank you."

She bites her lip and her smile fades. "Are you sure this will be okay? Murphy's so happy. I can't stand it if something goes wrong."

Feeling shitty for snapping at her because now I realize she was trying to distract herself with good news, I pull her into my arms. "It's going to be fine. It's really a formality."

"Thank you." She squeezes me tight. "Thank you so much for everything."

"Let's go make you an official family."

She peeks at herself in the full-length mirror. Heidi wanted to present a polished, mature image to the judge. She chose a conservative crimson dress, flats, and a sophisticated up-do.

"You look like Audrey Hepburn," I assure her.

She flashes a quick smile, probably not sure who that even is, and tucks a few stray hairs into the sleek chignon Trinity styled her hair into this morning.

We step out of the bathroom and I smile at the scene in front of us.

Someone—Heidi, I assume—wrestled Murphy into a deep navy

suit, complete with navy and burgundy tie. While his beard is normally kept neat and tidy, today every single hair is perfectly in place. Despite the grooming and the formal attire, plenty of ink peeks out, declaring he's still a badass. Something I assured him of when he showed up at our house fidgeting like a madman this morning.

Marcel's also in a suit—again, Heidi's doing, I bet—waiting with Murphy and Alexa.

Alexa looks so sweet in a little plum-colored dress, holding her dad's hand, I almost burst into tears.

Shit, I probably am pregnant.

Marcel's concerned gaze sweeps over me the minute I step out of the bathroom. "Are you all right?" he asks, taking my briefcase from my hands.

"I'm fine. Where'd Rock and Hope go?"

"Inside to grab a seat."

My gaze goes to Murphy. "Ready?"

"So ready," he says, flashing a huge smile. He slips his free arm around Heidi's shoulders and guides her into the courtroom.

Marcel leans down and brushes a quick kiss on my forehead.

"Thank you for doing this."

"Of course, I want to do it." My lips quirk into a half-smile. "They brought us together again. Now I'm able to return the favor."

His eyes light up. "That's right." He gives me a more critical look. "I guess I was so excited about our own news, I forgot."

I gasp and step back. "What're you talking about?"

He tilts his head and fits his hands into the curve of my waist. "Sunshine, I know every single detail of your body."

Heat races over my skin. How unprofessional would it be if I hustled him into the bathroom and—

"Save that thought," Marcel warns, turning me toward the courtroom.

A baby girl's screams pierce the air and Marcel laughs. "Sounds like little sister is *pissed*."

I laugh with him, then pull on his tie. "Give me one more kiss for luck."

"Happy to."

EPILOGUE #2

Teller

A few weeks later...

"Now can we tell everyone?" Charlotte asks as we step into the elevator.

"That we're pregnant or that we're having twins?"

"Both."

"Hell yeah." I whip out my phone. "I'm texting Murphy to meet us at the clubhouse now."

"Do you think we should wait and tell everyone at once?" She touches my arm. "Rock will want to know too."

"We'll start with Murphy and Heidi and work our way up."

"Deal."

At the bike, I stop. *Shit.* Should've brought the truck.

"Stop it," Charlotte scolds. "The doctor said it was fine for a little longer."

I hand over her helmet. "Enjoy your last ride."

"Enjoy *your* last ride," she mutters under her breath.

"I heard that," I growl against her ear, reaching around to grab her ass.

"Are you groping me in the parking lot?"

"Yes. I'd fuck you right now if I thought the cops wouldn't cart us away."

"Doctor get you horny?"

"No. Your hot, pregnant body did."

She squeezes my face between her hands and gives me a quick kiss. "You say the sweetest things."

"Sunshine, we better make these announcements quick or maybe we should stop at the house first so I can rut all over you."

She fixes her helmet. "Mmm. Such sexy talk."

Her mocking only gets me more excited.

"I have a confession to make," she says, as she climbs on behind me.

My hand freezes over the start button. "What's that?"

"I already told Carter."

I snort out a laugh. "You think I don't know that?" I reach back and pat her thigh. "Hold on."

Even though the doctor said it was safe, I take the slowest route home avoiding the busiest roads.

As we pass our driveway, I give it a longing look. But she's right, we should tell everyone now so I can have her to myself for the rest of the night.

Murphy and Heidi are waiting in the living room at the clubhouse with Wrath and Trinity. Heidi sets baby Grace in her bouncy chair and Alexa hands over her favorite pink baby doll.

"You're watching Grace?" I ask, bending down to say hello and kiss the baby's cheek. Alexa wraps her arms around my legs, refusing to let go until I pick her up. While she loves baby Grace, she's not always thrilled at the attention being taken away from her, so I'm careful to give them equal attention. In a few months, when there's even more competition for everyone's attention, she's really gonna be pissed.

"Are you playing big sister?" I ask Alexa.

Heidi chuckles. "Alexa loves having her over." She rubs her stomach and laughs. "I'm worried her sister's going to feel left out."

"They'll be fine," Murphy says, settling his hand over hers.

"Down," Alexa demands, making everyone laugh. As soon as I set her on the floor, she runs over to Wrath.

"Come here, you spoiled-rotten princess," Wrath says, holding out his arms.

Heidi raises an eyebrow at Charlotte, "So?"

Charlotte's bursting to share this news. "Yes!"

"I think I know the answer," Trinity says. "But, yes what?"

"Wait." I tap Charlotte's arm. "Heidi already knows?"

"Well," Charlotte hedges. "She kind of guessed."

Wrath groans, gesturing at me, then Murphy. "You two know it's not a competition, right?"

A slow grin slides over Murphy's face. "Of course it isn't. We're already winning." He points to Alexa and then rests his hand over Heidi's baby bump. "Two to one."

I bust out laughing and settle my hand against Charlotte's stomach. "Guess again, bro."

"Holy shit!" Trinity yells.

Heidi struggles to sit up and hug Charlotte. "No way."

"What?" Wrath and Murphy ask at the same time.

"We're having twins."

Trinity runs over and hugs Charlotte. "That's amazing. Are you excited?"

The girls huddle together to talk baby stuff. I nod at Wrath. "Sure you're not feeling left out?"

He hugs Alexa, who's still treating his lap like her own personal throne. "I'm good, thanks." He waves his hand at Murphy and me. "Apparently I'll have plenty to keep me occupied."

Outside, the sound of Rock's bike reaches us.

"Sounds like Mom and Dad are here." Wrath grins. "Go tell them your good news."

"Would you knock it off with that," I growl, sneaking a glance at Heidi.

I take Charlotte's hand and we go meet Rock and Hope outside.

Charlotte waits until Hope gets off the back of Rock's bike to approach. "How was the first ride, after...?" she asks, gesturing toward the house.

Hope rubs her hands over her ass and grits her teeth. "Rough."

Rock's clearly distressed to hear that and pulls her to his side, leaning down to whisper something in her ear. When he finishes, Hope's blushing and he's grinning.

He finally nods hello at us.

"You two look like you're about to burst. What's up?" Hope asks.

"You're going to be a grandpa," I tell Rock.

He groans and shakes his head, but his smile widens. "What'd I tell you about that?" Reaching out, he pulls me in for a hug. "Congratulations."

"Twins," Charlotte adds.

"Oh my gosh. Double fun." She wraps Charlotte up in a big hug. "Congrats."

"You coming or going?" Rock asks.

"Going. Told Murphy, Heidi, Wrath, and Trin." I gesture toward the clubhouse. "I'll catch Z and everyone else tomorrow at church."

"Sounds good."

We go through another round of hugs before Rock and Hope head into the clubhouse.

"You sure you don't want to wait and tell anyone else?" Charlotte asks.

"Nope. Trust me. Word will spread." I pull her in closer and lower my voice. "We need to go home and celebrate, Sunshine."

Keep reading for information on how to receive a free Lost Kings bonus scene!

NOTE FROM THE AUTHOR

I hope the second part of Teller and Charlotte's story was everything you wanted it to be! I'm still in love with it at this point and I hope you are too! Thank you so much for being open to the idea of a duet. I can't say I want to do this again any time soon.

As you know if you read my last author notes, with Beyond Reckless I worried readers would think Charlotte was too close to Hope's character because of the lawyer thing. And for Beyond Reason I wondered if people would think her story was too similar to Trinity's (even though it's vastly different.)

While I was desperately trying to finish Beyond Reason (having *half* the book already written is not the same as having the *whole* book written. When will I learn this!?) Hollywood was having a shocking-but-not-really-shocking scandal and #metoo was all over social media. For days, I was up to my eyeballs reading stories similar to things that happened to me at various points in my life. Some of them at the time I hadn't even realized were harassment or inappropriate or not even my fault. Worse, the people who *should've* protected me (teachers, relatives, employers, friends, clergy) *didn't*.

At one point I was like, whoa, I worked a ton of these issues into both books (hell, probably all of them if I go back and look.) So, no, I don't think having two sexual assault survivor heroines in my series was a stretch. Especially not in an MC series, which as people are so fond of reminding me "real MCs are much more gritty, gory, violent, brutal" or whatever. Yeah, no kidding, so is real life apparently. #metoo. But you found my books in the "fiction romance" part of the store, right? Not the "non-fiction documentaries section." I'll take my fictional, vigilante, badass-but not that bad-bikers any day. Real life is brutal enough.

I think my husband's getting a little scared of all my "why are men so disgusting?" rants. But it's also made him more aware. He's always had no filter and given zero fucks what anyone thinks, so he's not afraid to call out shitty behavior when he sees it at work or anywhere else. And I think that's important. Men aren't the enemy. They should be our allies. Sexual assault is a horrible crime against another human being, not something you only care about when it happens to someone you love. Right? Or are we too busy trying to ask the victim stupid shit like "what were you wearing?"

Back to Charlotte's story. So, in the original draft of Beyond-Reckless-Reason, I sort of went in the direction that Merlin was the one who raped Charlotte (it was one of those threads I left open to interpretation that my crit partners were like "No. Bad Autumn. You need to close that storyline.") But Merlin as the villain didn't feel right…it almost felt too…obvious. In the Beyond Reckless spoiler group (which you should totally join, because it's awesome) the consensus was that by the end of book #2, Merlin would be dead. (Damn you're a bloodthirsty bunch!)

We all know I hate to do what's expected of me, so that's when I knew it wasn't Merlin. But how could I redeem him, when he'd been so creepy? Well, I can't. People are complex. Not everyone is 100% good or bad. I know in fiction they're supposed to be more black and white, but we already know I don't like doing what's expected of me. And I already had it in my head that Charlotte's mother and uncle had some weird kind of relationship. And he was so mad at Charlotte's mom for criticizing her appearance at family dinner night…it made me think…

Dammit, I hate when my side characters have their own fucking backstory and shit going on! And no, Merlin is not getting his own story!

Maybe Merlin had been in love with Charlotte's mother first. Maybe he tried to do what his twisted brain told him was the right thing, even though it cut Charlotte so deeply. Also, I liked the idea of the ultimate betrayal coming from Charlotte's mother. Don't ask me why.

Who knows? Maybe Merlin really saw the error of his ways. Teller wasn't so sure, but he's kind of biased. I had a lot of fun writing their "chat" on the way to bury Keeper's body.

I had several people ask why Teller didn't beat Carter up on several occasions. I've written extensively about how important respect is in the Lost Kings world—and that's *very* true of real world biker culture as well. However, after the first punch in Reckless, Teller made his point. Besides the fact that Carter is Charlotte's brother and it would be disrespectful to *her*, I can't think of anything less "alpha hero" than to pick on someone weaker than you.

So, I realize I've written these badass bikers who also happen to have a trigger when it comes to women being abused—whether they know them—or even like them—it's a no go.. Yes, there's dirty talk and sex, but consent is always a huge part of that—at least I try to make it so. Dirty talk is fun if the other party is willing. Otherwise it's just harassment and kinda gross. So while my guys are crude, my ladies enjoy that crudeness and give it back. There is still always an underlying respect for each other.

I think one of my favorite scenes in Beyond Reason (and I have a lot.) is near the end, when Charlotte and Teller are being playful in bed together and she's grumbling that he's only supposed to wake her up on the weekends for sex. Good grief, if you put that conversation in a different context, it would be sort of disturbing. But for them, it's playful and teasing.

Ah, what's next? I'm not sure. I have this secret project I've been working on since June. I'm so in love with it, but it's probably not what I *should* be working on. One of those characters made an appearance in Beyond Reason actually. I think that's a land Murphy might visit. *Ahhh, Murphy,* how much did I love him messing with Teller in this book? He's such a sweet soul and a little bastard at the same time. I can't wait to write more about him one day.

I want to write my sequel to Bullets and Bonfires. And I'm still toying with finishing Objection (Mara and Damon's story) because I think it would be fun to see Hope before she met Rock.

But oh my God, I really want to write After Burn. Like I love this book and the whole idea and all the stuff that's going to happen in it so much. I'm afraid to work on it because I don't want it to be over with.

Z. I keep getting more and more persistent questions about Z. I love him. And I know the broad strokes of his story, and I think the rest of it will come to me as I'm working my way through After Burn. The events in After Burn will end up reverberating through at least the next two books.

Phew! I think these notes are shorter than Beyond Reckless-yay! Thank you for sticking with me.

I'm kidding!

♡ Autumn

REQUEST FROM THE AUTHOR

If you loved *Beyond Reason*, it would mean so much to me if you'd return to the place you purchased it and left a review. It doesn't have to be fancy or flowery. A few short lines are enough (just clicking the stars some vendors add to the back of the book, isn't the same.) It may seem insignificant, but reviews are a great way to encourage me to keep writing.

Thank you!

OTHER BOOKS BY AUTUMN JONES LAKE

SOCIAL MEDIA

Sign up for Autumn's Newsletter
eepurl.com/bOZj95
BookBub
bookbub.com/authors/autumn-jones-lake
Goodreads
goodreads.com/AutumnJonesLake
Instagram
instagram.com/autumnjlake
Facebook
facebook.com/AutumnJonesLake
Twitter
twitter.com/AutumnJLake
Lost Kings MC Ladies Facebook Group
facebook.com/groups/LostKingsMC
Pinterest
pinterest.com/autumnjoneslake
www.autumnjoneslake.com

autumnjoneslake.com

www.ingramcontent.com/pod-product-compliance
Lightning Source LLC
Chambersburg PA
CBHW072343020726
47506CB00004B/990